Drones is the first book in the **Maliviziati Series**.

Matalina heads the elite special forces of Baltonia, a small country near Switzerland, and where the Maliviziati maintain their secret society that opposes the Illuminati's various splinter groups that want to create a new world order. While she directs the most powerful special operatives in the world, she is very capable of going solo when needed. She was bred like her parents and theirs before to be the best warrior in the world. Unfortunately, her chosen mate, Bjorn, has turned against them, killing her sister in the process. She loved him earlier, and perhaps she still does. Still, when she finds him, she will kill him.

When a new faction attempts to release drones in America, Matalina has to respond to keep this from playing into the hands of those wanting to create a new world order. She soon learns that the leader of this group is one of Bjorn's operatives, Mario, a guy she should kill, but he is also the one person she needs to take alive to be able to locate Bjorn. With mercenaries flown in from Columbia to help this terrorist faction which was formed out of Afghanistan, this novel circles the globe as many players fight for eventual control of the world.

DRONES
BY
Johnny Ray
Copyright 2013© Johnny Ray

Published by
SIR JOHN PUBLISHING

ALL RIGHTS ARE HEREBY RESERVED
BY JOHNNY RAY

JOHNNY RAY

Johnny Ray is an award winning novelist who won the Royal Palm literary award for best thriller and is quickly making a name for himself as the master of the romantic thriller. He loves social interaction with his readers and can be found on

Twitter www.twitter.com/sirjohn_writer
Facebook www.facebook.com/authorjohnnyray.
He can also be reached by e-mailing at
sirjohn@wwisp.com,
Or you can just follow him on his blog at
www.sirjohn.us

for updates and future releases.

Johnny Ray's previous works include:

A WAR HERO RETURNS
Published by Sir John Publishing in 2013

JOHN RAIN–THE HAWAIIAN AFFAIR
Published by AMAZON DIGITAL in 2013

LITERARY AGENT–BEWARE
Published by Sir John Publishing in 2012

SCANDAL–THE DEATH OF A LEGACY
Published by Sir John Publishing in 2012

MODELS AND LOVERS
Published by Sir John Publishing in 2012

HER HONOR'S BODYGUARD
Published by Sir John Publishing in 2012

FOR LOVE AND VENGEANCE
Published by Sir John Publishing in 2012

THE SALSA CONNECTION
Published by Sir John Publishing in 2012

THE JOURNEY TO WHITESTONE
Published by Sir John Publishing in 2012

STALKING LOVE
Published by Sir John Publishing in 2013

Chapter 1

Matalina yelled and squeezed the slippery steering wheel harder as her thunderous airboat bounced several times over a marshy saw grass field. With the slimy, flying debris coating her dark sunglasses, blinding her vision of the men she was chasing, she tossed them to the floor and full throttled the motor.

She fought her way back into another stagnant smelling channel that weaved like the intestines of the swamp monsters, the alligators, that ruled this world. Still . . . she was too damn close to lose him now. She needed to avenge the death of her sister and complete her missions for the Maliviziati which had placed so much trust in her.

Although her earplugs did little to control the sound of the motor behind her that roared like a beast set free in the Everglades, she chased the fleeing boat ahead of her as they raced toward the west. She knew she needed to intercept these men before they disappeared or made it to a larger, much faster boat that would take them out into the Gulf of Mexico. Perhaps she should've taken the helicopter, as she had first intended. Damn–too late now! If she lost them, however, she knew she could make a run back to where she had hidden it.

Suddenly, she saw wakes ahead from a recent disturbance. Knowing that she was behind them again, she slid sideways while making another turn. After she almost missed the next fork, where they had veered to the left, she wiped her eyes again.

Then, with her vision slightly improved, she saw a large boat anchored in an open cove ahead. The luxurious yacht was about sixty feet long and had three decks. She knew it would be impossible to catch it after they boarded. Since her weapon, a Kimber Ultra CDP 11, was no match against the firepower she expected onboard, she executed the only advantage she had left–surprise.

Hoping they hadn't seen her chasing them, she steadied her airboat straight toward the back of their boat, hitting maximum speed as she heard the first bullet deflect off the front of her boat. She only needed a couple more seconds to make sure her boat turned missile would do its job of disabling their motor, or putting a hole in the hull.

Upon approaching fifty feet from the impact, she bailed out to one side and skipped on top of the water twice before she made it underneath. After she emerged, parts of the wreckage were still flying around, as smoke bellowed out of the back of their yacht.

As expected, she saw men who were armed with rifles and rushing to the back of the boat. Instead of fleeing and making for the shelter of a nearby channel, she quickly gulped in a large lungful of air, since she had a long deep way to go under the boat. One minute passed and then another, as her head started feeling dizzy, but she had no other choice but to keep going. Finally, she saw light above and swam for it. After surfacing on the other side, she grabbed a quick breath and went back under to swim toward the front of the boat.

The next time she emerged as quietly as possible

before she looked around. After she heard yelling and a few gunshots, she realized that some idiot was apparently firing wild shots into the water. She had to figure out a way onto the yacht before they figured out where she was. Without a lot to hold onto, she used her fingernails, which were coated in a special metallic material, to dig into the side of the boat as she climbed.

After making it onto the yacht, Matalina rushed to the captain's bridge to look for another weapon of any kind, since it would take some time to access her gun from its airtight pocket. All she found was a fillet knife in a side drawer. It would have to do.

Although she remembered seeing three men aboard the airboat she had been chasing earlier, she didn't know how many more were on this large cabin yacht. A quick movement in her direction soon answered part of the question as two men rushed at her, but stopped short when she pointed the knife.

In a deep South American Spanish accent, one of the men asked her, "Who in the hell are you?"

Matalina glanced at both, but didn't recognize their faces. Perhaps they were simply the hired muscle. Since they weren't wet, they had to be the ones stationed on the yacht. She calmly replied in Spanish. "That's not important. I came looking for answers."

With a snarky smile, he reached inside his pocket and retrieved a small pistol, which he attempted to point at her. Instead, he yelled with pain when she used the knife to slash out and cut his hand down to the bone, much like you would expect from a fisherman cleaning a grouper.

"You bitch!" He dropped the gun as the blood covered his hand and clothes. As he quickly backed away, he screamed again.

As the other man scrambled to retrieve the gun, Matalina snatched a handful of his long, black hair and slammed her knee into his face, breaking his nose. While he stumbled backwards in shock, she quickly smashed his head into the wall behind him, knocking him out cold.

She spun around to the other man, who had located an old shirt and was using it to stop the blood flowing from his hand. The other men onboard the yacht had to have heard the scream, meaning she only had a few minutes to get answers out of him. "Is Bjorn Rothschild here?"

His eyes darted from side to side, as fear registered in them. Still, he didn't answer.

Matalina repositioned the knife against his throat. "I don't have much time. Do you want to live?"

"Stop! No one talks about him and lives."

"So . . . you know him?"

"I just get paid to make deliveries–that's all!" He glanced at the knife. "I've never met him. I just know the name. He's not here."

Damn–she missed him again. She had moments left to get answers. "What did you deliver for Bjorn?"

"I don't know. Honest! These guys with the airboat came to collect a shipment we were hired to deliver. Bjorn's simply the guy who controls this area. Nothing goes on here without his knowledge and approval."

While she felt like he was telling the truth, she had to move fast. The others would find her soon. As he scrambled away from her, she saw him grabbing a knife from behind his back. Luckily, she moved faster and missed his jab. By catching his wrist, she extended his arm before twisting a tendon. She knew he would scream again. To stop him she butted his head, knocking him unconscious.

Matalina needed to know whatever it was that Bjorn was trying to sneak into America, especially since it might provide her with better information as to where he was hiding. She checked the confiscated pistol to make sure it was loaded and the safety was off. She was still outnumbered.

Knowing an offensive move was her best chance to survive and to get answers, she pushed toward the back of the yacht. With a floor above and one below, they could be anywhere. The battle fatigues she wore were heavy with water, and she needed to get out of them. After she unzipped the top, exposing her shell, she breathed better and could also now move much easier. Her cargo style pants had a waterproof compartment containing her electronic equipment she would soon need.

She rushed along a corridor, hoping to find something to hide behind as she reached a door. After moving from one side to the other to check out the outside patio area, which had a thick smoke hindering her view, she saw some movements. An additional smoky mist from a fire extinguisher they were using to fight a fire added to the hectic movements outside.

Matalina rushed forward, aiming the pistol at the first man she saw. He attempted to shift his rifle at her, but stopped as he stared at the pistol pointed at his face. However, he still held the gun pointed to the side. Since his hair was a dark black and his complexion denoted a South American heritage, she yelled in Spanish, "Drop the gun, slowly."

As he grinned, showcasing several gold capped

teeth, he gradually lowered the gun in front of her but stepped closer. She didn't have much room to walk backwards, which he seemed to understand. Instead of dropping the pistol as he leaned over, he swung it high, as if hoping to knock her weapon from her hand.

She stepped backward and kicked head high, catching him under his chin and popping his head back. With his windpipe crushed, he stumbled forward and fell to the deck floor, another death she would have to live with.

As two other men ventured into view, she refocused the gun at the first one's head. Neither of them appeared to be armed, but she wasn't taking chances. She waved the gun to signal for them to raise their hands. Again, she didn't recognize their faces.

The first man wore several pieces of gold jewelry and surprised her as he spoke English. "I don't know who you are, but you made a very bad mistake. Do you know who owns this boat?"

"I think I know exactly whose boat it is. The question is, however, where is Bjorn?"

The two men walked apart as she watched them step into confrontational mode. "Oh, I see you know of him. There'll be nowhere you can hide from him after he hears what you did. He's out to destroy anyone affiliated with any one world order type group, if that's someone you work for."

"I'm not part of any group like that, and much to the contrary actually, but I am the one, nonetheless, hunting for Bjorn, since he betrayed his country. Don't make me kill you, you're the only two left, and I need answers." She glanced at three wooden boxes stacked on the side that were covered in the fire retardant they had been spraying. "I understand you came to make a pickup. Do you want to tell me about it?"

"Screw you!" He grunted, as if he was still in control.

"Not today, you don't have the balls for it." Matalina stepped closer to the boxes. "Tell me what's in here. Now!"

Still no answer. They stepped further apart. They appeared to be ready to die for their cause. Still, she needed their help in transferring at least one of the boxes onto their airboat. This yacht wasn't going anywhere soon and her airboat was totally destroyed in the crash.

The response came seconds later when the man on the left side of her pulled a knife from behind his back and prepared to throw it. A quick shot stopped his hand before he could make the release. He dropped to the floor, holding his hand as he yelled.

"I want any and all weapons on the floor now. I don't have time to screw around all day." She watched them cautiously remove and drop two pistols in front of them.

"What now, sweetheart?" The mocking nature of the apparent leader of this gang asked.

"I want these boxes loaded onto the air boat. That's why you came, isn't it?"

"You have no idea what's in these–do you? Bjorn just stopped these from getting into the wrong hands, and he will not allow them to have them." His words confused her, but she didn't have all of the answers.

"Nope, I've no idea what's in them, but I do intend to find out later." She waved the gun toward them. "Let's get this done. I'll assure you that if they were destined to go to any new world order group, I will also make sure that doesn't happen."

After she watched him glance at new smoke coming from the engine room, he grinned as he complied. "As you wish." He raised his hand while he moved toward the boxes. Even though he was a big guy, over six foot three and weighing, she guessed, about two hundred and fifty pounds, he struggled with the boxes. He treated them with a lot of care, as if he was moving something breakable, or at least precious. Still, he gave no clue as to what they were.

Finally, they had loaded two of them while the smoke continued to thicken. With this causing such an attraction, she knew the possibility of someone else arriving soon was highly probable. How they planned to explain the gunshot wounds was their problem.

Suddenly, a small black helicopter zoomed over the boat as the man grinned. "I guess you never counted on Bjorn returning, did you?"

Was that true? Was that him? If so, she was a sitting duck. Time to get moving. Before she could react, she watched the helicopter make another pass overhead at what she guessed to be over three hundred miles per hour. The propellers on two stubby wings offered an interesting design, one she hadn't seen before. Was it military?

With a quick pistol whip across the side of the last man's head, she prepared to leave, knowing she would never get any answers now. In seconds, the deafening sound of the airboat motor roared to life. Without earplugs, she stood a chance of permanent ear damage, but she had no choice. She searched for the nearest channel she could find, hunting for anywhere she could hide for a minute. She remembered a cypress grove several miles back which would have to do. When she saw the small, black copter circle, she knew there was no way she could outrun it.

Unexpectedly, the copter veered off to the side and headed back to the yacht. Minutes later, she saw the clump of cypress trees. The boat scampered over the dry land until it reached some bigger trees. Would it be enough?

After killing the motor and searching for anything that would act as a cover to camouflage the boat, she kept glancing upward, knowing her hearing had been impaired at least for a while. Minutes passed, and she still heard nothing.

She located her smart phone hidden in the waterproof pocket. She needed help, but first she needed to mark this spot on her GPS. Whatever was in those boxes had to be hidden here for now. While it was a struggle, she managed to off-load the two boxes. Minutes later, she also had them covered with palm leaves and swamp grass as best as she could.

What happened to the copter? Was Bjorn, her mortal enemy, the guy responsible for allowing her sister to die, really on it? If so, she fully expected him to come after her. As such, the question became one of staying and hiding, or making a run for it.

She formulated a plan—a test of sorts. First, she searched the airboat for any more information she might be able to use, including the boat ID number. She could check later to see who it was registered to. In a small cabinet she found another set of ear plugs— good! She would need these in a minute.

After locating several small documents, she locked them away in the waterproof compartment of her cargo pants. Since these papers were all written in Spanish, and these men all looked to be from either Central or South America, she knew the trail would lead there somewhere. For now, she had to regroup before Bjorn found her, and where he had her at such a disadvantage. She needed to get to her copter if at all possible.

Matalina cranked the airboat motor again, knowing that Bjorn might be able to hear her. She had little time to get to the next place, which was possibly another mile or so away.

Making it under some tall, thick trees this time, she turned off the motor. Still, she couldn't see or hear any signs of his copter. What was going on? She decided to activate her plan as she retrieved her phone to send a distress message, one she knew Bjorn could trace. Since a rescue might come soon, he would have to know he only had a small window to make his move. Within minutes, she had staged her shirt and hat behind the driver's seat. If he wanted her, he would have to come and investigate on foot. She would be waiting a few hundred yards away.

As expected, the strangely designed copter, which gave the impression of a black scorpion, circled the area from high above and out of range of her pistol for sure. Would he try to take her out from so far away? Was he really capable of killing her? Was there nothing left of their love and destiny to be together?

As the minutes passed, the copter ventured closer. She could imagine a machine gun shredding the area with bullets. Still, she patiently waited, until suddenly she heard a loud explosion coming from the area of the yacht several miles away. A large plume of smoke soon filled the sky. What in the hell would cause such an explosion?

The copter stopped approaching and veered off, heading back toward the yacht. He had his chance to kill her, but he didn't take it. Would she have taken the shot if she had the chance instead?

She decided to use this last diversion to her advantage and headed for the swamp boat again, hoping to make it to dry land where she could find some kind of road. After she made it onto land, she rigged the boat to head back out, but this time unmanned. She still thought he might return. There would be another day.

As she watched the airboat race across the swamp, a feeling of being deserted swept across her. She suddenly imagined how her sister felt the day she had died after being left in the path of an invading African tribe who were intent on slaughtering everyone in front of them. To them, her sister was nothing more than another body in their way. But still . . . her sister's body had never been recovered.

Adelaide had been trained to be a warrior, just like Matalina. Her sister's passion to save those much less fortunate than her had placed her in harm's way one time too many. Still, all would have been fine if Bjorn had not attacked one group, inciting them into a three-day counter-offensive that swept across their land with so many men that the mere size of the attacking force could not be contained by anyone.

Matalina loved her sister. As a team they had been very powerful. Now, Matalina had to carry all of the weight of running what she knew was one of the most elite special forces in the world. But knowing that she had been bred to be a warrior, she never flinched when she had to go solo, which many situations dictated. Her compassion for humanity in general had been well established in her by the Maliviziati and her country. Matalina loved Baltonia, and she would do whatever was required to keep its secrets and to preserve its future.

An hour later, with the sun baking her in a salty sweat, Matalina made it to a small dirt road which was apparently used by four-wheeler and mud truck fanatics who loved to explore this area next to the Florida Everglades. Still, it looked much better than struggling through the swamps. As expected, however, she soon saw a flashing light coming from some kind of law enforcement vehicle.

The large, four-wheeled vehicle, a Ford Explorer, eventually pulled beside her as the driver side window lowered. An officer, looking to be in his mid-twenties, grinned at her while he removed his shades. "Hello, miss. You appear to be lost."

"Thank you for asking." She smiled slightly, but kept her teeth from showing. "I'm not totally lost, but I could use a ride." She waited as he opened his door to step outside. He had another officer riding with him who remained inside.

"How did you get out here?" he asked as he glanced around.

Since he asked in a friendly manner, she decided to return the courtesy. "I was testing out a new airboat I had purchased. It crashed, and I had to walk out."

"So . . . you're the one who made the distress call?

Matalina reached inside her waterproof pocket and retrieved a small cigar and a lighter as she watched him walk around to study her. Yes, she knew she looked a mess, and she felt like he had never seen anyone like her before. "Yes, that was me. I don't think the boat can be salvaged, but I'll have someone look at it later."

After he pressed a button on the mic attached to his shoulder, she heard it crackle as he waited for a better connection. "Yeah, I just located the person calling in the distress signal. She appears to be alright, and I don't think we need an ambulance. I'll bring her with us as we come out." His face soon reflected a serious overtone as he continued to listen. "I see. Please hold a minute and I'll ask her."

"We have a boat on fire several miles east of here. The boat appeared to have exploded. They have found several dead bodies in the water, and there doesn't appear to be any survivors. That's not where you came from, is it?"

Answering questions is one thing she didn't want to go through. She reached for her pocket again as the officer nervously placed his hand on his revolver. "Please relax . . . I need to show you something." She lit her cigar first before she reached inside her pocket again.

"What's this?" he asked, as she leaned forward and handed him her diplomatic card.

She needed his help, and she hoped he would also volunteer more information. "I think it's clear enough, and I hope we can keep this as quiet as possible." She blew out a puff of cigar smoke as she reached for her card. "I did hear an explosion, and I also saw some smoke." She paused to whistle. "That must have been one hell of an explosion."

He offered her a curious smile. "I understand the debris was scattered over a half of a mile. They must have been carrying some kind of high explosive on board." He stepped back and rubbed his chin. "I'll need to report this. Can you give me a second?"

"Sure, I understand. Please do what you have to do." She had expected this. Knowing this could take a minute, she turned to scan the skyline. Chances were that Bjorn had fled the area, and it would be a while until she could find him again. What was his involvement in transporting high explosives, or was it, interestingly, intercepted by him instead? That must have been what was in the crate she had left onboard. Still, she had two of the crates stored away. Would he come after them next?

She heard the officer talking, but couldn't make out everything. He was trying to describe her– interesting! Yes, she had short spiked white hair. Yes, she would be easy to describe in some ways, but impossible in others. On her father's side, her grandmother was Japanese and her grandfather was Swedish. On her mother's side, her grandmother was Russian and her grandfather was Mongolian. In each linkage, she had warrior heritage. Without any doubt, she was bred to be a warrior. Although her parents had hoped for a son, they had conceived two daughters instead.

The officer turned to face her again. "Can I see your diplomatic card again . . . just for a moment?"

"Why?"

"I can't remember the name of the country, sorry."

"It's Baltonia." Matalina needed the ride, but only had so much time to be distracted with small talk.

She watched him continue to discuss her diplomatic status with what appeared to be a superior. "Sir, she appears to be around thirty, and she is built like a female wrestler, including the white spiky hair of a counter-culture rebel of some kind. It would be hard for me to place which ethnic group she would fall in. She sounds European, but she looks like she's at least partially Asian."

One thing was for sure, she wouldn't be able to return for a while to see what was in the crates. She wondered if Bjorn knew she had taken two of the crates with her. Had he talked to anyone on board before the yacht exploded? The last question was the hardest one to answer. Did the yacht explode from the fire reaching the explosives, or did Bjorn, the guy who was at one time chosen to be her mate by the Maliviziati, destroy it to cover his tracks? Had he become that ruthless?

The officer turned to face her. "I was just told I have no authority to ask you any questions, and that I am to extend you all courtesies of a foreign diplomat. I've never encountered this situation before, so I hope you forgive me for not knowing the exact procedure I should be using." He offered her the pleasant good looks of a local guy who loved his job.

"Not a problem. Can I get that ride now?" She offered him a slightly flirty glance as if to say thank you.

Chapter 2

While waiting in her rental car for the marina that had rented the terrorist group an airboat to open, Matalina opened her computer. Since the odor of her cigar might ruin the new car smell, she respectfully lowered the car window. She clicked through one website after another, only to see how the story of the yacht exploding had been buried. After hitting one dead end after another, she watched the birds migrating above her, wishing she could be so free.

By using her computer the night before, however, she had managed to trace the swamp boat used by the thugs she had chased the day before to this marina. While the chances of obtaining a lead as to who they were would be hard, there was a small chance she might discover something.

Since there was still no sign of anyone opening the marina, Matalina called her mom to check in. Keeping a low profile and maintaining their secret way of life was the ultimate responsibility she had been commissioned with by the Maliviziati. Containing the mess from the day before had to be part of her mom's work or that of the CIA.

Her mom answered her private line on the first ring. "I was hoping you would call me soon. What happened?"

"I love you too, mom." The jab was intentional, but she knew it drew no blood. "I intercepted a load of high explosives being smuggled into America."

"That much I understand. Now tell me the who,

what, where and when that I don't know."

"I'm strongly convinced that Bjorn's connected to this, but I've no idea why, or what part in this he's playing. It's unlike Bjorn to be working with terrorists, so I don't know where and when they had planned to use these explosives. I do intend to find out soon. Still, there's a possibility he may have intercepted this and was stopping it."

"You have two weeks until you're expected to be here for the next international meeting."

"Mom, I remember . . . and I'll do everything I can to contain this problem, and have it eradicated by then."

"I hope so." The line went dead.

Her mom had never liked her being in the field. There was no doubt she still wished she had raised a son to be king one day. Matalina knew that accepting her position in the Maliviziati and becoming the future queen of Baltonia one day would be a challenge for her. It was a life she couldn't imagine. Still, that was her destiny one day–one day when all was at peace. Until then, she had to be the enforcer–there was no one else.

Eventually, Matalina walked into the front of the airboat rental company. She needed information on who rented the boat two days ago, and she needed to rent or buy another one to retrieve the crates she had hidden in the swamp. Since the weight of the crates concerned her, she also needed some muscle. Money usually managed to buy discretion in what she had to hire.

"Hello. Is anyone here?" Matalina walked toward the back of the shop, and she still saw no one. At the far back of the shop, the rear door stood wide open.

She went on high alert. Had someone else already been here? She located her PUD and clicked off the safety, but left it in the holster for now. "Hello?"

She rushed to one side of the door before she glanced outside–nothing. After shifting to the other side, she studied an outside deck. A body was lying on the ground. She quietly drew her gun out of its holster. She studied the older man on the deck, but saw no blood. Shifting her attention, she scanned the immediate area around her, most of which was swamp. A single channel led back into the everglades. While the dock had room for three boats, she saw only one.

When she backed to the man on the ground, she reached down to his neck. She located a pulse–good. Feeling safer, she reaffixed the safety to her PUD before she checked out the apparent shop owner's injuries. She shook him, but he didn't respond. After walking to the water, she removed a handful and splashed it on him. He groaned as she located the bump on his head.

Moments later, he roared to life, ready to fight. His eyes, a solid black color that burned like a piece of onyx, were smothered in a red stain.

"Take it easy. I'm not your enemy. I found you on the floor."

As he appeared to slightly understand, he gently rubbed the large knot on top of his head. "Damn it!"

When he staggered, she tried to steady him. "Here, let me help you."

He shrugged like he didn't want help, but within seconds he was on a stool next to a rail overlooking the dock. He raised his hand and pointed to the vacant docking station. "All I asked for was some identification. Damn asshole!"

"So, you saw who did this?"

"Hell, yes. I need to call the police."

Matalina stretched and glanced down the channel. "Did they say where they were going?

"Not exactly, but I saw them searching a map I gave them for areas to the east of here."

She thought they might be trying to locate where she had stashed the crates. She turned to face him again. "I can't stop you from calling the police, but I can help you even the score, that is, if you're interested."

She watched him raise his head to examine her. "There were three of them. And all of them large, well-built men."

Matalina paused for a second before she asked, "Was one of them Swedish looking, with long blond hair?"

He looked surprised with the question, but answered quickly. "No, they were all black haired men who spoke Spanish."

She pointed to the one remaining boat. "I can use your help, or I can do this on my own. It's up to you. How much for the boat?"

He winched. "This is my last one."

"How much?"

"No shit . . . you plan to go after these dudes?"

"I can also pay you for the one they made off with, if you're able to handle it discretely."

A change in attitude crossed his face. "How much?"

"Enough, but we don't have much time. Are you interested?"

"Yes, but money up front."

"You got it!"

Minutes later, Jake, the owner, had loaded his boat with an arsenal of his own, a Smith and Wesson and a sawed-off twelve gauge he had loaded with buckshot. These boats were his livelihood, and from his looks she assumed he was a full-bred local Indian, one that had never been run off his land. She felt a bond with him that was hard to explain. Her family, like his, was fighting for traditions the world wanted to destroy–a one world order that had to be stopped.

When Jake was finally ready to get underway, she gave him the GPS coordinates to where the men would most likely be found. The location of the crates wouldn't be disclosed until all was clear. She assumed the false location she had given to Bjorn had been relayed to this group. Although he still might be close, she doubted it. At least she knew he wasn't on this boat they were chasing.

While Matalina doubted they could find her hiding place, there were no guarantees. This time she needed to take one of them alive. She needed answers. Surely, she thought, they could give her something she could use to find Bjorn. The first item of business, however, would be to locate their boat.

As they approached the area, she motioned to Jake to kill the motor. Trying to sneak in on someone with a motor that roared like this would be impossible. She needed to bail out and have Jake make a circle to offer a diversion. Her weapons were secure, her mind focused, and now was the time to act.

"Okay, I understand," he finally replied, "but if I see'em before you get to'em, their asses are mine. The damn gators will have a good meal tonight."

She couldn't blame him for being mad, but she needed one of them alive. She had to move fast. "Drop

me here. I think they're on the far side of this Cypress
grove. Draw their attention, and I'll get behind them."
She jumped ashore before he could object.

This time she was packed with everything she
needed. While she didn't want to kill these men, she
was determined to get answers. Even though she had
been trained to kill, she still preferred to avoid it,
unless it was completely necessary. Unfortunately, that
had happened all too often in her missions.

Although she didn't know all of the details,
anyone who was smuggling military-style explosives
into America had terrorism written all over their
intentions. She started clearing her mind of her past
hunts for Bjorn as she raced across the small marshy
island. From the sound of the airboat, Jake would be
around on the other side soon.

After pushing past the foliage of a palm tree, she
searched the open space ahead of her and double
checked the GPS reading. The marked location was
less than two hundred yards ahead of her. A hundred
yards further she spotted their boat on a knoll near the
far side of a small pool. Still, there was no sight of the
men, but she could hear Jake's airboat closing in. He
had to have their attention.

Matalina drew her pistol and pushed forward until
she saw several men attempting to hide behind a small
clump of trees. The diversion had worked as planned.
With the roaring airboat speeding toward them, they
had their guns drawn and pointed at it.

Matalina fired several shots above them before
she yelled, "drop your guns now!" As they all turned,
the men slowly lowered their guns, but didn't drop
them. She fired two more shots in the ground in front
of them. "I mean now!"

One man tossed his gun to the ground, while both of the other men raised their left hands higher to indicate they were complying. As they lowered their guns to the ground with their right hands, they defiantly bid their time, but finally complied. None of them turned to face the airboat that ran on ground behind them.

Jake soon jumped out of his boat and raced toward everyone. He made no excuses as he headed for the biggest one who briefly grimaced before Jake pistol whipped him. The man dropped to a knee, but remained conscious. Matalina stepped closer, pointing her gun between his eyes. "I guess that's called fair payback. It hurts, huh?"

"Who are you?" a man on the far right finally asked.

"That's not important. I need answers, and Jake needs to be compensated for his damages. Do you work for Bjorn?"

"Bjorn?" The guy looked confused, but she had expected being lied to.

"I know he's involved, so let us drop the dumb looks." She watched the guy that had been pistol whipped scramble to his feet. "We all know the chances of making it out of here without being eaten by an alligator are slim to none."

Glances between the men passed valuable information she picked up on while the guy speaking English continued, "I've heard the name, yes, but I've never meet him. I think he knows our boss. That's the best I can offer you."

Really? She lowered the gun to his knee cap. "I think you can do much better."

"Wait, I'm just a guy trying to make a few

dollars! This bullshit isn't worth this crap. I'm a shrimper who hasn't made a good living since the BP spill here. We were told to find a crate located on this spot . . . and to make sure no one knew we were here." He glanced at Jake. "Sorry about the smack on the head."

Jake moved closer to him. "Fuck you." Jake spit to his side before glancing at Matalina. "I say leave'em."

Instead, Matalina cocked the pistol, her attentions clear. "Tell me where I can find Bjorn?"

"Don't, please! This job isn't worth this shit." He rubbed the cut on his head received from Jake before he opened his palms in a display of asking for mercy. "I've heard of this guy. . . Bjorn, but I've never seen him. He lived somewhere close to here, and he had some dealings with a guy named Zafar from the Middle-East somewhere. I understand that nothing goes through this area without Bjorn's permission."

Had she missed him again? "You said *lived*. I'm pretty sure he was here yesterday."

"Maybe. I don't know for sure, but I heard he was moving." He shifted his eyes to the other two men who were intensely studying him. If he was selling out Bjorn, his life might be worthless later if they told on him. Still, they volunteered nothing. She would concentrate on them after this one stopped talking. They had the information she needed.

"Okay. I need to know where his base was here, and where he moved to."

"I think he had a house on the Faka River, but I don't know where. I promise." While the frantic look in his eyes indicated he was telling the truth, she at least had some information to go on.

"And where is he moving to?"

As he opened his mouth, another guy stepped behind him and stabbed him, making him yell with pain. With a quick reflex she fired, hitting the guy with the knife between his eyes. While the two fell to the ground, the third guy located a hidden gun and turned to fire at Jake, hitting him in the chest before rushing behind him as if to use him for a shield.

The slight clearance to his head, however, was all she needed as she fired once and connected to his forehead. As he fell backwards she rushed to Jake, his face was distorted in pain and blood covered his chest. He wouldn't live much longer. Killing innocent people was the one thing she had tried so hard to prevent. She should haven't have involved him in this. "Jake, I'm so sorry."

"Don't worry about it. I had . . . good life." Those where profound words, coming from a man who was in pain and dying. She wished she could have known him better.

"Is there anything I can do for you? I'm in your debt."

His eyes glanced to the side. "Don't let'em gators eat me."

"I promise." She watched him smile as his stare froze. His death would be another one pressed in her memory forever. She would make sure he had a proper burial and that any family he had would be well taken care of. She owed him that.

She suddenly heard a groan coming from the man who had been stabbed. He was still alive. She hurried to turn him over. He was yet another guy swept into a world that could've been avoided, and another death she would have to live with. While many people thought she had no heart–she did. She carefully found the knife in his back and removed it. "How are you?" A dumb question, but it was her only way of determining how bad he was. With the amount of blood he was losing, she knew he didn't have much chance of surviving either.

As he tried to speak, he spit blood. She held his head higher, giving him a chance to breathe. "If Zafar hears I talked, he'll kill my family."

"Tell me what you know and I'll try to help them." She knew he would die soon. "I have resources."

"In my wallet, you'll see many things, including how to reach my family." He spit blood one more time as he closed his eyes and muttered something in Arabic.

Matalina glanced at the depressing surroundings of the swamp as she raked her teeth over her upper lip. She had made promises she would keep, but first she needed to gather her thoughts and evaluate what she had learned. While she thought she had found his hidden lair, it looked like others had as well. With the area becoming such a hot bed, she realized Bjorn might have had no choice but to move on. Still, who was it that was sneaking high explosives through this hidden cove? She closed her eyes for a moment. She also needed to understand what they were intended to destroy?

It would take some major work on her part to get all of these bodies on the airboat. If she left any of them, the gators, bears and cougars would soon have a feast, not to mention the buzzards that flew above. But . . . before she left the swamp, she had to find the crates she had hidden and destroy them. She would use the first airboat taken by the other men to make the trip around the cove to the other side.

Minutes later she used her GPS to fine-tune the location. Nothing! Someone had beaten her to the explosives, but who? She had stopped the men who were hired to find it. Now, were they simply a decoy?

A possible answer stunned her as she heard a major explosion and new plumes of smoke rising above the swamp. She jumped back into the airboat and cranked the motor, knowing she wouldn't have long to investigate what was going on. When a small land-bridge blocked her way, she gunned the motor, quickly plowing over the top.

Eventually, Matalina raced along a stream toward the bellowing smoke ahead of her. After she ran the boat on land for a hundred yards or so, she jumped on shore and pulled her pistol. However, she saw no one around. After following the smoke, she soon discovered a house, which was shattered to pieces and burning. With all evidence of this place destroyed, she had little doubt that this was Bjorn's place.

She also realized that any information in the crates leading to where it had came from, or who was behind it, was also destroyed. Suddenly, she stopped and listened harder as she detected the sound of a small plane coming in her direction. After rushing for cover, she waited. Would it land nearby? More importantly, who was onboard?

Matalina watched the small hydroplane circled twice before flying to the west. She had to get back to the bodies and take care of all evidence of her being in the swamps. While she had taken all wallets and anything else she could find on the men, she had no time to analyze this information yet. The authorities would have to be arriving there soon.

She pushed the airboat to carry her back to the dead bodies as fast as it could go. From there, all she had to do was trade boats and race back to Jake's place. She circled the small island looking for the other airboat–nothing. Had she gotten lost? She rechecked the GPS on her phone. No–this had to be the right place. She soon found tracks of the airboat, but that was it. That was damn fast!

Matalina knew she needed to get airborne to do any good as she raced back to Jake's place, and where she had left her rental car. To clear a scene like this required professional help; much like Bjorn would have access to. Still, she had heard he was long gone. So . . . who was behind this?

Chapter 3

Matalina eventually arrived back at Jake's boat rental place. Unexpectedly, the airboat she had gone out on with Jake was docked to the pier. As she pulled next to it, she realized the bodies had been removed. A closer look further suggested it had been completely wiped clean of all blood traces. These guys were good.

Still, Matalina tied on, and since they could still be close at hand, she found her pistol and stalked toward the rear entrance. The backdoor stood wide open. She checked both sides of the door before she ventured inside. Jake was lying face down behind a small counter he had used to book reservations. The three men had been staged in front of him to make it look like it was a holdup gone bad.

This was the kind of setup many first year forensic students could even recognize, but anyone worth anything at all would soon learn the bodies were moved, and that one of them had a knife wound in the back. Still, it was enough to establish a diversion, if the right money was involved.

Matalina checked the register and saw a small amount of money left, but she knew he didn't need much to operate. Since the chances of finding any receipts to lead to a suspect would be problematic, she now felt glad she had paid in cash, which reminded her–where was the money she had given Jake?

Since Jake's computer was still working, she decided to check for any details left on it. She got lucky, as several credit card usages showed from earlier. After copying them to a flash drive, she removed a small canister and fingerprinted the three men. That information would be critical in finding out who they really were later. Since she assumed the police would show any time, she decided she would rather spend her time looking for Bjorn or the others responsible than answering questions.

More dead bodies left behind only made her more determined to complete her mission to stop the world from changing. She had a major mission she needed to accomplish. Was this part of what Bjorn was after also? He had formed his splinter group, unwisely, but they still had some common enemies. What was his connection to all of this?

Chapter 4

The flight aboard her rented plane through the crystal blue skies above the Everglades was fruitless, with no signs of the boat or any other private planes anywhere. As expected, however, it wasn't long until the sound of her small plane's engine was overpowered by a coast guard helicopter and the voice of the pilot who ordered her to leave the area. They had to have many unanswered questions of their own. Hacking their computers to find out what they knew wouldn't be hard, and it would be one of her first things she planned to do after she returned to the Maliviziati owned condo in Miami.

The wallets these men had on them proved to be a mixed bag of leads. Two of the three were from Columbia. The one who had been knifed, the one that gave her some information, was from New Orleans. Could they have been recruited by Bjorn or this new guy, a Zafar? For some reason, she didn't think so. Were they simply a diversion to keep her busy while Bjorn, or one of his henchmen, destroyed any trace of them in the Florida Everglades?

Matalina soon went to work searching for any connection to Bjorn by hunting for ownership information on the property where the house had been destroyed. It was on one of the last private pieces of land before entering the Everglades. The direct access it had from the Faka River to the Gulf made it a perfect place for him to hide. Yes, she knew that he was aware that she was after him. This wasn't the first time she had come close, and it was amusing how he still managed to keep his operation together.

Finally, she found the owner information in the tax records. It was a dummy corporation based in Sweden. Not very original, and one she knew he meant for her to easily find. What kind of message was he trying to send her?

As far as she could determine, Bjorn had never operated in Columbia or had connections in South America before. She decided to switch her searching activities to the small hydroplane. There couldn't be that many operating inside the Everglades during this time period.

Fifteen minutes later she found the information. The plane was registered to a Carlos Rico, the name of the man who had been knifed. She also managed to track the last known location of the plane to New Orleans. After seeing the name of the pilot listed as Carlos Rico, she retrieved the wallet Carlos had on him when he died. The photos didn't match. He had no passport on him. With the last bullet to the face apparently fired after he had been hauled to the rental office, possibly to cover the fact he had been knifed, his true identity would be hidden for a while.

Now, were the planted leads to Columbia the truth, or were they another false trail? A quick check of the passports of the other two men indicated that at least the photos matched the people she had shot. Then, she received the next big shocker. Both men were originally from Afghanistan and had degrees in physics, with specialization in aerodynamics.

Two hours later. Matalina had researched these men as best she could on the internet. They were part of a small corporation in Germany that built small drones; one that even the CIA had used on occasion. With her interest peeked, she went inside the CIA files to find more. It seems that this was a renegade group the CIA had hoped to infiltrate and failed. For the last three years they had disappeared underground. How were they connected to this?

It dawned on her what they could have on their minds. Oh . . . shit! Drones armed with high explosives would be hard to sneak into America, but building them here might be impossible to detect until it was too late. Still, she knew this was all speculation on her part. With leads going to New Orleans and Columbia, she had to decide which would be more important to follow first. Being an immediate threat to the security of the United States, she had to follow these leads instead of chasing Bjorn for now, that is, unless he was deeper into this than she thought. Drones could also be a major threat to her country.

The quick trip to New Orleans might help, but she knew the truth she wanted was probably in Columbia or Afghanistan. She hated people losing their life needlessly, especially when she was the one that had caused their deaths. There was also something special in this guy, Carlos, who begged for his life. She pinched her thigh, a habit she often did when she was mad at herself. She should've seen this coming when he opened up to her.

Carlos had given her a name, Zafar, and one she hadn't concentrated on until now. She searched for the name on the internet, and as she somewhat expected, he was also from Afghanistan with ties to the Fischer Design Group, the same aerodynamic consulting firm the others worked for.

The chances of such a small operation pulling this

off were minute. The CIA would be all over it. Thinking back on the data file she read, she wondered which operation inside the CIA had more information. She had favors she could use, and this was the time to call them in. Since she had little time to waste until the trail would vaporize, she found her phone and sent a message to be contacted in New Orleans the next morning. These off-the-record meetings were tricky, but necessary.

The next call was to Executive Worldwide Jet Services, a company specializing in catering to the wealthy and in return they asked very few questions. She would keep them on standby after getting to New Orleans, since she didn't expect to be there long, and wanted to get to Bogota, Columbia as quickly as she could to follow the trail leading there.

As soon as she finished making the arrangements, she received the results of the finger print analysis she had requested. She blinked her eyes, as she hadn't expected such a fast response. What she received was somewhat unexpected. The three fingerprints didn't match any known persons. The three men identified in the documentation she had removed from them had also been entered into the computer. All of the documented men had fingerprints on file, but she didn't have a match with fingerprints obtained from the dead men. As such, all three men were imposters, or had fake documentation. Why would someone plant such documentation on them? Were these guys used to hide the identity of others?

The information in their wallets all became suspect now. Were the references to Columbia a trap to lure her there? She felt like she was being played. Yes, tomorrow she had many questions for the CIA.

Would they be cooperative? If they wanted info from her, they had better be.

Chapter 5

As the private jet landed on a small air strip south of New Orleans, Matalina hoped to get answers before she went downtown. A car was supposed to be waiting for her. Before landing, she had studied several small canals on the side of the airstrip where the float planes were moored. Since she had counted less than a dozen planes, she hoped it wouldn't take long to identify the one that was used in the Everglades. She needed to find out who it belonged to, and how to find them.

Dressed in her army-styled fatigues, she was prepared to do battle as she marched off the plane. While she expected the men in the float plane might have disappeared hours ago, she never knew for sure. Her white gold jewelry sparkled in the sunlight as she walked to the office. Even her matching white gold painted fingernails seemed to glow in the vibrant morning light. The extra coating she had added on the flight was firmly set, just in case she needed this weapon.

Since the front door of the office was standing open, she stopped to survey the area. After glancing inside, she saw the aftermath of a small fight of some kind. A brusque old man was standing behind a large counter, wrapping a white cloth around his hand.

He stared at her, but glanced away, offering a disgusted smile, before he asked, "What do you want?"

Matalina leaned closer to inspect his wounds. "I just landed here. The pilot will be in shortly. What happened to you?"

The short, white-bearded man glanced outside toward the parking area where the small jet was sitting and the pilot was busy chocking the tires. "Don't get many nice jets like that landing here." He studied her as he continued to wrap his hand. "You're not smuggling drugs into Naw'lings, are you? I don't allow such shit."

Since she didn't see a driver who was ready to take her into the city, she assumed he hadn't shown yet. "Not hardly. But . . . I need some information. You had a plane land here from Florida yesterday afternoon."

He stopped wrapping his hand. "What of it?"

She offered a small, compassionate, but closed lip smile before she continued. "I need to know who owns that plane, and who was on it."

"Since you sure to hell don't look like the police, why do you think I'll answer any questions for you?" She watched him study her short, white-spiked hair.

"I asked nicely." She smiled for the first time to let him see the white gold capped teeth before she let her jacket move to the side to reveal her pistol. The desired effect immediately registered on his face. "I hope we can keep it that way."

"What is it with you fucking people?"

"I assume that is from those who flew that plane." She pointed to his hand, again offering to help him.

He squinted, twisting his jaw before he continued with a slightly softened attitude. "That plane belongs to a guy named Carlos, but I haven't seen him for a while. I thought maybe he had gone on a trip in it, but these assholes flew it back in. I went out to help them dock it and was told to mind my own business. They told me to not call the police or they would be back. I tried to reach Carlos, but no answer."

"I see." Matalina opened her side bag and located his wallet. After removing his driver's license, she handed it to him. "Is this Carlos?"

The old man glanced at the license and paused. "What are you doing with this?"

"Looking for answers," she volunteered as she waited for an answer.

"He hasn't been in here for a while, but I don't think that's him." He shook his head for a second. "However, I can't be for sure. He's a shrimper who stays by himself most of the time. I think he must be from somewhere in the Middle East, but who knows these days. I never saw him wearing one of those turbans or anything, but he had a peculiar way about him, if you know what I mean."

"I need his phone number and the directions to his place."

"You know I'm not supposed to give that out." He leaned forward. "You never answered how you got his wallet."

"I took it from him after he died." Matalina dropped several hundred on the counter top before she motioned to his bandage. "I assume the ones responsible for his death are the same ones you ran into. I need to catch them before they disappear."

He laughed. "I don't think these are the kind of men you want to run into, honey."

"On the contrary. I think they have information I need." She glanced again at his bandaged hand. "I assumed a little revenge would be something you might want."

He glanced at the money. "Do the police know

about Carlos?"

"They do, but they have bad information. They assumed he was killed during a holdup, one that I think was staged by those who used the float plane." She leaned closer and focused on his eyes, a deep brown that showed signs of a troubled past. "I don't have a lot of time, since my car will be here soon. The pilot will stay behind until I return."

The guy turned to watch a large, black town car pull in front of his shop. "I don't know who you are, but you didn't get this from me–okay?" He pulled out a card file and starting looking through it. "He hasn't answered his phone all day, but this is the address I have for him."

Matalina accepted the piece of paper with the address on it. She dropped two more hundreds on the counter. "As you said, this meeting never took place." As she walked away, she wondered if he could be trusted. In any case, she knew to hurry and to be careful.

Thirty minutes later, Matalina located Carlos Rico's house hidden down a long, winding dirt path. She saw no vehicles around, and the dirt had no signs of tire prints. It looked like it had been abandoned for a long time. "Stop here," she told the driver. "I won't be long."

The driver glanced over the back of the seat. "Are you sure you're going to be okay in there? It looks like it needs to be torn down."

"I'll be fine. I need to hurry to downtown New Orleans, so I won't be long." She adjusted her bag and waited for the driver to open her door as images of her future life as royalty would dictate. Even if it was her destiny, she wasn't looking forward to it.

The wooden front porch rested on concrete blocks spaced about six feet apart. Upon closer examination, the entire house appeared to be built on these piles of blocks which were about three feet high. It must have been constructed this way to make sure the local flooding didn't get inside the house.

The front windows were so dirty that she couldn't see inside. Although this seemed to be a wasted trip, she moved to one side and knocked on the door. No answer. She reached for the knob and twisted it with ease before she opened the door. "Hello?" Again, no answer.

Matalina paused for several seconds to allow her eyes to focus. She saw a light switch and flipped it, expecting the power to be off. Surprisingly, an overhead light came on. It wasn't abandoned after all.

She studied many dirty plates in the sink, as well as several bottles of empty whiskey bottles lining a small table. She next walked over to the refrigerator and opened it to see several six-packs of beer and half eaten meals stacked on top of each other.

Matalina started searching for any kind of drawers or places where paperwork of any kind might be stored. Nothing. She walked back to the bedroom which consisted of a mattress on the floor and a steel cased gun cabinet on the far wall. After she found it locked, she started to look for a way to open it. Shooting open the lock wouldn't be smart, since many people stored the ammunition in the drawers.

After glancing out the back of the shack, she saw a small boat shed on a small bayou with a boat beneath it. Maybe she could find something there that she could use to open the cabinet. She opened the back door and walked across the small backyard. Since this boat wasn't big enough to go shrimp fishing, she assumed he owned another boat somewhere else.

While searching for anything she could use, she found a spare set of keys to the boat attached to a small cork, something many fishermen used to keep from dropping the keys into the water to be lost forever. She noticed another key on the ring. Could it fit the gun cabinet?

With only one way to find out, she headed back inside where she saw various scratches on the gun cabinet, indicating she wasn't the last one interested in what was inside. The lock turned with little effort. As expected, the drawer was layered with twelve gauge shotgun shells, some boxes of forty five shells and a half of box of thirty-thirty shells. Below them was a nice hunting knife made with a deer antler handle and a manila folder. It wasn't dusty as she would have expected from one stashed there for a long time. Since it appeared to have been recently added, she flipped open the cover in anticipation. The letterhead of the Fischer Design Group matched the aerodynamic firm she had seen earlier. While flipping through the contents of the file she saw many designs of what looked like small planes of some kind. Since this would take a while to digest, she folded it once to make it small enough to fit inside her side bag.

Suddenly, a gunshot rang out. She hit the floor. After crawling her way on the floor to the front window, she glanced outside. Her driver was lying face down in front of the car. The shooter had to be out there somewhere, and she had no clue how many others were with him. Since any chance of these paper thin walls stopping any bullets were slim to none, she had to make a move. After grabbing the keys, she ran out the back door and raced for the boat. She hoped it would crank fast, since she had nowhere to hide, and they had the upper hand at the moment. As she jumped onto the boat, she heard the assault of bullets on the shack.

A quick slash with her assault knife freed the boat from the tie to the dock. The boat stuttered as she tried the first time. How long has it been since it was used? She pumped the choke and tried again. Black smoke blew out of the engine as it cranked. There was no time to properly warm up the engine. She threw the throttle forward. Several bullets whistled through the Cypress trees as she made the first turn.

After making it to safety, she throttled down. Since she didn't come here to run, she had to find a way to double back without being seen. With every turn looking the same, however, her sense of direction soon disappeared. She rushed under a large Cypress tree and located her smart phone as she killed the motor. An aerial view soon oriented her as she planned her next move.

When she heard a small buzzing sound above her, she glanced upward to see a small toy-like plane making circles. She had no doubt it was trying to find her. She jumped from the boat into the knee deep water and made for deeper cover. Minutes later, the drone accelerated, as if it had a rocket propelled burner attached. The boat exploded with a loud crash that scattered all of the swamp birds around her.

That was close, she had to keep moving. Then, she saw another one circling the area. She ducked behind some grass and waited. As it flew on her side of the tree, she braced her right hand and placed her best shot at the object, which was less than three feet long and maybe four or five inches wide. She missed. She fired three more shots. One of them connected, causing a massive explosion in the sky.

Now, would there be more?

Matalina had taken no chances by constantly staying on the move, rushing from one clump of trees to another. Hours later, she found her way back to the shack. No one was there, including her driver or the car. Someone had cleaned the scene.

Without any other options, Matalina started to walk along the small dirt road leading from the cabin. Suddenly, a blue flashing light on top of a four by four vehicle rushed toward her. While this would be a good time to flash her diplomatic card, she decided to wait and see what information she could obtain first. Who called them? Also, what could she really report? The body of her driver and the town car were gone.

The emergency vehicle slid on the soft sandy surface to a stop in front of her. A national park enforcement officer soon emerged on the other side with one of those "who in the hell are you" looks.

With a quick change of plans, Matalina opened her chest level pocket to retrieve her diplomatic card. She didn't have time to waste trying to give details. "I assume someone must have given you a call?" She handed him the card and watched a cocky smile cross his lips.

"No, I haven't received any calls, but I heard a

loud explosion a few minutes ago and thought someone might be dynamite fishing."

"Listen, I don't have a lot of time to explain, as I'm supposed to meet with someone with the CIA in a few hours. Can you arrange for a ride for me into the city?"

"CIA? There're no cabs that operate this far out. The best I can do is to get you a ride on the bus heading to New Orleans." He glanced toward the dirt path of a road. "How did you get here, anyways?"

"I had a driver, but obviously he's not here anymore." While that was a true but sidestepping answer, it would suffice for now. Still, this officer might have some answers to what was going on. "I was looking for a guy named Carlos who lived in a shack at the end this road, but no one was there."

"It doesn't surprise me. I've like almost never seen anyone here. I think this is a place he fishes out of, but I think he lives in the city somewhere." He glanced at the card one more time before he returned it to her. "Since you mentioned the CIA, is there anything going on here I need to know about?"

"I don't think you'll have any more problems here, but you'll have to ask someone else for that kind of information. I'm simply trying to find him to ask a few questions." Carlos had mentioned a family, and how more information in his wallet would help her. She needed to examine it better. Were there hidden clues in it?

"I see. It's just so strange to see the big expensive truck he drives parked in front of such a rundown shack."

"Yes, that would be nice to know." That answered part of her questions. This place had apparently been used as a hideaway, perhaps a safe house for some reason. As soon as she had a chance, she needed to take a better look at the file she had grabbed earlier. "When is the last time you saw him here?"

"I don't think I ever met him face to face, but I assumed that was him in the black Escalade." He raised his hand to ask for a moment. "Let me check with my supervisor for a minute and see if he'll let me give you a ride to New Orleans. Do you have a name of the person you're meeting with?"

"Nope, but I'll make contact when I get there." She lied, since she had met this guy, Nelson, several times, but she knew to keep his name confidential.

His friendly smile soon faded. "Let me see what I can do." Matalina knew it wouldn't be long until he returned to the shack to investigate. The multitude of bullet holes would be hard to miss.

She discretely listened as he made a call. Whoever he was talking to was never specifically addressed, as he simply related the fact that he needed to give someone a ride to New Orleans. While this guy had a badge on his chest, he had never shown any identification. Had she been taken in again? While he had admitted hearing the explosions, he had slyly hid hearing any gunshots earlier.

Since he appeared to be playing her, she decided that two could play the game. He replaced the phone and grinned. "It looks like you have a ride."

She knew if she stepped inside his car, he would attempt to deliver her to others. That wasn't going to happen. "What did you say your name was?"

"Jason–why?" He turned to face her.

"And what's your middle initial?"

His pupils immediately dilated. She had him. He

appeared to sense it and reached for his pistol, only to be kicked backwards into the side of the truck. She grabbed his wrist and twisted hard, forcing him to drop the gun.

His free hand struck out at her, but it was easily blocked by her raised arm. After he regrouped and threw another punch, which she avoided, it allowed her time to grab his hand and pull him off balance long enough for her to twist and shove her hip under his middle. With a quick lift, he went flying over the top of her to land on the dirt. Being such a soft landing it did little to cause damage, but it did give her the upper hand at the moment.

While still holding his wrist, she extended it and twisted again. Although it had to hurt, he didn't even yell once. Showing no weakness was the mark of a trained soldier. Still, she wasn't about to release him for a while. He had answers she needed.

After becoming tired of the standoff, she snapped his elbow and regrouped in front of him as she removed her own pistol. "I'm not sure what all's going on here, but I'm pretty damn sure you're going to tell me."

He shot her an evil grin as the sound of several trucks roared off the main road and toward them. With no time left, she hit him hard enough with the pistol to knock him out before she glanced inside his truck to see the key in the ignition.

After jumping inside, she turned the truck sideways as the tires threw sand and swamp debris into the air. Being such a narrow road, she knew it was soon going to be a deadly game of chicken as she ran directly into the path of the oncoming trucks.

Matalina focused on the two trucks, hoping to

formulate a plan. While one of them pulled to the side, the other one rushed forward, eager to take her challenge. As the distance of close to one hundred yards shrunk, she had images of a suicidal terrorist that would love the chance to die for his cause. Seconds before she made contact, she sharply veered to the right. He attempted to match her movement. After another quick fake movement to the right, she jerked to the left and received a glancing blow to the side of the truck.

With one more truck to go, she slammed the pedal to the floor. Before she engaged this last truck, however, she saw a small clearing on her left, which she decided to take. The main road had to be close. Seconds later when she saw a small fence blocking her way out, she had no choice but to floor the pedal again and crash through it.

The playing field was now even. She turned the truck sideways and looked for cover. She had them cornered, and they would have to face her firepower. Again, the unexpected happened. A small black copter, one she had seen earlier, and one which barely made a sound, flew overhead and landed near the cabin. Would they come after her again or would they make a run for it?

She decided there would be another day and jumped back into the truck. This is one time she needed backup as she lifted the handset and yelled mayday. With a quick look in her rear view mirror, she saw the copter chasing her. It had to be military of some kind, but one she had never seen before. She yelled mayday again.

A voice responded. "Who is this?"

"It doesn't matter. I'm in Jason's truck, and I'm

being chased by someone in a black attack copter who is trying to kill me."

"Please identify yourself."

"Screw this," she yelled, as she tossed the handset to the side and turned onto another small road, looking for any cover she could find. As soon as she ditched the truck, she watched the copter pause for a second, hovering in place. Then, as if it had jet propulsion, it raced away, disappearing in seconds. Had the pilot heard the call for mayday?

She waited several minutes before she returned to the truck, where someone was yelling over the radio for her to answer. After retrieving the handset, she decided enough was enough for today. "I'm back. This is an emergency. Please pass me on to the CIA. I need to talk to Nelson, the head of the New Orleans field office."

After talking to Nelson, she had decided to avoid heading on to New Orleans. After all, that's where her attackers might expect her to be heading. The CIA copter arrived moments after she returned to the small airstrip where she had her pilot waiting for her. She had to get her files onboard before she met with Nelson. The jet would be considered a closed box, and one they had no right to inspect. Whatever she found must be important enough to risk many lives in stopping her from seeing it.

From her brief review of the file, she knew the trail led to Columbia. Although she wasn't sure why, she felt like she would know soon. Talking to the CIA was always a battle of wits, since they wanted to receive information and not give it. However, this time she had information to give them, but would they listen? Since she also needed their help, she breathed in deeply as she headed to the small airstrip office where they were waiting for her.

She recognized Nelson before she got close to him. He often carried a special sense of arrogance about him she didn't care for. Two other men, dressed in dark suits and wearing dark glasses like his, flanked him, but stayed ever so slightly behind him.

He removed his glasses as she neared him. "Hello, Matt. It appears you've been very . . . active lately." Matt, short for Matalina, was a name many people knew her by in the intelligence community.

"I've been getting my exercise the last few days."

"I just heard you filed a flight plan for Columbia." Nelson pointed to her jet. "Do you have any idea what you're getting yourself involved with?"

"Not totally, and I was hoping you might be able to fill in some blanks."

"Matt, what I'm looking at is several suspicious shootings, destroyed property everywhere, and more missing people. I think I have a lot of ground here to hold you for questioning."

"Nelson, we both know that holding me for questioning is the one power you don't have."

"Oh yes, the diplomatic immunity card. You do know those annoying little details can be pulled and you sent home, never to return again, don't you?"

"You can try, but instead, I have information I think you might want to investigate while I'm gone, you know, doing your job for you." She knew she was pushing the limit with him, but he seemed to like it in a weird sort of way. It was as if they understood each other's position, one that was hard to control with various oversight committees breathing down his neck, something she didn't have to worry about.

"I can only imagine what you have onboard you're taking out of the country."

"And as you know, you have no authority to see what's enclosed in a box, which is what the jet's considered to be."

"I know the rules." He glanced around before he continued. "Matt, you asked for this meeting. Are you going to tell me something I don't know?"

"I would consider a trade of information a normal negotiating tool."

"That would all depend on what you have to offer, and what it is that you need."

"Fair enough. I assume you know someone is trying to smuggle high explosives into the country."

"While some factions are always trying to get through, I think we have a pretty good handle on who these sources are and how to handle it." Nelson yawned. "Tell me something I don't know."

Matalina decided she needed to be the one asking questions as she shifted into a more aggressive mode. "What can you tell me about these . . . factions that were trying to kill me today?"

"Are you suggesting you need to report a crime?"

"It takes a lot of effort to clear a crime scene, doesn't it? Still, if you don't need information on how these explosives are going to be delivered, I guess we don't have much to talk about."

"As you know, one of our biggest challenges is to keep the general public safe and . . . shall I say, calm."

"I have a trail going to Columbia, and one only I can follow. I need information on a guy named Carlos.

Without this background info on him, I doubt there will be much to report after I go there." She deliberately held the last name for now.

"Is it alright if I ask why you want information on this one guy?"

"He appears to be a central part of an arms smuggling ring."

"Really! I hate to disappoint you, but the guy I think you're referring to here was one of ours. He had infiltrated this ring to some extent, but hadn't reported much progress to us."

Matalina stopped for a minute to analyze the new information. "I saw one guy die who I thought was Carlos. Do you have a photo of your man?"

She watched Nelson hesitate. Relinquishing the identity of a man undercover was dangerous. "You know I can't do that."

"Okay, let me approach this in a little a different way. Do you have photos of the three guys killed during a reported robbery in the Everglades?"

"Since that's public knowledge, I'm sure we can do that, but it might take some time."

Matalina shook her head. "Allow me." After retrieving her smart phone, she searched the net until she found the report in the morning paper. With photos of all three in the article, she turned the phone to where he could see it. "Is one of these Carlos?"

"I recognize one of these men, but none of them are Carlos."

With the wallet containing all of the information on Carlos safely protected on the jet, she wondered if she should trust them with what she found. "In such a case, I'll assume your man is still alive. It would be good to know who he is, so we can work together on this."

"Not possible . . . I'll assure you." He nodded for the first time. "You mentioned you had information on a delivery system."

"I thought that might get your attention. Since stopping any panic is one of my objectives also, I hope we can work together on this one thing."

"I'm listening."

"In return, if I give you a name, can you give me all of the files you have on them?"

"I wouldn't guarantee all, but I'll see what I can do. What do you have?"

She decided to proceed with caution, since she wanted additional information on what they knew. While the dark glasses he had replaced prevented her from studying his eyes, she had other subtle clues she could use to see if he was lying. His voice being recorded by her wire would be analyzed later for stress. "What do you know about me being attacked by a couple of small drones?"

"Drones?"

"Play dumb with me here and we can end this conversation now."

"And why would you think we would be using drones to attack you?"

"I never said *who* was behind the attack. I simply asked if you knew anything about it."

His hesitation indicated that he wanted to stall her. "Since we're the only one in America with any kind of drone capabilities, I think it would be natural that I make such an assumption."

"There's a saying in America that I like. Assume is a fancy way of saying that you have a belief that makes an ass out of you and me. Am I right?"

"That's close enough."

"I think we can also use another analogy in describing how Americans usually have one major Achilles heel. Arrogance can be a serious weakness."

"I guess we can debate for a long time the thin difference between arrogance and self-confidence. I'm not sure what you saw, but I can assure you that we haven't used any drones to attack you. Why would we?"

Again, she used her smart phone to show a photo of the drone in the sky that was hunting for her. As she allowed him a small glimpse of the object above the skyline of the cypress trees she was hiding under, she stopped. "In such as case, I would . . . assume . . . that you have a renegade group in America, or some serious competition entering your domain."

"*Assume . . . ing* that you have my attention, what is it you want from me, Matt?"

"I'm willing to forward this photo on to you if you'll share anything you learn about it."

"And what else?"

"I've the name of a company that may be the front in this operation."

"You still didn't mention what you wanted in return."

"Simply the file you have on them. I would find it hard to believe you know nothing about them."

"I'll need clearance to do this, as you might *assume*."

"There's one other thing. I don't need this company to vanish before I get more information, which might happen if they know we're on to them. I'm on my way to Columbia in a few minutes to follow their trail. I need at least seventy-two hours to

track them down without you blowing my operation."
She ran her hand through her short, spiked hair. "Mess
this up and you won't get any more information on
what I find out there."

"Obviously, we try to operate as discretely as we
can. A public panic of any kind is what we strive hard
to avoid. You should also know that we have assets on
the ground in Bogota."

"That, my friend, is our one common goal." While
they had different reasons for doing so, this one
interest held them together. His objective was to
protect America from any and all foreign threats while
making his bosses back in Washington look like they
were in control, thus keeping them re-electable and in
power. Her objective was slightly different in that she
wanted nothing to develop that would give any
governmental powers the excuse to move forward with
a new world order.

"Matt, it's been nice talking to you, as usual, in
spite of the fact that this conversation, you understand,
never took place." He motioned for the guys with him
to back toward the black sedan behind them. "Even
with you going to South America for a little vacation
time, I hope you check your e-mail from time to time.
I know I'll be checking mine."

Chapter 6

After safely leaving American airspace and studying the cloud cover below her, Matalina stretched out in the large beige seat aboard the private jet she had hired to take her to Columbia. A soft Italian ballad played over her earphones, giving her time to analyze what she had obtained so far. After lighting her small cigar, she blew a large puff of smoke, the smell of which she hoped the ventilation system would eliminate so that the crew aboard would not have to deal with the resulting irritation. If not, she really felt sorry for them. She inhaled another drawl of her tasty little cigar of which she had earlier dipped the butt thereof into her Turkish coffee.

Pausing for a second, she wondered who this Carlos person actually was. Did someone fake their death using the apparent sacrifice of another man? One thing was for sure, if the CIA wasn't involved, which she still doubted, this new group had to be extremely well-funded and organized in order to be able to clear crime scenes like they had. Although Bjorn's involvement remained a mystery, he apparently had a run in with them also. She now suspected he was long gone, and while she wanted to get back on his trail, this new development took precedence for now.

She used her computer to do more research. She had been told that everyone on the boat that had exploded had been killed. After doing more research, however, she found nothing about the boat explosion, not even so much as a tweet. This group, or the CIA, was very good at covering their tracks.

Still, the question remained about what caused it to blow up. She knew she had caused major damage when she crashed her airboat into it, causing a fire on board, and that the crate that remained behind had high explosives in it. More deaths she was responsible for. This ate at her, even though she knew their deaths may have prevented millions of deaths in the future.

The other possibility was that it was destroyed by someone else wanting to make sure all links to them were destroyed. Could a drone strike have been ordered against them as well?

The captain admitted knowing Bjorn, but refused to answer any questions as to what his involvement was. One explanation would be that Bjorn had established an operation there, a place to hide, until others stumbled into his territory.

Whoever this group was, they had made it perfectly clear they didn't like her messing with their affairs. Since they had a shot at her earlier, she assumed they were more interested in getting the explosives back first, since only after they had them did they launch the drone attack on her. For some strange reason, she wondered if they used this as an excuse to test their drone capabilities, making her a guinea pig of sorts.

The thoughts of the explosives reentered her mind. What kind of explosives were they? She would have the small sample she had managed to grab analyzed soon. While they were powerful, there weren't enough of them to cause major damage. Was panic their main objective?

Finally, she had the drones to worry about. Background information on the aerodynamics company would help, but just how much cooperation she received from the CIA would be questionable for now. Her search on the internet yielded little clues. The only address was in Columbia, and in a small town called Pasto. While the president of this corporation was a Hamza Masoud, a name she suspected was also a fake, she kept searching for Arabic names on the net tied to drone development.

After doing many combinations with the name, she spotted one she recognized. Since Zafar had an aerodynamic background and had studied in Germany, she focused her attention on this guy who was born in Afghanistan. There were no records of him after he graduated, other than him being listed as the president of this one company. She eventually realized, however, that all three names did fit together somehow.

Matalina opened her e-mail account and sent copies of the drone she had taken photos of to the CIA and also to a lab back in Baltonia. While it wasn't clear, anything she could learn would help. She also sent the name of the aerodynamic company to the CIA.

Knowing that she would be there soon, Matalina closed her eyes. While the future of the world was so uncertain, she knew her role in it. She had been bred for her work, and trained by the best. Sure, her parents were hoping for a son. Now, they had to wait for a grandson. Bjorn had been selected as her mate not long after she was born. Just like her, he had been bred to kill in the name of self defense for her country and her secret society, the Maliviziati, hidden away in the mountains of central Europe. With him being ten years older than her, he had learned much, and he was also trained by the best before they were first introduced. His training was ruthless, and his demands on her were beyond comprehension for anyone not born into the life she was so lucky to have.

With a few minutes left, she opened her smart phone again and called home. They would want some kind of update. Her mom answered the phone in a whisper.

"Hello, mom. I only have a minute until I land in Bogota, Columbia."

"I see. Is that where Bjorn's heading?"

"I don't think so. It appears that he was at least slightly involved with this, and I'm still not sure to what extent. I'll go after him again soon." She decided to confess. "I think I'll need some backup on this mission. This faction is large and well organized. I also need to learn as much as possible about drones."

"I can assemble a team for you. Can you send me more details of what you need?"

"Sure, but it might be later today. I don't think I have long to discover anything here. I think they're planning on erasing all evidence of being here soon."

"Matalina, we have another problem here and would like you to join us as soon as you can. While you're here we'll arrange everything that you think you need to finish this new mission. This will also give me time to arrange for the top minds in drone warfare to be brought in."

"Thanks, mom. I love you." Matalina laughed as she ended the call, realizing that her mom had smoothly adjusted into her role as queen. Would she be able to follow her mom and do the same one day?

###

Matalina knew she had to go through channels to get into Columbia, but her diplomatic card would save her a lot of time. As was usually the case, she expected little help, and offered no more than what was needed to gain entrance into their country.

As the pilot pulled next to a gate and began to shut down the engines, he looked over his shoulder. "How long do you plan on being here?"

"That's hard to say, but perhaps for a day or two. You can return to the states as soon as I'm cleared. I'll have someone else come to get me."

He looked a little confused, but nodded his head. "It was nice to be of service to you."

Matalina knew she had to return home soon, and only pilots working for her government were allowed to come close to Baltonia. The final trip inside her country would be by helicopter. Secrecy was imperative to keep their way of life secure. It wasn't just their life, as the whole world depended on them to maintain a balance of power, and to stop the one world order from becoming a reality. Baltonia had been this balancing force for over fifteen hundred years.

The Columbian custom officers stopped next to the jet. Their striking uniforms were bold enough to get her attention. After they welcomed her to Columbia, she handed them her diplomatic card that they scanned and recorded on a form they had with them.

The two standard questions came soon enough. What was her purpose in being there, and how long would she be in their country. While it was almost laughable, since she could tell them anything, she decided to be nice. "I'm not sure, maybe a day or two.

As far as why I am here . . . well, it's not clear yet. I'm here looking for answers."

"Such as?"

"I need to know more about how a company located in Columbia does business with the United States. It would be good for me to have a short meeting with your foreign trade minister, if possible."

"I'll put in a request and see what we can do, but this is kind of short notice to expect much."

"I understand, but my questions are preliminary and not too demanding." She hoped that would satisfy him for a minute. "I also need to arrange a private tour guide, a local pilot, to show me the country."

"There're many here that I'm sure would like to handle your business." He handed her diplomatic card back to her. "Is there a particular line of business you're interested in?"

She decided to drop a bomb shell. "I'm interested in the aerodynamic industry."

"Really! We don't have much of a thriving aerodynamic industry here."

"You do have your own air force and an airline company based here, so there is some." Matalina placed her card back inside her side pocket, sealing it airtight. "Like I said, this is just a preliminary trip to Columbia, and one I plan to use to assess the possibility of investing here."

Appearing satisfied, he motioned to the other guy with him. "We still need to record the reason for your trip."

"No problem. The jet's leaving as soon as I'm cleared. It was contracted just to bring me here. I'll have official air transportation to take me back to Baltonia."

"I see. In knowing that, we'll make this quick, and get the pilot back on his way."

A few hours later, Matalina had managed to rent a car and evade any tails that anyone could have placed on her. The location of the Fischer Design Group's building was on the far side of the city. Although she doubted there would be anyone there to answer questions, she could always hope.

After she pulled in front of the Fischer Design Group building, which looked plain and simple, and not one she would normally think of being a high tech type company, she paused. The part that was the most confusing was that if this group wanted to keep their missions hidden, why have a company address at all?

Even if sitting and watching might be productive, she had no time for such. She eased out of the driver's seat and prepared to get answers. The street looked deserted, so what she had to do would be easy.

She stopped to knock on the door. With no answer, she reached for the handle. The door was locked as expected. While tempted to pick the lock, or simply kick the door in, she decided to check the back of the building first. She glanced around the top of the building as she walked, just to make sure there were no video cameras. In the back of the office building, she found an attached small warehouse with darkened windows which prevented her from seeing inside. Still, it looked vacant as well. Was she too late? Had they moved on, or had the building already been cleared of any information of their operation earlier?

Minutes later she found a way inside by way of a

delivery door that had been left ajar. Security apparently wasn't a major concern of the owners. The place had scattered machinery that appeared to be in working order. The floors were well swept, and the overall appearance was one of a well run operation.

Still, it gave a feeling of being deserted. She saw no signs of anything being produced, or any inventory of raw materials. She searched the disposal bin to only see many tubes and small pieces of plastic parts. What she really wanted was sketches or working prototypes of what they were producing. Could they be developing drones, as she had assumed? Absolutely!

For the next hour she roamed through the building. The bits and pieces of information she found added additional questions she wanted answers to. All computers and paperwork had been removed. She felt sure they had produced something here, but they had already moved it to another location.

Finally, she found more small clues like a piece of an address to a place in eastern Tennessee, and a reference to a mountain village in northern Columbia. While it looked like they were producing the bodies here, the propulsion system and the explosives had to be handled in another location. She had no guess on how many they had produced here.

The central office, where she assumed engineers had designed the drones, had been stripped of all paperwork also. The design tables were cleared. Still, she wondered. She found a few sheets of drafting paper and laid them on top of the table. With a small amount of graphite she rolled it over the paper, hoping to get any impression from any indentations left on the table. Whatever they worked on last might be there.

She strained her eyes, as she eventually saw a

design materialize. It looked like a small plane. This would be all she needed to confirm what she had suspected. She went to work on the other drafting tables until she found more leads she had hoped for, several phone numbers. She would have to analyze and research these later.

While she was distracted in obtaining this information, she barely heard the front door close. She wasn't alone any more. She turned and pointed her pistol in the direction of the door as three men walked in, two of them armed.

The one who was unarmed had on a well-tailored, double breasted suit and a bright red tie. The gold around his neck and in his mouth indicated he was wealthy, but had earned his money the rough way. He grinned as he glanced at her pistol before he spoke in Spanish. "I see we meet. From what I understand, you're the one who has been killing my men."

It looked like she had finally found someone who could give her some answers. She needed to keep him in play and talking, knowing that she could take the two men on either side of him out at any time. "I only wanted answers. They're the ones who made bad decisions. Perhaps I can get answers out of you."

"I heard you would be here soon. The answers you want are complicated, as you can imagine. There're many different special interest groups at play." He paused, as if amused by her defiance in front of him. "I'm intrigued in knowing more about you. To have so much power supposedly behind you, why do they send you out to do a man's job . . . and by yourself?"

As she expected, he had been given the basic information on her, but nothing more. Did that come from Bjorn? "I take it you've talked to Bjorn about me."

"This name keeps coming up, but I've never met this guy. One day I hope to. It sounds like we have some common interest." He placed a hand in his pocket before he continued. "Is your operation in the arms business?"

"Nope, that's an easy question, but since I answered, then answer one for me."

"Since you'll never be able to tell anyone, ask away."

"I can tell you're trying to build some kind of drone here. Do you care to enlighten me?"

He paused for a second as if in thought. "This space was rented to a company that did aerodynamic research, and just like many tenants, they didn't stay for long. That was too bad, they paid well."

She wondered if he was the owner of the building. If so, getting his real name later would be easy. "It does appear they left in a hurry. I hope you were paid up front. However, I do have a question I hope you'll answer. Why here?"

"It would make sense that they wanted a place to test their designs without being seen. No one uses my part of the country in the jungles without permission."

Matalina edged her hand toward her vest as she watched the men tense with her slow movement. "You can relax. I assume it's okay if I have a smoke." She removed her small carton holding her favorite cigars. "Do you care for one?"

"Thanks, but no. I prefer my own." He squared his shoulders in her direction. "You know it's bad for my business to have it known that a girl killed my men and I'll have to make an example out of you."

"You can try."

He motioned for one guy to move closer. It was time to get his attention. Within the blink of an eye she fired two shots, one at the hands of each man holding a pistol. Their guns went flying, followed by screams of pain coming from both men. As the one on the right reached for a backup, she kicked him in the middle of his face, possibly breaking his nose. As he stumbled backwards, the other man looked on as if trying to decide what to do next. Her pistol raised at eye level made him freeze. "Please, don't shoot!"

As the leader backed toward the door, she refocused on him. "Going somewhere?"

He stopped and grinned. "Who are you?"

"A girl with an attitude and questions. Shall we continue?"

"Perhaps, but you're a dead person. You'll never leave this country alive."

She decided to push forward while she had the chance. "How do I find Bjorn?"

"I don't know. I told you that I've never met him."

"Then how do you communicate with him?"

"Just like the jungle here is my domain, the Florida Everglades are his. Call it . . . professional courtesy."

It was all fitting into place. The drones were being tested and built here and smuggled into America by way of the everglades. Still, all she found smuggled was explosives. "It's not like Bjorn to be part of a terrorist group."

"I never said he was part of any terrorist group."

"Which is what you are, right?"

"I wouldn't call us that. We're only trying to

defend our rights to do business. That's all. This guy, Bjorn, is an obstacle we ran into. I think he has been convinced to relocate."

"And would you know where that might be?"

As he started to answer, a barrage of bullets ripped through the room. She hit the floor as she saw him get hit in the head, knocking him backwards. Seconds later, all was quiet. Was that it?

She rolled over and saw where one of the other men had also been shot. The third one had disappeared out the door they had come in from. As she went after him, she heard him yelling while he fled the building. A lone shot made her realize the attackers were still outside. She scurried for cover on the far side of the room. One quick glance over the top of a small cabinet area confirmed he had been shot while attempting to leave. How long did she have until they mounted another assault inside the building?

With another quick glance she noticed blue and red light flashes bouncing off a car parked on a side street in front of the building. Were the police already on the scene, or were they the ones who had fired at them?

After glancing around the room, she saw nothing substantial to hide behind, so she decided to work her way to the back of the building and the way she had entered. She stopped by the two men who had been shot long enough to remove any papers they had with them and their wallets. Any information she could obtain might help.

Moments later, she eased out the back door that, surprisingly, had no backup covering it. Surely, the police would've thought to do this. Since she knew they would be there soon, she walked along an alley until she found a way back to the main street. With her black hood covering her hair, she turned to study the activity in front of the building. They were in a standoff situation, obviously waiting to see if anyone else was inside.

As she moved further away she still had one main question. Were they the ones shooting, or were they the ones responding to a shooting? She glanced at her car that was still parked close to the building. Would they be able to trace it to her? Since it was about a half block away, she didn't think so. Nevertheless, she would make arrangements to get it later.

As she walked away, she knew that she was going into the jungle soon, but that she needed to wait for her team to arrive. While they were getting prepared, she also needed to do some aerial reconnaissance. Since it was too late to do that today, she searched the net on her phone to find a place to spend the night. She needed time to put some of the pieces together.

Chapter 7

Matalina finished smoking another cigar of which she had continuously dipped the butt thereof into her Turkish coffee. After tossing the butt to the ground, she slowly finished her coffee before she walked around the six passenger Cessna one more time before she loaded the rest of her gear. The pilot, a Pedro Moreno, started to object to the heavy load, but changed his mind when she handed him more cash. The sweat popping out on his forehead confirmed just how nervous he was. "Lady, are you sure you want to go there? It's not safe. I know much more beautiful places to show you."

Matalina knew how to fly, but she needed someone who knew the hidden world beneath the jungle. Flying directly over the various drug lords operations would not be smart. Hopefully, this pilot would know those locations. "I need to get a feel of the land and see for myself what it's like there. If we run into any problems we'll immediately leave. Is that okay?"

"Okay, we'll see what we can do, but please trust me when I avoid some areas while pointing to them from a safe distance."

Matalina knew the trail led to the jungles of Columbia. From her research the night before, she had already identified the man who owned the building. This owner also worked for several drug cartels there, providing them with any manpower they needed, often in the form of hired killers. He was a wealthy businessman who owned many properties in Columbia. Someone didn't like her talking to him, but who? The police report was vague in reporting how he had been killed in a gangland-style shooting. There was no mention of her being there.

The part that kept her awake all night was the fact that she had been in the sights of killers many times, but they had always withdrawn instead of attempting to finish the job. Why was this?

Her gut feeling was that Carlos had been used to smuggle something into America and was then eliminated to keep it a secret. She understood how Zafar's grudge against America could be exploited and his help obtained. Since the building owner had mentioned the jungle before he died, there must be more there. Perhaps this is where the explosives or the drones had been moved. His land holdings in the northern part of the country were easy to locate on the tax records.

She had a lot of territory to cover, but she thought she had an idea of where to start. Still, this was an area that the drug lords wouldn't like her flying over. Even finding a pilot who would take here there had proved to be difficult. Worst of all, she was sure that word of her wanting to fly in these jungle areas would get back to them, and they would be waiting for her. Drawing their fire to flush them out was risky, but she was prepared for this. If she had to bail out of the small plane, she had a small parachute that would come in handy. The team she had assembled the night before would be able to retrieve her if needed.

Moments later, the small plane lifted off the ground and quickly gained altitude. Matalina knew that Pedro would feel more comfortable flying high, but she wanted a closer view. Still, she decided to slowly push him. From the air she saw what she was facing. What was she thinking? This would take forever to search.

An hour later she knew she was wasting time at this height. "I need a better view." She pointed to one area she had marked along a small river.

"Hmm, that's a bad area, not too safe."

"I understand, but I can see all I need in just one pass." She produced more cash.

"Okay, but just the one pass, please."

"In such a case, let's make it a good one. Also, make it slow enough so that I can see everything." Since he had accepted the money, he would have little choice in agreeing now. She hated using him, but she needed to draw their attention. She knew they were waiting for her somewhere.

Although seeing the area was very unusual, it produced nothing she could use. She would have to get on the ground to see any better. At the end of the river where it trailed off into the mountains, she pointed to the left. "Let's circle the mountain here and see what is on the other side."

"That area is isolated and just has one small airfield. The original tribes still live there, but no others venture anywhere close."

"Isolated is what I'm looking for." She watched him proceed with caution. On the far side of the mountain she could see nothing, but wanted a closer look. "Can you take us lower?"

He casually pointed out his window. "There's nothing to see on this side, but as you wish."

She looked for the small airfield he had mentioned. The solitary spot where there was a break in the forest landscape was ahead. When he saw it, he slightly veered off to the right. "Please, let me have a closer look at this spot."

As he complied, she watched him glancing around, studying the area below them. With him covering the left side of the plane, she concentrated on the right. The runway was short, and only an experienced pilot could land and take off from such. Perhaps it was used most of the time by helicopters. "Do you know why they have this here?" She pointed to it again.

"The drug lords in this country have many places they have used and abandoned. I think this must be an old base from sometime in the past."

"It does look rather forsaken." She mentally marked it on the map, since it might prove to be a good place for her team to establish a base later.

Suddenly, something that looked like small birds at first started to scatter under them. Rather than flying in a group, they separated in many directions as they soared along. Seconds later, she realized what was happening as she pointed at them for Pedro to see. "I think you were right to avoid this area. I'm sorry. Do you think we can outrun them?"

Pedro hesitated for another few seconds as they watched them climb. "I think these are small model planes. They won't be able to match our speed."

"Pedro, these are drones! I have already seen them in action. I think they have a rocket propulsion system attached to them."

His reaction was instantaneous, as he quickly rolled to his left and went full throttle. "If that's true, I doubt they have much of a range."

So far, all was going as planned, but perhaps it

was too easy. They wouldn't have given away their hiding place, knowing they had no chance of destroying the plane. She searched for others, ones that the pilot may have inadvertently flown into range of from a pre-planned ambush. Her presumption soon proved right as she saw the smoke trail behind a small missile heading right at them. With her left hand she reached over and pushed his stick forward, sending the small plane into a dive while banking to the right. Pedro glared at her for grabbing his stick, but soon relented as he watched the approaching missile.

It would be close. If there was a lock on her plane, it would be over in seconds. As the missile gained speed, the plane edged out of the path, missing a collision by mere feet.

With the added speed, she glanced at Pedro. "Sorry about that, but we need to climb out of their range now." As he fought the plane to gain attitude, she searched for more drones. At first, she thought it was over, but then she saw another streak of smoke to her right. "Bank left–now!"

As he did, she lost sight of the missile which disappeared under the plane. She held her breath and rechecked her jump suit. She might have to bail any second. She started to breathe out when she felt the bump, but instead of a loud explosion, all she saw was a large burst of light.

Pedro arched his eyebrow as he studied his instrumentation. "I think we're okay. We have to run for it now."

"Agreed!"

With each passing mile she felt safer. The airport at Bogota wasn't too much further. Surely, they wouldn't attempt such an attack so close to the capital.

As she heard Pedro making contact with the tower at ten miles out, asking for clearance to land, she leaned closer. "No one is to know about this attack . . . agreed?"

"I have to see what kind of damage is done to my plane. It might have to be reported."

"I'll pay for any damages, but I want all evidence we recover–deal?"

"Deal." Pedro's hands were now visibly shaking. She closely watched him as he trembled, knowing that she might have to help him land. "Lady, I don't know who you are, but I hope we never meet again."

Matalina smiled as she placed a hand on his shoulder. "Don't worry. I won't bother you anymore." Again, she had placed an innocent man's life in danger, but at least this time, he was still alive.

After Matalina emerged from the Cessna, she dropped to the ground to check the bottom of the plane. A black scarred area caught her attention. This had to be where the small drone hit them. The fuselage looked stable but defaced as if a small blow torch had seared the outside. The explosion wasn't powerful but hot. She remembered how the trail behind the drone had disappeared just before they banked. This exhaustion of fuel must have slowed it just enough to keep it from penetrating their fuselage.

She used her knife to start exploring the area of impact. A small amount of the missile was embedded in the lower fuselage. Somehow she had to find a way to remove this section of the plane and have it analyzed.

She watched Pedro crawl under the plane with her. "Wow! That was close." He was still shaking. She knew he might not be safe for a while. They would track him down. She needed to help him escape and find a new identity, but first he might be able to help her a little more.

As she slid out from under the plane, she raked her lower teeth over her upper lip. "I'm so sorry to have placed your life in danger, but I've a deal for you."

"I'm listening."

"I'm putting together a team of people to go back into the jungle." His eyes darted around as she spoke. "I want you to go with us. Your knowledge of the area will be very valuable to me."

"You're crazy."

"You stay here and they'll find you, and they just might kill you. You have a much better chance of survival with me. After this is over, I'll help you relocate to another country."

"What about my plane?"

"Consider this my plane now, and I'll buy you a much better one after this is over."

"You can do this?"

"Absolutely! Now help me get this part of the plane removed and safely stored somewhere. I need to have it analyzed."

With the chances of the mountain site being cleaned and abandoned soon, Matalina knew she had to hurry. An assault by air would be suicidal now. The dirt bikes would be the fastest way to get inside the jungle stronghold, where she suspected they were making the explosives, and then perhaps assembling the drones as well.

She needed to know how many they have made already and where they had been shipped. Bjorn may have intercepted some of them, and may be even on to where the next batch had been delivered. It wasn't too unlikely that he might just be an ally this time around. However, that still remained to be seen. Since he had turned traitor, she couldn't trust his motives any more.

The team consisted of five men from Baltonia who had been specifically flown in for this mission. Even if Pedro could help with his knowledge of the area, he wasn't a military-type guy who was capable of joining in on any fighting that might break out.

From the maps obtained by satellite, there were three routes into the area, but all of them looked challenging. Teams of two would hit each one. Pedro, who had some experience on a dirt bike, would stick with her. Since there were many drug production operations in the area, they needed to be careful and move through the area as fast as possible.

She wasn't sure which route the men from the drone assembly plant would be using to leave, which is why they had to cover all of them. As soon as one of the teams made contact, the others would have to find a way to join them. She knew this would take strong communication skills from everyone on the team.

As she rounded a sharp bend, she spoke into her mic. "Okay, guys, it's time to check in. Let's use short but precise messages. I'll go first as Team One. It looks like we have some hill climbing to do on our side."

"Team Two reporting in. We're on the other side

and encountering a lot of mud. I doubt if they'll be coming out this way."

If this was true then she knew that Team Two could rejoin them soon.

"Team Three here. We're on a trail that looks like it has been abandoned for a long time, but it's not too hard to use. If this continues we'll be making good time."

If this was also the case, she realized she was on the most likely one they would use. She slowed to study the climb ahead. It was going to be a challenge, and one better suited for a horse than a bike. She hoped this would be the worst of the trail in front of her.

After a quick glance at the men behind her, she attacked the incline with dust spraying everywhere. When she was almost half of the way up, her bike slipped sideways and fell over with her on it. She repositioned it and tried again. The slick mud made it stall again. She backed off on the throttle and tried a slightly different line to the right. It felt like she was only inching forward. Still, she was gaining on the hill. Finally, she hit a firm footing and accelerated for a few feet to a point she could take a small breather and reassess her route to the top. She had no doubt she could make it, but she worried about the others, especially Pedro. At the top of the next small hill, she found a place to rest and watch those below her make a run at it.

With a hand signal for Pedro to come next, she waited to see if he could make it. She needed him. His bike slipped over when he hit the first rough spot and his motor died. "Get up, you have to keep moving," she yelled as loud as she could.

Pedro attempted again and fell almost at the top of the next small ridge. He surprised her with his strength and pushed the bike the extra five to ten feet to a spot where he could readjust and prepare for the next ridge. With the next being the worst section to climb, she offered more encouragement. "Come on, you can do it."

He gunned the motor and attempted the incline with much more confidence, but he suddenly hit another rock he couldn't get over, causing his progression to come to a complete stall. Getting moving again would be hard. She pushed her own bike to the side and started to descend the hill to help him climb the rest of the way.

When she yelled for him to wait, he apparently didn't hear her as he made another attempt. The front of the bike hit the small boulder again and went over the top, barely missing him as it crashed down the hill, and over a side cliff. Damn, it would be impossible to recover.

A minute later she reached him and offered him her hand to help him above the knoll that gave him so much trouble. He looked embarrassed as she attempted to make him feel better. "Don't worry about it, you can ride with me."

As they made it to the top, where she hoped they wouldn't run into any more hills like this one, she waved at the other team member to join them. He scaled the hill with ease. He waited for her to tell him how they would handle the problem. To carry Pedro with them, they would have to make room on the back of her bike. Some of her equipment would have to be reloaded on the team member's bike. They had to move fast.

She spoke into her mic to let the other two teams know she had been delayed. They had reported having a much easier path now. With all three paths having different degrees of difficulty in traveling to the outpost ahead, she understood why they had built the small landing strip there. It would also make it easier for her to surprise them. Once they secured the base there, she could order in a helicopter to take them back out.

A couple of hours later she calculated that they were all within a few miles of the base operation. They would all have to walk in from there. No one had seen anything. Her satellite report showed no one had flown in or out of the post either.

She decided to give the order for everyone to move in closer and take up positions where they could better monitor the operations. Even with the thick canopy of tree tops above her, she glanced above her often when she found openings, hoping there were no more drones in the air. She could imagine one being loaded with an infrared camera and locating their heat signature. The bikes would definitely be hot, and they would prominently stick out.

"Listen up. We're all close now, and I know they have some drone capabilities. If you see any at all, report in and take cover. We can assume the control center is inside one of the buildings. Our best chance of success here is to take it as fast as possible."

As all members checked in with their positions, she turned to Pedro. "Here, take this. You might need it." She handed him a Glock twenty-one. "Stay close."

Team Two reported in next. "We have contact. There's movement around several buildings."

"Good. Spread out and wait for us to get there.

81

We're not far."

Team Three reported in next. "We have problems. Take a look in the skies. I see many of these small drones circling the area. I think they're on to us."

"Damn! Take cover. Try to hide your heat signature and get ready for an assault. We'll have to move fast." She motioned to Pedro. "Make for that small cliff and hide under it. Use any leaves or other debris you can find to hide. We'll come back for you."

"I want to come and help you. I don't mind fighting."

"The best way to help us now is to keep us from being discovered. Here's a radio also. We might need you to act as a command center for communications. I have a helicopter we can call on to help get us out of here."

He finally agreed as he accepted the radio and rushed toward the cliff. "Let me know what I can do. I also have a score to settle. They're the ones who have ruined my life here."She knew that, and she would make sure he would be properly relocated. She owed him that.

Suddenly, she heard a small buzzing sound above her. Had they found her? After taking cover, she waited until the sound had disappeared. With quick hand signals she sent Pedro on his way and the other team members in a direction to the left. They had to split up.

Minutes later, she heard a small explosion on the other side of the building. She assumed the worst and that one of her men had been killed. Since it was time to attack, she ran forward toward the back of the building, looking for any cover she might need on the way.

After closing in to within fifty yards of the largest building, she saw movement. Several men who were carrying rifles had climbed on top of the building. Two others were concentrating on the direction of the explosion. Before they realized they had been attacked from all sides, she had to get closer. A fifty yard dash carrying over one hundred pounds of gear would take all of her energy, but she had no choice. Seconds later, a quick glance to her left confirmed that her team member was also closing in.

The two men spotted her as she made the last run across a small opening. She dropped to one knee and fired, and immediately hit the first one with several shots. The second one hid behind a chimney top before she had a clear shot. As she waited, she knew this would soon expose him to her other team member.

Then the unexpected happened as another drone streaked across the sky, taking out her team member. She saw some movement from him on the ground, indicating he was still alive. To save his life, she had to act fast. After pulling an explosive from her belt, she rushed forward, hit the five second timer and threw it on top of the building.

The guy behind the chimney ran away from the charge, but stopped to fire at her. He missed. She didn't, as the explosion rocked the top of the building. Did it take out the other men?

With another drone positioning to her right, she had no time to guess as she ran for the door to the building, throwing her weight into it, knocking it open. The drone exploded into the side of the building as she rolled forward on the floor.

As she regained her footing, she heard more gun shots from the top of the building. Somehow, the men there had evaded her charge, and were engaging her men on the other side of the building. She would help them in a minute, but first she had to find out who was controlling the drones. They had to be in a room somewhere in the building. She glanced at a lot of paperwork and drone parts scattered around the room. She had hit the mother lode, but first she had to secure the location and stop any more drone attacks on her men.

With a single door leading out of the room, she rushed forward and kicked it open, but moved to one side, anticipating some gun fire in exchange. There was none. After darting inside, she saw many computers, but no one in control of them. Jumping into one of the chairs she went to work accessing the computer, which was being remotely accessed.

Overriding the remote access, she watched a control panel giving her access of the drones. She saw images of her men in the photos, they had been targeted and she had intercepted the firing button just in time. She clicked on a home button, assuming that would bring them back to their base. She waited and watched the camera shift in direction before going blank. An explosion suddenly confirmed they had been destroyed instead. Had she been overridden?

At least her men would be safe. She yelled into her mic, "The drones have been destroyed. Try to take the men on the building alive. We need them. I'm in the lower part of the building now and have it secured."

"Matt, we see no more hostiles on top of your building, and we may have already eliminated everyone there. However, we have new movement in a hangar-looking building to your north and next to the small runway. Do you want us to intercept?"

"Do you see any kind of aircraft there?"

"If there's a hangar door, it would be on the other side of us. I definitely saw movement there a few seconds ago."

"Cover me in case there's anyone left alive on the top of this building. I need to make sure no one is preparing to make a run for it." She paused. "Also, someone check on my partner, he got hit, but he was moving."

Seconds later, she made one last glance around, hoping to have more time in a minute to analyze this place. Bullets shattered the side of the building as she made her run toward the hangar. One man on top of the building yelled that he wanted to surrender as he tossed his gun to the ground below. Good! Still, she had to make it across the opening to the hangar.

After making it half way across to it, she heard a helicopter engine roaring to life. She ran harder as she watched a small black copter, one she had seen before, rush along the clearing while gaining some altitude. She stopped and fired, but she knew it had escaped her range. She would love to know who was on it. Now, was anyone else inside the hangar?

She rushed to the side of the building and edged along it until she reached the hangar door. The voice of one of her team members soon confirmed that he was approaching from the far side. She would give him a minute to get in position.

Finally, she yelled into her mic. "Okay, let's go in together." She immediately saw him when he rounded the other corner. She dropped to one knee and leveled her pistol as she glanced inside. No one was there. The hangar was covered in drone parts scattered all over the floor and several work benches. She also noticed one additional small plane that either had been abandoned, or was used as a backup.

As she started to relax, her team member rapidly pointed to a blinking light. She had little doubt what it was. "Run!" she yelled as she knew she had been set up.

The expected explosion shattered the building and knocked them to the ground seconds after they had rushed away from it. The back of her head hurt from something hitting her. She fought to stay conscious. She studied the other guy who lay lifeless next to her. Was he dead?

As she struggled to sit, she saw the small black copter returning, as if to see if the job had been completed. It swiftly cut her off and made her a sitting duck in the open. Where were her men? She tried to stand, to find her sidearm, but she had nothing available to defend herself with that she could find.

Then, she heard a voice behind her, Pedro. "Stay down." She watched him level the gun in the direction of the incoming copter. Seconds later, he emptied the magazine as he fired at the copter. One or more of the bullets must have found their mark, as the copter veered to the right. Otherwise, it appeared to be undamaged from the bullets.

After recovering, she forced her way over to the other man and felt for a pulse. Nothing. "He's dead." She felt the back of her head and studied the sticky sensation of blood. How bad had she been hit? She glanced around for the copter and finally saw it disappearing to the east.

She yelled instructions to the other men on her team. "Get out of the other buildings now. These guys love to play with explosives." Her body felt weak, but she had to help get them out. Several steps later she felt herself stumbling, but luckily for her, Pedro reached under her and helped her toward a group of trees on the far side of the building. What remained of her team pulled the only survivor with them as they rushed from the building.

As expected, another building suddenly exploded. Debris flew in all directions as she hit the ground again. Had her men gotten far enough away? She turned and looked through the smoke. Good! She saw them moving. They were alive, but hurt.

With a new burst of energy, she quickly managed to cover the distance to them. After a quick assessment, she knew they had also received injuries from flying debris hitting their backs, but it didn't appear to be life threatening. They still needed medical attention. She called for her copter to come get them, since the chances of the black copter sticking around now were remote. She assumed from the size of the blast that some kind of governmental agency would soon arrive.

The man they had captured was in much worse condition. She had to keep him alive. He had answers she needed. She lifted his head and yelled at him in Spanish, "Talk to me, how are you?"

His eyes focused on her with a deathly stare. "I don't want to die."

"Listen, I'll do what we can for you. I have help on the way." Then she saw the blood coming from his leg, where a major piece of broken wood had penetrated his thigh. She started to remove it, but reconsidered, knowing it might add to his bleeding.

Matalina yanked the medical kit from the back of

her team member's pack, looking for something to use to stop the bleeding. With her knife she sliced open his pants to have a better look. She had to stop the flow of blood. Using the remnants of the pants, Pedro used them to keep pressure on the wound, hoping to stop the flow. "Hold this, and I'll be back in a second," Pedro yelled, as he grabbed her hand and directed it to the wound before he continued. "Trust me."

Minutes later he returned, holding some red clay he had retrieved from a nearby hill side. "This isn't going to be pretty, but it'll keep him alive." He used the mud to coat the area around the wound. True to his words the red covered clay absorbed the blood and made it look much worse, but she knew it would stop the flow soon enough as he kept coating it on top of the wound.

Her helicopter pilot called in to check on them. "We have medical personnel on board. What are we looking at?"

"We have multiple injuries and several dead. Someone needs to stay here while you make several trips. We also have one guy in critical condition that I need to keep alive. He'll need some blood and a doctor to remove a piece of wood from his leg."

"Understood, we'll be there in about ten minutes."

Since she wasn't sure how much she would get out of this guy later, she decided to push for some answers now. "What's your name, and what do you do here?" Even though he was in pain, he attempted to resist telling her anything. He moaned as he glanced at his leg. "Listen to me. I'll try to save your life. Just remember, it was your people who tried to kill you. Do you want to live?"

While he acted like he understood, he hesitated.

"My family, they will hurt my family."

"Trust me. They'll come after your family one way or the other. If you truly want to help your family, tell me what you know." As his eyes glazed into another world, she slightly shook him. "Hang in there and talk to me. Help is on the way."

He glanced at her with glassy eyes. "What is it you want to know?"

"I want to know who is behind this operation, and exactly what you're planning to do with these drones." She waited for an answer, knowing he might die any minute.

"I only know that it's this guy from Afghanistan who forced me to come here. He has been here several times, but I've never been allowed to directly talk to him."

This confirmed part of what she had assumed earlier. "What are you planning on doing with these drones?"

"I heard they're going to be used in the United States. My job is to test them here. They want us to find a way to increase their range by using upper air currents."

Was this the truth? "That would take a lot of expertise and money to design. What are you planning on attacking?"

"Several places . . ."

He faded away again as she violently shook him. She had to know. She clicked on the mic to check on the inbound pilot. "How much longer?"

"We'll be there in a few minutes. Are you sure the area is secure?"

"I think so, but keep your eyes open."

She glanced back at the guy who was still

breathing, but now unconscious. He had to make it. As she turned her attention to her men, she knew they all needed medical attention, all of them, including her.

Chapter 8

As Matalina glanced out the side window of her jet, she recognized the mountain range which descended into the small landing strip just north of Lake Como, Italy. The puffy white clouds radiating in contrast to the bright blue skies made her relax. She felt at ease, listening to the gentle hum of the engine, and just knowing she would soon be home to the sweet smelling mountain air she loved. Maybe it was her medication, but a dizzy sensation swept across her as they descended.

After landing, she would take the governmental helicopter to her castle compound in Baltonia. This is the way the Maliviziati had hidden their mountain top fortress for years. Although there was only one highly guarded road in and out of her country, this mountain fortress had many caves that extended for hundreds of miles in all directions.

Minutes later they were onboard and flying low along a river leading into the mountains. This would make tracking them almost impossible. After landing, the copter would be rushed into its mountain hangar, a large complex that had been created to hide their entire air force, one she hoped they wouldn't ever need, but available if such ever became necessary.

The brief stay in the American hospital she had been flown to had stabilized the wounds to the back of her head, but the small concussion she had received would take much longer. Although this had given her time to think, she knew the trail would be long gone before she got back on it. Time was the one thing she knew she had little of since they could now be reestablished somewhere else in the United States.

The guy they had captured was alive, but unconscious after he had slipped into a coma from the lost blood. While he would hopefully recover, he would be a special guest in her country for a long time. Later he would be resettled, but only if he cooperated and helped her learn more about this imminent attack on America, and anywhere else they planned to attack.

While the two weeks back home would give her some time to recover, she knew she had many other duties she had to attend to. Being paraded as the princess of her country was something she hated, but something she knew she had no way of escaping. She had never been a girly girl type and hoped that another person could take her job there. Still, she knew it was her destiny, just like it had been for her mother.

Also, it wouldn't be long until she would be called on to produce an heir to the throne. That had been so carefully planned, long before she was born. However, with Bjorn's actions, the future of her country had been shaken. He now posed a major threat to their way of life, their very existence. He knew much about the Maliviziati, which had grown into a small country hidden inside the mountains of central Europe. Their money had made this possible for over a thousand years. The actual connections of many of these families went back to the creation of their secret society–the Maliviziati.

The royal limo was waiting for her as she stepped out of the copter. This one had been specifically made for her, highlighting her love for white gold. Only a few knew of her exploits into the world that she lived when she ventured outside the compound. Many expected her to be the charming princess who would be queen one day.

In this hidden society of the Maliviziati, consisting of the super rich from around the world, she knew many of those here lived much different lives in their alternate country. This was the place to relax and bind together for the mutual benefits of those of the same wealth and beliefs. Decisions were made here that affected everyone around the world. Many of the central families here had been at war for over one thousand years with those who eventually formed the Illuminati. While a few members of the central families lived there year round, citizenship was granted only to those specially chosen to be a part of their society.

Matalina relaxed as she walked into her stateroom inside the mountainside castle. This was the one place she felt like she could truly rest, which was something she needed to do to be able to fully recover.

Still, when she was here she needed to stay in shape and perfect her skills. Vic was her trainer, a guy she looked forward to seeing again. Of all of the men in the world, he was the only one who could get the best of her in hand-to-hand combat. Still, this was what he had spent his life perfecting, and he also had the genes from his past, much like her, that gave him a superior advantage. She needed his special skills, since Bjorn had betrayed his country, and most importantly–her.

At thirty, she knew she still had some time to do what she did best. She had served as the enforcer, the special operative, the one person who could go where no one else could. She had been trained to kill since she was able to walk. Her country, Baltonia, was extremely important to her, and she would do whatever was required of her to preserve it.

Several maids scurried about to take care of her. In this domain she wasn't expected to do anything for herself, which was so different from what she did outside these walls. Allowing others to do this for her had always been hard, but something her mother had taught her that would be expected if she wanted to be queen one day.

As she allowed herself to be undressed, she studied her room. A large spa on the terrace slightly above her had a great view of the mountains. From the movements of several maids, she knew it was being prepared for her, but first she would receive a full massage. A table was ready, and an oriental-looking woman was standing ready to give her full treatment.

A female doctor walked over to her first. "I think I need to take a look at your wounds first and see what needs to be done."

Matalina laughed as she glanced over her body. Some princess! She had battle scars everywhere. Even the best cosmetic surgery in the world couldn't hide all of them. The glue from the bandages stung her forehead as he removed her dressing. While she hated to admit it, she was lucky to be alive this time. The wounds to her back were painful, but healing well. Although she wished she had time for more cosmetic work, she could easily hide this and work on it later. She only had the two weeks to heal, and to somehow become an expert on drones.

As soon as the doctor finished the dressings, Matalina allowed her body to relax as the massage started. The fingers felt so nice as her muscles melted under their touch. Being pampered had its rewards, but she knew this wouldn't last long. Still, she knew this would be good in speeding her recovery.

With her mind floating, as if lost in time and space, she remembered the good times with Bjorn before he had changed. She fought to avoid thinking about how he had ruined her world, concentrating instead on their past. They had been lovers for over seven years. Within the next year they would've been presented as a royal couple, giving him the future title of king.

His hard muscular body had fulfilled her on many occasions. Yes, the physical connection was intense, but it was the inner connection of their minds that was even more so. They had been so careful not to get her pregnant. As things worked out, she could only be so thankful now.

She felt herself getting wet just thinking about him. The magical fingers on her back didn't help. This woman was paid to do anything she required, but she had never allowed another woman to give her sexual satisfaction. This would now be Vic's job later. He had so usefully stepped in to fill the void after Bjorn had turned traitor.

Matalina slowly squirmed as she drifted deeper into her hidden world. Thoughts of making love to Bjorn returned. Despite everything he had done, his past would be hard to erase. How could he have done what he did? She would love to know, to ask him, but she also knew that she would hesitate from doing what she had to do when she found him–kill him!

###

It wasn't until later in the evening when she was finally given admission in to see her mother, the queen. The formality of such meetings is what had her hating this life, but she knew it was expected.

At last, the staff was excused and the doors closed, giving her the chance to drop the facade. "Hello, mom."

Her mother quickly lost her composure and rushed to her. "Matalina, I've been so worried about you. Are you okay?"

"I'll be fine, and I just need a week or two to heal more." She kneeled to allow her mother to stroke her hair.

"The council will be meeting in a few days, and they'll have many questions for you. They're concerned about what they have heard." Her mother reached for a glass beside her. "Do you want something to drink?"

"Brandy would be good." She gave her mother a hug. "I don't think they're going to like what I have to say, but they need to know."

"I agree, but they all have faith in you, and I think they'll be inclined to give you whatever support you need." She walked to a cabinet and poured her daughter a large brandy. "I've managed to bring some of the top minds on drone technology here this week, as you requested. This is a threat we need to quickly address. They also will be installing a new laser facility on top of the mountain here to destroy anything that comes into our airspace, but it'll take a while to become fully functional."

"I agree that we need to push this forward as soon as possible, since Bjorn knows our defense systems well."

"Matalina, you don't think he'll try to directly attack us again, do you?"

"I don't think so, but I don't know him anymore either. It's just a matter of time until I find him. However, I need to stay on this new threat for now. I thought he was involved, but that's even questionable for now. I know he ran like hell when he found out I was after him."

"You know your father will want to see you before the meeting that starts the day after tomorrow."

"I understand how he wants to be properly prepared. Is he here?"

"No. He's in Germany, meeting with several people. He has to convince many that he's completely in control of this situation that's making many people nervous."

"I'll be ready to tell him what I know and what I need when he's ready."

Matalina ventured into the training facility. While she wasn't completely healed, she still needed to stay in shape. The equipment there was all world class, with a biofeedback computer monitoring her every move and output. Since the results could be compared to her earlier records, she had to work hard and she knew it.

It was time to start stretching and warming up to get ready for her first real test. Just how far could she run at full speed? What was her limit? In a life or death situation, she had to know. She knew the best test would be the dreaded four hundred meter. Vic would be there in a few minutes to get her started.

After ten minutes of stretching and preparing her muscles, she watched the door open and Vic walk in, dressed in all black, the color he preferred to wear. She realized she had missed him much more than she wanted to admit. His body was extremely well-toned, and perfected for the job he had been given. Although she directed the activities of the most advanced Special Forces in the world, he was the one who trained them. In fact, when she was gone, he was left in complete charge of them.

In keeping with his no nonsense persona, Vic marched toward her, making him one of only a few that wasn't intimidated by her. They had worked together for a long time. If anyone could find a weakness in her from her injuries, it would be him. Then, it would be his job to eliminate it.

"Hello, Matt. It's good to see you made it back. How's the head?"

"Healing, but it should be fine soon."

"I talked to the doctor earlier. We agreed that any hand-to-hand combat is out of the question for at least another couple of weeks, maybe a month. It would be too dangerous."

"I wish I had that kind of time, but the trail will be gone soon and an attack using some drones might happen before then." She could smell his presence as he moved closer. "I'm required to be here for two weeks for some meeting. I'll use this time to heal, do research and form a new team to help me."

"We have the records on your past physical performance, so this should be a good indication of any loss of your abilities." He pointed to the equipment. "We've made some new advancements that I think you'll find interesting. Are you ready?"

"Yes, I need to know what my limits are." She allowed the machines to check her stats. Her weight was one hundred and thirty nine pounds, height measured five feet and ten inches, and her body fat was six percent. Next, her blood pressure came in at one hundred and ten over seventy, with a resting pulse rate of fifty seven. She laughed, knowing there had been no changes in her readings.

While she knew she had the genes for an Olympic gold in many sports, she had dedicated her life to her family and her country, and most importantly, to the Maliviziati, all of which she loved. As the machines analyzed all factors, including a small blood sample and her oxygen conversion rate, she waited for the final results. The mobile readers would be worn during her test.

Vic walked with her to the start of the track that was an even one hundred meters. She would have to make four circles. Each would be calculated as to percentage of her maximum speed. While most men in their best of shape can reach speeds of sixteen to eighteen miles per hour, she had been clocked at over twenty many times. The top recorded speed for any humans was clocked at twenty seven miles per hour by Olympic sprinters Michael Johnson and Donovan Bailey during one of their Olympic competitions. She beamed as she remembered setting the record when she went through CIA training several years ago at twenty five, not far off the mark of the best in the world.

When she was on a mission she often had to move fast, be it either running for cover or chasing someone. Knowing exactly what she was capable of was often a matter of life or death. She toed the starting line with the pent-up of energy of a cheetah and waited for the word to start. Every aspect of her test would be analyzed.

With a portable reader, Vic glanced at her. "We have everything ready and emergency medical personnel standing by, just in case." He motioned to the side room where a nurse studied them.

Matalina closed her eyes for a second before she breathed in one last breath and exploded onto the track. No one, not even she, could run full out for four hundred meters, but she would give it her best. For ten seconds she pushed for her top speed, a critical part of the analysis later. Trying her best to maintain it she pushed on without too much stress.

She made the first lap, hoping she had a good time, but now concentrated on the next lap, which started to stress her muscles some. She knew her time was slower, but still good. As she crossed the line on her second lap, she glanced at a clock for feedback. At twenty one seconds, she was doing great. Now, came time to fight the pain, as the third one hundred lap destroyed most who attempted such high level speed.

The acid quickly built in her muscles. She had to block it, as she imagined herself in the field, being shot at while she raced for cover. Each leg hurt as she pushed on. She had to press on as she could see the time slipping away. Her speed had slowed too much. Just ahead, she saw the line and the clock ticking off the time. Her vision was too blurred to make it out.

As she neared the line, she saw Vic running beside her, yelling at her like a drill sergeant should. "Come on, girly, push it! What's to matter with you? Your pussy got you sidelined? Can't make it with the big dicks? Want to quit . . . girly?"

He knew how to push her buttons. She hated being called girly. And . . . she really hated being referred to as a pussy, especially when she competed in a man's world. She pushed on, giving it her all to pass the line. Now, the real test began–the last one hundred meters. Just being able to complete it after such a fast speed would be a test of what she was really made of, and often the difference between making it to safety and being shot in the open.

Vic continued to run beside her. He wasn't going to allow her to coast. Her heart beat faster, there was nothing left to give her energy but pure lactic acid she was drawing on. Her speed dramatically slowed, but she kept going, grasping for air just to keep her lungs from burning.

Finally, she could see the end of the last lap ahead. Knowing she could collapse after she crossed it, she moved on, not giving her muscles, her lungs, or her heart any choice. Vic continued to yell. "Come on you weakling, don't you die on me now, girly!"

The word *girly* did it as she pushed on. As soon as she crossed the line, she felt like falling to the floor, but he caught her and held her with his rock hard muscles, reassuring her that he wouldn't let her fall. What would her time be?

Several minutes later they finished the last circle in a slow walk. She saw a small bed waiting for her. A little time to recuperate would be nice. She knew she had to wait until she had fully recovered before moving on. The amount of time it took her was also an important thing to know.

As she recovered, she slowly reopened her eyes to see Vic smiling at her. "For a girly, you weren't so bad." She forced a small smile.

After standing and stretching for a moment, she glanced at the monitor and the results. The first lap was ten point two seconds; the second lap was twenty one point three seconds, with the third lap coming in at a remarkable of twenty nine seconds. She was fine with the last lap, which was well over a minute since her job was simply to make it. Her top speed burst at the beginning was twenty three miles an hour, a speed only an elite few men could match.

So far, her injuries hadn't affected her performance, but this only presented the first of many tests she had to complete. Next was swimming, and she had to start this within the next few minutes. The distance she had to cover was one thousand meters. Additionally, she had to swim this in full fatigues.

Minutes later, she could feel the burn in her legs again, but her arms were still strong. She pushed on, drawing on every reserve she could find. With him in the water yelling at her again, she managed to finish. Her time was seven minutes and two seconds. Still, it was a great time.

It would be good to have time to recuperate, but Vic pushed her harder as he had the nurse assistant hook new monitoring equipment to her. "Okay, girly, it's time to do some pushups. You got one minute, so let's see what you're made of."

This was one of the tests she enjoyed, since her upper body strength was always good. One minute later she recorded one hundred and twelve pushups. She rose to her feet after she finished, shaking more lactic acid from her arms. "What next?" She glanced at him, knowing she could stand on her own.

"As you wish, sweetie. On your back, you have one minute to give me some sit ups. Come on! Don't take all day, girly."

She breathed in deeply as she dropped to the floor and rolled on her back. Over the next minute she counted out one hundred and eight. Not bad, but she had done better before.

"Matt, we can keep going, but I think we both know you're in good physical shape. However, I still want to check out one more thing. Since you received a concussion, it would be good to see if this has affected your balance any." Was he referring to a balancing beam, or a drop in the water where she would have to find her way out? She waited as she watched him studying her. "Are you sure you don't want to wait until your head gets better?"

"The tank may have to wait, but we can try some other tests."

Walking the beam was the easiest of tests, except when they added complications. This beam shook, and rotated at various times. A mirage of lights was also added to distract her. Each movement would be analyzed.

Minutes later, she was on the beam and ready. At first, it was fine, and then she felt her balance off center. She stumbled, but managed to climb on again, and again she lost her balance at the first sign of difficulty. Had the injury caused problems with her balancing? Eventually, she had to agree that it had. She might need more recovery time than she had thought. She definitely needed more testing and time to recover.

Vic had her do many more tests while evaluating her on each one. There was nothing wrong with her core strength. This was a new feeling that she had never witnessed before. Finally, he smiled at her and directed her to stand in front of him. "Okay, girly, I think this will answer many questions. It's time for you to pretend to be a ballet dancer."

With Vic close to six foot five, he towered over her. She knew what he had on his mind as he lifted his hand high above her, waiting for her hands to join his. A small edge of nervousness crossed her thoughts as she reached upward and felt him using his strength and guidance to spin her like she was a top for over a dozen spins. When he stopped, he let go of her, but she knew he was close.

She staggered to her right, and then back to her left. She lost her balance and staggered twice before she felt his arm around her, giving her support. It was almost a minute before she recovered. It felt like she had been on a heavy night of drinking.

He softly spoke as he rubbed her shoulder. "I'm not sure if this is from the blow to your head or you're developing an inner ear weakness. We'll need a doctor to do more tests and see what can be done."

This wasn't fatal in her ability to carry out her missions, but it was a weakness she needed to work with. She wasn't perfect, and she had some other weaknesses like bright lights that blinded her for a period of time until she could focus, thus the need for her sunglasses. "This is a bummer."

"I think we need to wait for the doctor before we continue. We have two weeks to work with you." He reached around her to hug her. "I want you to be safe, and the only way to do that is to make sure you're in tip-top shape."

"Thanks. The doctors want to do some other tests on me tomorrow. I'm sure all of this data from today will help them." It felt good having him hold her, a submission she allowed no one else. That is, since Bjorn disappeared out of her life. He was also the only guy she had sex with now that Bjorn had betrayed her and his country. They both knew it was extremely important no one else ever knew of their affair. Additionally, she knew how important it was to not get pregnant. The baby she produced would be king one day. The father of her baby would be chosen by Matalina's father. While this was much different from other girls around the world, and especially for those living in America, she never questioned this. She had simply accepted this as the way it was since she was a small girl.

Still, she was growing more and more dependent on the ecstasy generated by having sex with Vic. Their meetings were full of lusty emotions that weren't restrained by demands on the other, but a full understanding of giving and receiving earthly pleasure to each other. "Vic, I need to take a long bath and have some good food before I see some advisors. I'm expected to see my father tomorrow morning."

"I understand." He kissed her cheek, holding his lips close to her for an extended time. "I know you're tired and sore from your last mission."

"Yes, but I want you later tonight." She hesitated in using the word she really wanted to use–need, but it was honest. She needed his attention.

"As you wish. I'll never disappoint you, my princess."

"You never have." Princess! He seldom called her that when they were alone but used it as required in front of others. "A princess is what I am, and what I have no control over. Tonight, however, I want to be the most wicked woman you've ever had–

105

understand?"

"Perfectly." He grinned, showing off his brilliantly white teeth.

###

Later, as Matalina stepped into the tub, she felt the hot water, relieving the sore muscles she had pushed to the limit today. It was time to shut out the world for a while. These moments alone were the only personal life she had ever known. It made her almost feel embarrassed for taking them. The perfumed water cleared her head, making her relax even more. Still, there was simply one real reason she allowed herself to be pampered–she needed to heal as fast as she could.

In a few hours she would be meeting with some of the top intelligence people in the world. They would all be demanding answers, tough ones that she couldn't give at this time. These were citizens of Baltonia, but people who also retained dual citizenships in other countries. Their network of cooperation centered here.

She selected some small fruit pieces and enjoyed their freshness before she added some of the different cheeses chosen for her. The soft Italian music lowered another layer of her tension. She knew the tune but not the words, despite hearing it many times.

Although she was naked in the tub situated in a large room, she felt safe and secure. She had never thought of herself as sexy or desirable. On the contrary, she assumed it would take a very hard up guy to want her. While her breasts were firm, there wasn't too much to them, and not like the sexy goddesses she had seen in the world outside of Baltonia, the trophy wives she had seen on the arms of some of the most wealthy and powerful men in the world.

The spiked white hair she felt comfortable with had to be covered during the meetings and public appearance with a blonde wig that made her look like a fairytale she had no interest in. She knew the demands placed on who she was, but could only suffer through it for so long. She preferred action and adventure to looking like a silly little sex object.

Even the veneer covers she had to wear over her white gold capped teeth had to be made special. She had the tendency to bite right through most of them. Her teeth were a weapon that had served her well on many occasions. Still, she remembered the time she had been captured, forced to grind her teeth to stubs as she chewed her ties in two in order to escape. The easiest part to cover was her nails. A coat of enamel nail polish would easily hide the white gold alloy she used to turn them into lethal weapons. And even when she had them covered, she still had them available if needed.

There was one more reason for the night of pampering. In a few days she would also be tested for any mental weaknesses. She doubted anyone could ever capture her alive, but if they did and attempted to torture her to gain information about her family, country, or the Maliviziati, she knew she wouldn't break. To her this was much more valuable than her own life.

Moments turned to minutes as she enjoyed the soft warm water. Sex with Vic was always a powerful erotic experience. She wondered what it would be like to one day actually sleep with him all night. Would that be asking too much? More importantly, would it cause her to become more dependent on him than she could effectively control? She didn't need any more weaknesses.

Eventually, all good things must come to an end. She had to dress for the meeting. She was sure they were all waiting for her.

The large meeting room that had been selected tonight had been specifically designed for this kind of meeting. All fourteen spaces had been filled. Each location was equipped with every electronic device imaginable. The room was also extremely well monitored in case any problem arose. The security outside their castle was on high alert, in spite of their country never having faced any challenges in the past. A retreat inside their mountain complex would stop even atomic bombs from reaching them. This was perhaps the most fortified place on the planet.

The walls, covered in amber, made the room glisten in a modern display, while retaining its historical reverence. Electronic gadgets were always useful, especially when they could be kept out of sight until needed. She had been given the seat in the center, not so much in honor, but in respect to the fact she would be the focus of attention.

This meeting was formal in many respects, but it was still simply a briefing before the more serious ones that would be held over the next two weeks. The meeting was to be held officially in Italian, which she knew everyone understood.

She stepped forward and acknowledged everyone by name as she made her way around the table to her spot. These were the real controllers of the world. Their advice was taken as sacred by not just the kings and dictators around the world, but by those advising elected countries that considered themselves to be free countries. Everyone there, as their parents before them who had fought the predecessors of the Illuminati, now continued the fight against its splinter groups with their lofty goals and ambitions for a one world order. By far these were honorable men who had the interest of mankind at heart, with many of them having direct linkage to the beginning of the Maliviziati. They had all seen the evils of a one world order. The visions they adhered to made them fiercely opposed to any groups like the Illuminati and its plans to rule the world. Both respected the power of the other to some extent, since neither side wanted another world war, or being exposed to the general public.

The Maliviziati had done a much better job of hiding than the Illuminati inspired factions had. The two opposing secret societies had learned to coexist in some respects, but fight it out in other ways around the world. Stopping any infiltration into their country had been a demanding job, but one they had achieved with a stiff hand. Those allowed to come here to live had to be specifically invited.

Finally, Matalina made it to her seat as she waited for one elderly gentleman to hold her seat for her. This was such a farce, since she knew many of these men knew she was a warrior and one of the best operatives in the world. However, to keep peace and observe traditions, these charades had their place.

She briefly checked her monitor before she spoke. "Gentlemen, it's so good to see everyone. I wish I had more information to give you on my latest mission, but it's one I need to pursue heavier inside the United States." She watched everyone focus on their monitor. "You'll see the various men on your screen that we've connected to this plot to use drones in America. If you have more information on any of them, your help would be appreciated."

For the next hour she went over the men she had suspicions of being connected before she waited for their input. While she gained some insight, she also had other names added to the file. Almost like a damp fog hanging over the room, she felt the tension mounting of one impending question, and one she didn't have a good answer for. What was Bjorn's connection in all of this?

Vanhesson, the German financial mogul, eventually added to the meeting. "Raising the kind of money required to succeed at this plot of using drones has to be a daunting task. That is, unless one of the Illuminati splinter groups isn't involved. Therefore, I'm inclined to believe they are . . . at least in some fashion. This might be the perfect way for them to persuade many governments to yield control to a central one."

Matalina glanced at him. "Agreed, but do you have any direct knowledge of them doing so?"

"No, I don't . . . and another possibility exists. They could have backed this on a side note hoping that it would never be traced to them. It could be financed by a single member of their committee of silent hands. If this had the full backing, it would be much better financed and I would've seen evidence of it." He paused for a moment. "Additionally, the main guy we seem to have in our sights was trained in aerodynamics in Germany. He was gifted and appeared to be obsessed in becoming the best. I think I know why."

"If so, this could help." Matalina thought she knew the answer, but she would love to have it confirmed.

"It was several years ago when Zafar lived in Afghanistan. A drone attack there missed its target and hit his house, killing his entire family. He watched them die. They say his mother was buried under the rubble where she cried out for hours until she died from a loss of blood."

"I know that had to be tough on him." Matalina added.

"When he attended school in Germany, he had made many friends who were sympathetic to his past. I can only assume they're working with him." He retrieved a handkerchief from his pocket and wiped his forehead before he entered a code into his panel. "These are all known associates he made when he was there. I hope this helps."

"Thanks." Matalina watched the files flash on her monitor. She saw almost forty new people she would have to research and memorize. She studied each one in detail. Suddenly, she stopped. One of the men she recognized. Do we have photos of Mario earlier? If he now worked for the CIA, this complicated everything. However, in reality, was the CIA playing him, or was he playing the CIA? Since she didn't know, she decided to keep this information private for now.

"There's one more source that still worries me– Bjorn." Vanhesson turned his attention in both directions before he continued. "I know we all hate to discuss this, but the facts are fairly clear. Since he knows he made enemies here, it wouldn't be unreasonable to believe he might be looking to build a new power base."

"Although this has been discussed many times, it might be good to analyze the new information obtained on this mission." Matalina motioned for him to continue. Many of these men had developed good relationships with Bjorn earlier. It was his actions that got him expelled from the group. During many meetings earlier, his motivations have been questioned and discussed. It always centered on if he was doing what he thought was best for the Maliviziati, or for himself. There was a lot of evidence to support both arguments.

"I'm glad to hear you say so. I'm, for one . . . still trying to understand him."

"First, I think everyone here knows how I feel, since he's responsible for the death of my sister. Still, to be objective, I'll share what I can from this mission." She reached for her glass of water before she continued. "I had obtained word he was in the Florida Everglades. We all know he's in hiding, and this would be a good place to do so. In the process of tracking him, I ran across explosives being smuggled into America. I should have the full analysis of what kind these are in a few days. I can say that they're a military type, but not American made."

Another man asked a quick question. "Were you actually able to make contact with him, or in any way document that he was there?"

"I never *actually* saw him there, but one guy told me he was there earlier. He also acted very scared of him. There's a strong possibility that someone accidentally intruded into Bjorn's place. However, there's also the possibility he's the one who gave safe passage for these smugglers."

Vanhesson spoke again. "I think we all know Bjorn wants a more direct confrontation with any new world order group and all who support them."

Matalina didn't like having to defend Bjorn, but she knew he was frustrated in not being able to follow his own beliefs. "This private war with the Illuminati and its fractioned groups has lasted for centuries, and the best we can ever hope for is a balance of powers. An attack on them will simply play into their hands of increasing governmental protection and control."

"I think the people in this room will agree with you, but Bjorn is . . . shall I say . . . more of a dreamer who thinks he can bring these new world order groups to their knees with a full attack on their power."

"And we all know how his first full attempt in Africa went. Millions of innocent people were slaughtered in one of the largest genocides in history. Africa has many natural resources that can be exploited, and by those who place no value on the lives of the people who live there." She watched many of the men lower their heads in respect. Bjorn's actions had torn the council apart in many respects, but made it stronger in others. The ensuing battle for control of the central council of the Maliviziati was fierce, but Bjorn had been defeated and banished from Baltonia. Exactly how many men he had taken with him wasn't clear, but she had the name of his four main supporters. They were all on her list to find and bring to justice. They all represented a threat to the Maliviziati.

While Matalina kept asking questions and obtaining additional information, she spelled out in detail what she needed. "We need to increase research on laser protection systems, not simply for here but for everyone. I think we all know this is just the first wave of drone attacks that we have heading our way."

Vanhesson stretched his arms. "I think we all know Germany has a lot of interest in this new technology, and we'll do everything possible to build these new systems, but it takes money and time."

"I think I speak for everyone here that we've little time, and all of us are willing to spend more to double or even triple the research. While you're working on what you need, I'm putting together a team to go back after this renegade group which I now suspect is assembling in the States."

Another man, a military leader from Russia spoke next. "Isn't this a job the CIA should be doing? It's their turf."

"I'm sure they're doing what they can, but there're several things to consider. The Illuminati descendants, especially those of the Freemasons in America, would love to see an incident occur that the government there could use to push for more governmental control. While this group of terrorists I'm after is apparently looking for revenge and a way of having drones removed from warfare in the future, I think they're also leading the way for others to see the potential use of drones against other nations."

"I understand. I've many assets available for you in America if you need them."

"Thank you," Matalina replied with a smile before she turned to Vanhesson. "I think it would be good for me to make a quick stop in Germany to discuss drone technology there. I need to know as much as possible so I can finish this mission."

"Matalina, you know you have my full support."

An hour later, the meeting ended. Now, she had to

be able to put all of the pieces together and brief her
father tomorrow morning. As she closed her eyes with
the last man walking out the door, she knew she
needed a diversion. Time with Vic would be perfect
tonight.

When she had called Vic, he acted as if he had
anticipated her call. As always, this was expected to be
nothing more than a physical release for her. However,
satisfying him also never bothered her, since the fact
of doing such made her feel even more so in control.
Next to having sex with Bjorn, he was the best at it.
He was much bigger than Bjorn, which added to her
pleasure.

As she knocked on his door, she pulled the white
robe closer around her. The slight chill sweeping
through the castle made her wish she had told him to
start a fire in his fireplace. His bed was comfortable,
but thoughts of the bare floor in front of a raging fire
sounded perfect for the night.

The massive dark oak door to his room squeaked
as it opened. She patiently waited for him standing on
the other side to acknowledge her. He wore a white
towel wrapped around his waist. His body, which
looked like it had been chiseled out of granite, glowed
with a healthy tan that surprised her. Had he been on
vacation somewhere himself?

"Vic, thank you for seeing me. I think you knew I
would be calling on you." She winked.

He raised a finger to his lips. "There's no reason
to say a word. It's my job to keep you in the best shape
possible. You don't need to have any frustrations or

distractions from hindering you."

"Thanks." Okay, so he admitted the obvious. This was just part of his job, and it wasn't love, but pure sexual satisfaction for her. He didn't even offer her a smile as he reached for her hand, pulling her inside his room.

"It's chilly outside tonight, so I started a fire. While it builds, what would you like to drink?" From the fresh smell of his skin she knew he had just finished a bath, apparently getting ready for her. With his bright yellow hair still slightly wet, a closer look at his face revealed smooth skin which had been recently shaved. For a lover, he had never disappointed her in making himself totally irresistible to her.

"Brandy would be great, thanks." She was ready to jump his bones right this minute, but she knew she had all night. She never drank too much, but tonight brandy would be great.

She settled in a Queen Anne designed chair which was next to the fireplace as she watched him place a small table in front of her. After he walked to a small bar area on the far side of this sitting room, he retrieved four brandy glasses, two of which he filled with hot water and carried to the table first. Interestingly, he offered her a small smile, a rarity.

After returning to the bar, he lifted a canister holding the liquid gold and smelled it first before he made the perfect pour. If the glass rested on its side, the brandy would extend to near the edge of the rim. His walk back over to her allowed the towel to slightly separate as he walked, making her want to see his giant tool she needed tonight.

"It should be ready in a minute." He leaned the glass holding the brandy on its side so that it would rest on the one holding the hot water. As the intoxicating smell of the sweet brandy filtered over to her, she closed her eyes for a second to concentrate.

She had too much on her. This diversion into a purely physical world of lust would do her good and she knew it. Although some citizens of Baltonia expected her to be a fairytale princess, waiting for her charming prince to sweep her away, she knew it would simply be a matter of time until her father would inform her who that might be. Until then, she needed to fulfill her needs as a woman, so be it with Vic.

Several minutes later, she opened her eyes to see Vic patiently waiting for her. The brandy had to be warm by now. As he handed her the glass he caressed her shoulder, tenderly massaging it at first before he increased the intensity. "You look tired."

"Mentally, I guess I am, but it's also frustrating that I'm stuck here when I need to be back on their trail in America."

"I'm sure that will happen soon enough. I'm putting together a team for you now. You need to be prepared to cover a lot of territory this time. I have one of the best explosive experts on the team, several pilots who are experts in aerodynamics, and one guy who is a top notch sniper."

"Good, when will the team be ready?"

"Within the week. I want to work on getting this coordinated and up to speed based on all of the data we have to date. I know you still need to do some more healing, and we need to do some memory testing. I still have some concerns about your concussion."

"Don't worry, I'll be fine." Matalina dreaded this much more than the physical test she had often

117

subjected herself to. Still, they were invaluable in letting her know what her limits were.

With his face maintaining the same solemn, but pleasant charm, he lifted his glass toward hers. "Good enough, we'll worry about it later. The fire will be making the room much warmer soon."

She touched his glass. "Vic, thank you for taking care of me and never demanding anything in return."

"Perhaps I should be the one saying thank you, since you're one of the most fascinating women in the world." Vic's eyes had always illuminated in this brilliant blue color that had the ability to penetrate most people around him. She often wondered, amusingly, if he might be partially bred by arctic wolves that had such intensely blue eyes.

Matalina relaxed as she held the brandy that had been produced not far from the castle. "*Interesting* is a good word, I guess, to describe me. I know I'm not the typical sex goddess many men of the world desire." She ran her hand over the top of her head and brushed the spikes of hair on top, as she thought about the day she decided to cut her hair. Establishing who she was had helped to define her, a female warrior with an attitude. It wasn't so much that she was antisocial–far from it.

Vic snuggled closer to her side. "I guess that depends on what a man, any man, wants in a woman. The inner beauty of any woman far outshines the outward appearance. At least it should, if the man has any substance to him." Of course Vic would think like this since he was one of the most athletic men in the world, while also being very mentally demanding of all of those he trained.

Matalina raised the glass of brandy to her lips and

tasted the heat, a true creation of a work of art. Many people could make brandy, but only a few could bring it to its ultimate quality like this. As the brandy slipped down her throat, she felt the first rush of heat spreading across her body. "Well, what I am, I am." She closed her eyes for a second and drank in a much larger sip of the liquid gold.

"Relax as long as you wish, my princess, we have all night." Vic gently lowered the robe off of her shoulders and massaged her bare skin. His fingers were strong, but sensitive to every fiber of her muscles. He had the incredible ability to play every single muscle with just the right amount of pressure.

"Ahhh, that feels good." The hard training, the days of battle in the field had all built muscles, but often resulted in scars she would have to live with forever. She knew there was no one else in the world she would allow to touch her like this. In this ever changing landscape of evil coming from the various Illuminati splinters, she couldn't let her defenses down. Still, she needed this time of bonding with the human race to let her know what she was really fighting for.

As she felt Vic slide behind her and massage her with both hands, she knew what he was doing. To prepare her for the intense love making they would enjoy later, she needed to clear her mind of all worldly distractions. She heard the fire crack with a sudden blaze of light which barely registered through her partially closed eyes.

As expected, she felt the robe lower to her hips. The warmth of the fire and heat of a lotion Vic had applied to his hands kept her more than warm. He worked in the lotion first over her shoulder and then

119

along the full length of her arm, stopping at her hand to grasp it slightly, as if a lover would to reassure his partner that they're connected and can trust each other.

Was he trying to put her to sleep? She hadn't had a deep relaxing sleep in a long time. She had hoped for sex, but how could she resist this?

After he worked the other arm, he skillfully removed her robe and forced her to stretch out on her stomach in front of him. The same magical tonic soon covered her entire backside, where he worked his magical fingers over every muscle. Eventually, he concentrated on her feet. With all of the trauma they had suffered, she hoped he would be gentle here. He must have understood as he continued to pamper her.

She must have drifted off to sleep for a second or two until she felt a cooling mist sprayed over her. She knew the reason for the mint smelling lotion. It was time to revive her, to bring her to an enlightened stage.

Vic soon centered on her rear, squeezing it forcefully, working muscles that needed attention. As she felt her mind clearing, she turned onto her back and glanced at the towel he had on. She slightly arched her brow, as to ask when he planned to remove it.

"I hope I don't disappoint you. I know you want tonight to be special." He dropped the towel, revealing his massive manhood.

"Vic, you've never disappointed me." She kept looking at it, as if she had never seen it this large before. As she reached for him, he returned the attention to her. He had her wet and ready in seconds as her level of arousal hit afterburners. The internal heat he had her generating vastly outperformed the lotion he had used earlier.

He laughed. "I'm glad." He leaned forward, as if

to give her a gentle cozy kiss, before he gradually kept building the heat behind his strong rugged lips which massaged her even stronger than his fingers had worked on her body earlier. The moisture in his lips overpowered any lotion he could have selected. But . . . there was more–the scent. He smelled so manly, so earthy that she inhaled his aroma, intoxicating her senses deeper with each passing moment.

With one hand increasing her heat below and one teasing a breast, she again realized just how fantastic a lover he was. When he parted his lips and slipped a tongue across her lips, it felt like he was going to devour her with a rasping rush of taking her completely under his control. His tongue soon slipped into her mouth, a dangerous move for anyone who knew just how powerful her jaw and teeth were. Should she bite him . . . slightly . . . teasingly?

He removed his tongue before she could decide, apparently knowing just how far he could push the limits. Without pausing, he moved on to her most sensitive place, the nape of her neck, which exposed her to a vital weakness anyone would search for during battle. However, this wasn't a battle. This was a trusted relationship.

She was ready. He had to know that. Just how far was he going to take her until he allowed her satisfaction? She squeezed his manhood hard enough to get his attention. "Vic, I want you, and I want you now!"

"Good." He paused for a second to secure protection, something they both knew was extremely important. Any child produced would be king one day.

"Yes, very good."

"Enjoy, my princess." He had no reason to

121

proceed gently. That wasn't what she wanted. She spread her legs as wide as she could, allowing him to slide on top of her. His body was massive, but hard as a block of granite. He also offered the one thing she needed, consideration of his heavy weight, as he used his elbows to support the crushing effects it would have on her.

"Vic, tonight, I'm simply a woman who wants to be completely satisfied." As she guided him home, she felt him thrust forward, as if he had finally lost control. His size hurt for a second before explosive signals to her brain overrode everything. She yelled, but not out of pain, but with an ecstasy she had suppressed so many times in her life.

He was strong, powerful, and perfect for her. Much more than she could ever admit . . . publicly. Still, she had him tonight.

CHAPTER 9

The royal guards, dressed in elaborate uniforms of purple and white, designed by the best tailors from Milano, were on both sides of her as she marched in to see her father, the king of Baltonia. Her shoes clicked on the stone floor before coldly echoing off the walls of the castle. Even with the modern designs and technology below them in their fortress hidden there, the castle above retained its unique character of a medieval fortress or abbey, including the musty damp smell that overrode the last remnants of her morning Turkish coffee she wished she could have enjoyed more.

When she becomes queen, this farce of royalty would be removed. Damn it, he was her dad! Still, this was his court around him for now. Many of these never knew the real side of her, Matt, the woman who was much more warrior and operative than this helpless, princess girl type pushed upon her. If there was a way to avoid this future, she might take it.

While sitting in a large chair in the center of the far side of the table, her father stared at her as she entered. He had been bred, just like her, to assume this position. He had been a mighty warrior, a man of action, earlier. Now, he was a mighty administrator, judge, and arbitrator of the peace. One day she hoped she had time to talk to him about his past.

After he stood to welcome her, the guards turned and left, leaving only about ten other people in the room. Her dad looked to be in extremely good health

123

at sixty-five. She hoped he would remain so for a very long time, and this would give her more time to do what she really liked, and what she was best suited for.

Her father pointed toward a chair that had been reserved for her. "Hello, Matalina. Please have a seat." She knew her mother usually used this chair. He wanted to talk to her alone and she knew why–a future husband.

Several of the men around the room glanced at her. There were no women in his inner circle. When she became queen, that was something else that would definitely change. "You look good, father." She selected her words carefully, knowing that everything would be criticized by this inner circle as they made recommendations to her dad on her future.

"I've been briefed on your last trip. There was a lot of collateral damage that had to be covered. If all of this is true, we might be facing some major challenges in maintaining a stable world that we see as the best for everyone."

"I agree that this takes precedent over all other operations." She reached for a file she had with her. "This appears to be the central figure in our current problems. He's an Afghanistan national who has apparently prepared for this mission for a long time. He's highly trained in aerodynamics, and that makes him very dangerous."

"I understand, and we've ordered intelligence from many sources, but tried to do it with discretion. I think we all know how many governments will use this to their advantage and ask for further policing powers."

"That's exactly the problem, but I think we have auxiliary problems that haven't surfaced yet. While this guy is focusing his energy directly against America, his knowledge and expertise may be utilized by others with a wider target."

"We know this operation is expensive. What have you learned about who is behind this?"

"This is the one piece of information I don't have yet. We have one terrorist we captured and hope to get info out of, but we have nothing yet. The others I've managed to find haven't lived long. It's obvious they want to cover their tracks. They're also extremely well trained on cleaning scenes and controlling the media."

"That sounds like the CIA in operation. I know you occasionally meet with them. We also have had some contacts, but it appears they're holding many cards they're not disclosing."

"I think it's a combination of many factors. They know much more than they're telling, but I also think they're being played by one of their own." Matalina handed him another photo. "The CIA thinks this man that I refer to as Carlos Rico is a plant inside a group of terrorists, but I'm suspicious that it might be the other way around, and that someone has tried to hide their identity by faking a death."

"I'll see what I can find out for you on him. What else?"

"I also know you want to know about Bjorn. There's some evidence of a connection, but it's not clear. I even see a small chance that he stopped the explosives from making it to the source in America. Somehow the explosives I found were destroyed by someone. If it's not Bjorn, we might have an unknown ally this time."

"We have one of the most advanced laser protection systems in the world here, but it's one Bjorn

125

knows well. If he obtains this new technology in drones, he could use it against us."

"Do you think Bjorn really wants to wage war against us?"

"I think he has already tried once, but was defeated. However, he would love to be king."

"If I had married him, this would happen automatically, so why the play for power?"

"There's a lot of differences from being in control and being a figure head with no power. He's a strong headed guy who can be a major threat to us even now that he has been banished from Baltonia and any contact with the Maliviziati."

"You know that it's simply a matter of time until I find him and destroy him."

"With his resources, that might take a lifetime, and you do have other duties to perform. You're the only one who can claim a direct linkage to the throne, and your mother and I aren't getting any younger."

"Father, you're just sixty five and have many good strong years ahead."

"I wished everyone on the committee shared your opinion. I've been asked how much longer we can leave you working in the field as an operative."

While an operative was a good modern word for a warrior, it failed to capture what she knew was her true nature, the one she was born to live. "I think we should both have twenty more years to do what we're doing now. That's plenty of time to accomplish missions that can't wait. Until I have a child who matures, we'll be left without an enforcer to run these operations."

"The word is that after giving birth, the child can be raised for you while you're still active. This might be the only way."

Matalina closed her eyes at the cold impression his words left in her heart. "Even that would mean I'm out of action for several months."

"I understand, but it might be the best course of action, otherwise, you might be pulled early, and I know you don't want that. Additionally, you'll need to produce several children, since we've seen firsthand what can happen." He chuckled briefly as he recovered. "We both know that a son would be much better."

"We can talk about this later, but not now. Too much is at stake."

"I just need to give the committee word of what to expect."

While she didn't really want to know the answer, it did feel like the best time to ask it. "Since Bjorn's out of the picture now, do I have any rights to ask who has been selected to replace him?"

"Matalina, I know you're seeing the world in a new light and how many foreigners view our practice, but it's still tradition here. This isn't the time to expect a love child, but one selected to lead the most powerful group and country in the world. Even if it's more of a secret society, Maliviziati has operated this way for centuries."

"I've no problems with traditions, and you know I love my country. I just know that it'll be hard to replace Bjorn with his background and genetic makeup."

"You're much smarter than most people. As a father, I also want you to be happy and have a good life. Being queen will be different for you, and it's something you'll have to adapt to then."

"Father, you know I'll do what I'm called upon to

do, but first you have to give me time to find and destroy not only Bjorn, but all of his followers."

She watched her father shift in his seat as he refocused on that problem. "Bjorn did take several of his closest friends with him, all men who could cause major problems for us as well. Tell me what you know about where they are, or what they're planning."

Matalina was prepared for this and reopened her file she had with her. "Eric, the Swede, is thought to be somewhere in the northern part of Europe. The last I heard was that he was attempting to recruit and train mercenaries for his own private wars."

Her father glanced at the photo with disgust. "This is such a shame, since even his father has turned against him. At first, I had my doubts, but after talking to his father many times, we have all concluded that Eric has completely been expelled from his father's world." He returned the photo. "Still, how would Eric be able to fund such an operation?"

"I'm sure finding people to finance his operation wouldn't be hard. I wouldn't put it past some of the descendents of the original Illuminati members to be behind some of it."

"Do you absolutely think Eric has converted this much?"

"I knew him well earlier, and this is hard to swallow, but I also saw how Bjorn changed." She placed the photo in the folder and selected another one. "While he's a threat, he's not the biggest one by far."

He accepted the next photo. "Armando."

"Yes, he was born as a descendant of several kings, men who have power, but not nearly as much as when Spain was a powerhouse. It's his mother's side that has been so good for him. She's Greek. Building a life in the shipping business was a natural for him, but he felt frustrated with the restrictions placed on him by his parents and grandparents. His interest was more in building battleships, both small and large ones. His specialty was high tech boats used by special operations around the world."

"And what's the latest you have on him?"

"It's sketchy, but I have sources that say he's in Asia somewhere, maybe even in China, working for the government."

"Do you believe this?"

"No, not really. I think this is all a screen, and I've not told anyone else. I think he's in the States, and either in San Francisco or Portland." She moved closer. "I don't want him to know that I'm on to him. As soon as I complete my current mission, he'll be my next target. I want to take him alive for one reason, since I think he'll lead me to Bjorn."

"We'll get back to Bjorn last. Again, I've one lingering question which is . . . who is financing him?"

"If he's able to produce such a boat, he would have many people who would want such, even the CIA." She waited for her father's response which never came. "We have some sources and may have to use them to get answers, since this will be at a high level."

"I'll see what we can do." He glanced at the folder. "Who's next?"

"Andrew, the Frenchman, the guy who has supposedly had his own parents murdered. This is the one guy I would have thought would be involved in the drone attacks, since he was last seen fighting in Libya. He lives and breathes fighting. Psychotic is too mild of a word to describe his behavior. He's a certified lunatic."

"However . . . if I recall, you insisted on having him cover your back many times during some earlier missions."

She flinched, knowing this was true. "There's no doubt that he's good at what he does. I also know the reason he followed Bjorn was that Bjorn gave him many more opportunities to fight. I think the truth may come out one day that even Bjorn couldn't control him."

"How much of a threat does he present to us?"

"On his own, very little. There're no hand-to-hand battles here. He's not into political wars where there are no fierce battles. Now, he could cause us many more problems by creating unrest around the world. This is another guy many new world order groups would love to have under their control, and for this reason, if none other, he has to be found and destroyed as well."

"I think you're suggesting a death squad be used in doing this."

"In this case, yes, especially since there's no way of controlling him."

Matalina reached for the photo before she presented the last one. "That brings us to the last guy who followed Bjorn. Mario has always been a rebel, but one who knows how to make contacts and manipulate people. There's no doubt he wants to be one of the richest men in the world, much like his father was at one time. If any of the guys who followed Bjorn were now financing the other projects, it would be him. He knows how to find and attract money. This is the one guy who isn't a physical warrior. He fights his battles through others who he pays to do his dirty work. As such, he could be operating anywhere, but I've heard he might have a place in America he uses often."

"What you're showing me is a worldwide chase that might take years to accomplish."

"I never said it would be easy." She glanced around at the others who never offered a word, but appeared to be listening. "What I hope is that when I find one member of this group, I'll get info on the others. They all have to be communicating to some extent. They all know that they will be hunted until they're found, and thus will be in hiding most of the time. Allowing them to feel safe will be the best way to keep them from going underground much deeper."

"That all brings us to the central figure in all of this. Do you think Bjorn is still their leader, as you suggested, or has he lost all control over them?"

"I'll say it's debatable, and hard to say exclusively. When everyone feels the heat, they could band together again, and as such, I think he'll be their natural leader again." She raked her teeth across her upper lip. "I do think that once he's eliminated, the others will fall quickly. He's the smartest and the most deadly of all of them. He's also the one with a vengeance against us, and will one day come back after us, after he has fully recovered and built a new team. I may be wrong in this, but that's the assumption I'm going on now."

Her father returned the last photo to her. "I should've asked earlier, but how's your head healing? I heard you barely escaped a blast while running from a building loaded with explosives."

"It's healing well, but it needs more time before

I'm back to full speed and ready for another mission. Like it or not, I don't have much time to get back on their trail. They're working on some special equipment to help me until it's fully healed. I hope to be checking it out in the next few days. They also have a full range of mental tests for me to make sure I have no loss in capacity. These exercises also make me much more mentally alert, so I look forward to them."

She decided to hide the one condition that she now faced, her inner ear problem that was making her dizzy. In her work she needed perfect balance and focus. An expert had been flown in and would see her tomorrow morning. She could only hope this was a temporary condition.

"As always, we're depending on you." He stood and walked over to her before he briefly kissed her cheek and offered her a fatherly hug. "I hope to see you some more before you leave." Was that it? Would there be no private time that she could really talk to her father? She raked her teeth over her upper lip one more time in frustration. If so, she was ready to get back on her mission and away from the castle.

###

She had slept well the night before and felt eager for her training and test today. Her ability to identify and record vital information from a scene was critical. These tests would start easy, as if they were practice rounds before they pushed her to the limits.

She recognized the testing room she had been in many times before. Every aspect of the stimulus and her reaction would be recorded and analyzed. She closed her eyes and rested until she heard a voice on the monitor speaking. "Hello, Princess Matalina. Are you ready to get started?"

"Let's do it."

As the screen suddenly flashed in front of her, she closed her eyes to avoid the loss of vision caused by such a brilliant light. They had blindsided her with this one, but it was something she needed to know. Bright lights often did this to her and it was one of her weaknesses she had learned to work with.

"Sorry about that, but we needed to know how much you're affected by bright lights now." The brightness quickly lowered before it increased in intensity, but much slower this time. Several minutes later, this part of the test was over.

She was given several minutes to relax her eyes before the next test. The screens around her placed her in a virtual room. She attempted to remember every detail before she closed her eyes and forced the images to remain deep in her memory. She opened them again and compared her thoughts, adding new details before she completed the process.

A voice alerted her that this image would end in five seconds. She attempted one more time to remember all details. "Okay, on each new image one item will be added or one item will be deleted. You'll be timed to see how long it takes you to identify the difference."

Thirty minutes later these light exercises were over and she felt like she had done well. Next, it would get more challenging. The images were flashed in front of her at shorter and shorter periods of time. She had to call out all of the items she could remember. This time she would have to wait for the analysis to see how well she did. The last part of this test was images of men. Sometimes the name was written below the image, and other times it was spoken.

Several minutes of distraction were introduced, and then she was tested on matching them up. To make it harder, the names were always foreigners, making the challenge even more difficult. She concentrated harder, hoping to score high on this part.

With one more session left this morning, she breathed deeply. She had been trained in many languages since the day she was born. This was both a good thing and a bad thing. By not having a central language to focus on, she had to rethink each time a language was presented to her. It also made building a full vocabulary difficult.

Each time she was asked a question in a different language, and each time she was expected to answer in the same language. Adding to the difficulty was accents she had to distinguish and adopt. This part of the test she knew she was stumbling on. Was it from the head injury? As the test ended she felt mentally tired. She needed a break before she went over the results.

After walking back to her room, she closed the door and walked over to a large window, one where she glanced out over the mountain range to see a large hawk circling above. The freedom of such mobility inspired her to follow the bird making each circle. To be above it all and not have anyone to report to made her envious.

There were many times she felt like she had the burden of the world upon her shoulders. The importance she played in maintaining order in the world was actually only known or appreciated by very few people. It wasn't that she wanted fame and glory, she didn't–really. It was more of the fact that she felt frustrated in doing most of it herself and that she couldn't share the responsibility with anyone else. She missed her sister. She missed Bjorn.

Yes, she thought she had found a soul mate earlier, one that would be perfect. Then, he did the unthinkable; he sold her out and her country–but why? She would love to have answers, but she knew that would probably never happen. If found, he would be killed on sight. A ten million euro reward would be paid to anyone proving they had killed him, with no questions asked. Additionally, that person would become a national hero in her country and within the Maliviziati. As such, his true story would never be known to the world, but to those that mattered the most, he would become a legend.

She had to stop thinking about it. These meetings would be over soon and she had to concentrate on her current mission, which would take her Germany in a few days. There would be another day when she could get back on Bjorn's trail.

Chapter 10

After landing in Munich during the cool of the evening, Matalina puffed on one of her small cigars, but otherwise wasted little other time in doing anything else. Her limo driver used blinking lights and Baltonia's diplomatic flag to rush her through the noisy traffic around the airport to a hastily created meeting that she hoped would give her more information on drone development in Germany, and more importantly on Zafar, who had studied there. It was extremely important for her to learn how much he knew, who he had associated with, and thus, any and all connections he had made.

She studied Dr. Werner Fritz, a slim man with black rimmed glasses, who had the typical nerdy look of a college professor, as he walked into a meeting room that had been prepared for them inside the airport hotel. "Hello, Matalina, I'm glad you could make this meeting."

"Thank you for seeing me on such a short notice."

Since she had been invited there, the security was tight, not just for her but for the people she would be talking to. There was no delusion in the pressure forced upon them for not having all of the answers. If terrorists had developed advanced drones they could use as weapons, they would be one of the first targets.

As soon as the door closed, everyone had a seat except Dr. Fritz, who was flanked by two men who were either military guards or intelligence officers. Even though the information exchange might help each other, there were national interest secrets that would remain hidden on both sides of this meeting.

Dr. Fritz spoke in German. "While we all know why we're here, I think a short presentation of what we have will be invaluable. I'm sorry if some of this is redundant."

True to his words, Matalina watched many clips of information she already knew. However, she did see small pieces of information that might be useful, like more photos of Zafar taken from different angles. As she looked for distinguishing marks or characteristic identifiers, she had to memorize every aspect of his face in order to pick him out of a crowd. He had grown his black hair slightly long, and had it hanging like a mop around his shoulders. His beard was cut short in contrast, but it retained the same deep dark black color.

Matalina finally pointed to one photo asking for it to be blown up. After they granted her request she saw a small scar to his chin that extended to his lip. "Did he receive this during the drone attack that killed his parents?"

Dr. Fritz answered. "It's assumed that he did, but we can't verify that he did." He motioned for another photo to be displayed. "The only other identifying mark he carries is a small tattoo on his right arm, the name of his mother written in Arabic. We know this was added when he was going to school in Germany."

Instead of waiting for the presentation to continue, she asked, "Do you have any knowledge that he specifically went to school here to learn this drone technology?"

"It would appear so, but you have to remember that going to school isn't a crime. As far as we can tell, however, he never had contact with any military facilities here that would've given him any additional training."

Dr. Fritz motioned for the presentation to advance to highlight the companies that were well known to be developing drone technology. "As I'm sure you're aware, only America and Israel have drone capacity utilizing full-sized drones. Since that might change soon, the rest of us are working hard on micro drones, something we now think he might be capitalized on as well."

"The evidence that I've found would support such. While these small drones wouldn't have massive firepower, I can see many other uses for them in the hands of terrorists."

"Precisely, and that's why the full Security Council is meeting. A drone can be programmed to hunt for one specific individual, and that wouldn't take too much of a payload to accomplish its mission of assassination."

"Even if this is a possibility, I think we can rule out being highly developed at this time."

"Why is that?"

"I've come under attack now several times by these mini drones, and I've forwarded part of the drone that was found for your analysis. I hope you have had time to do so."

"We have and we'll discuss it more shortly . . . and we'll share what we do know." He pointed back to the screen. "I think you'll find this informative as well."

Since she might receive some answers to her questions, she decided to be patient and watch the rest of their presentation. As she already knew, the major companies involved in this research and development were the giant companies like Northrop Grumman, and Boeing. The list also included General Atomics and Aero Vironment. The only other company she could imagine involved in this, and the one who wouldn't want to share their technology willingly was Israel, which had made major technology advances inside their Aerospace Industries while developing the Heron.

She saw no mention of some of the other players, such as the German company EMT, the British BAE Systems, the Dassault in France, or even the Selex in Italy, but she assumed they would be discussed later. In particular, she wanted to hear more about the Talarion Program being developed in Germany.

When the presentation restarted, she refocused on the information provided. An extensive list of all known associates was presented. Many of these were just other students in his classes, none of which could help him finance such a venture. This is where she hoped to find some kind of connection to the old Illuminati families, which had the funds to exploit such. If not them, she knew that some terrorist group might have centered in on him. While this may have started as a personal vendetta, it could've grown into a political war of which it would've been easy to recruit him.

After not making any connection, the presentation turned to what she definitely wanted more information on–the analysis of the drone that had been recovered. It had only left a scalding burn on the side of the plane. Had the explosive payload failed?

Dr. Fritz started speaking as the photos started to display on the screen. "The fuselage is nothing more than common plumbing piping, which can be readily found. We can assume, however, that the missing parts were much more complicated, carrying either a computer chip or receiver for remote control, maybe even both. Based on the designs you provided us with, there wouldn't be much space available for a cargo."

"Still, the drone was able to intercept and strike the plane I was in."

"That much is obvious, and from what I was told, you came close to outrunning the drone. As such, the drone has a short operating range." He asked the guy next to him for the frame to advance on the presentation. Inside the tip we found something we weren't expecting. It consisted of a hardened metal alloy that was apparently designed to penetrate its target."

"That had to add to the weight the drone carried."

"It would also account for why the explosive was a flare type material designed to ignite whatever the tip breached."

Now she understood. "So your assessment is that they had hoped to hit a gas tank onboard her plane." Her evasive movement had in fact saved their lives. "Apparently, they have found a good use for micro drones, but one that would require high skills in controlling such a crude design in the fuselage."

Dr. Fritz continued. "The place they had in Columbia offered them a great location to test their drones, but there's little doubt they've moved it to another location. It will be imperative to find it as soon as possible."

"That much, we can both agree on." She needed more information. "Based on the designs I sent to you, what would you guess to be their range?"

"No larger than they are, it would be safe to say

the most would be a few miles. The problem is that since they're so small, they can even be launched from the back of a small van."

A man on his right, Olaf Joachim, motioned that he wanted to speak. Matalina waited for him to step forward. "I've one more theory they might be working on. The designs you sent to us had all of the earmarks of a glider. As such, if it could be released high enough or given a way to climb into the upper atmosphere, it could stay there for a long time, waiting for the perfect moment to launch an attack."

"Again, wouldn't this require a large amount of sophistication?"

"Yes, but it's a theory we need to consider them using." He paused for a second. "I was one of his teachers at the university where he studied. He's a smart individual, and totally dedicated to mastering this field."

Matalina raked her teeth over her upper lip before she asked a question she wanted answers to. "Since he was a foreign student from a country we all know to be hostile to the rest of the world, how did he get admitted to the university here?"

"He didn't come by way of Afghanistan, but rather by way of a school in Italy where he had exceptional grades in his undergraduate field of mathematics and computer design. We didn't have the background information on him then that we do now. He had managed to completely hide his past. Being an orphan gave him the perfect way to do that."

Now, she thought she could make a connection. Still, she didn't want to give away her advantage and have it sent to the wrong person. Could Mario have recruited Zafar, or perhaps even located him for just such a mission?

The meeting lasted throughout the day, only giving her small bits of information here and there, but all would be utilized. She had no doubt she had to get back to America and find a place they could continue their testing while establishing their sleeper cell close to whatever target they had selected.

Finally, she stood. "Gentlemen, you've been most helpful. I hope to gather more information soon. Since we know this to be a growing problem in the future, we all need to see about funding a major project in providing technology to neutralize these small, micro drones. When we get back together next time, it would be useful to see what you suggest." She glanced around the room, knowing she needed to get prepared to do war with an enemy she had to find first, one who would definitely be waiting for her to find them, or perhaps even baiting her into another trap.

As she prepared to leave, Olaf offered her one more suggestion she would have to consider. "If they're planning on increasing their gliding skills, they'll need a lot of wide open spaces, and somewhere the winds are constantly blowing."

Since she knew this was a possibility, she would have to consider it. Especially, since one of the shipping invoices she had intercepted earlier was from Arizona. That would be her first stop.

Chapter 11

Just like the constant flow of a raging river stream, the high winds relentlessly whistled across the barren prairie of Arizona, unhindered in their eastwardly march. The dry heat reminded Matalina of the Middle East, with its choking brown dust blown into the atmosphere, robbing any redeeming blue ambiance from the sky above. The only difference she saw was the lack of Turkish coffee in this wasteland. She had no intentions of drinking dirty water.

Realizing how one man's hell is another man's heaven, she knew how this area was also well known for attracting avid glider pilots. Still, it was also isolated enough to offer the perfect cover for testing drones.

She studied the office in front of the mini storage facility, which corresponded to the address she had recovered from the Columbian operation. The low level security offered to the space renters made her think she had made a mistake in pursuing this lead, but she only had a few options for now.

She parked her car in front and walked inside. Going through all of the units would take time she didn't have. She needed the manager's help in finding the unit Zafar had used. Since she had been blindsided several times earlier, she had no intentions of finding another bomb waiting for her.

When she saw a manager, or perhaps the owner, behind a glass door, she opened it and walked inside. His face frowned as he studied her. "What can I do for you?"

"I need some information."

"Such as?" he asked, as he leaned back into his chair. His biker style clothes revealed a guy who had seen many days of trouble and action. The tattoos covering his arms also suggested time in prison at some time. She removed several hundred dollar bills from her pocket and dropped them on the table. With no emotions showing, he pocketed the money. "I'm listening."

"You received some shipments here recently from South America. I simply need to know exactly what it was, and which unit they're stored in."

His eyes slightly dilated. "I get many shipments here. Many people pay me to accept packages for them, and I'm not one to ask many questions. You know what I mean?"

"That can be admirable, but it can also be . . . stupid." Yes, she selected a fighting word, and one that would get under his skin. "You have no clue that you might be storing enough explosives to level all of this, do you?"

For the first time he nervously glanced around him. "It's still not my business to ask questions. I'm just a storage facility." He glanced to his right. "Listen, sweetheart, just the same, the shipment happened several weeks ago. They've never come back since they came for their shipment. It's still leased to them, but we assume it's empty."

Confirmation of the shipment answered her first question, but he had to know more. "I see."

Before he could say anything else, another guy walked out of a back room. "Jim, you dumb ass. You need to keep your mouth shut. These guys might come back." The big bulky Mexican looking dude turned to face her."You sure don't look like the police, so why are you sticking your nose into all of this?"

"That's not important." She watched him arch his back and shifted to his full six foot eight height as she turned to face him. "I offered some money, and I can offer more, not to mention . . . I did ask nicely for your help."

He laughed like a small mountain about to explode from a volcanic eruption. "And . . . ."

She stepped forward, with one hand grabbing his neck and the other his balls, sending him a message he wouldn't forget any time soon. As he attempted to swing at her, she dug in tighter, sending blood streaming down his neck. When she thought he had had enough, she released him. "You don't really want that kind of pain again, do you?"

The first guy grunted, and then moved in defense of the bigger guy. "We have a way of handling bitches like you around here. That was a big mistake, sweetheart."

She caught his fist in her hand where she squeezed it, breaking bones in the process. He yelled with pain as she twisted his wrist, forcing him to the floor. With the big guy reaching for a drawer she assumed held a weapon of some kind, she decided enough was enough, and quickly leveled her PUD at him. "I simply want answers."

He squinted as he studied the size of the opening staring at him. "Okay–enough. Who are you?"

"Not important. I want info on who rented that space."

"Someone who offered much more than you did to keep this quiet." He pointed to a file cabinet. "I have no name, but a receipt I signed when I accepted the shipment. That's the best I can offer you."

"It's a start." She pulled a photo from her side pocket. "Is this the guy you dealt with?"

She watched him study the photo. "No, not him, but close. These Arabian guys all look the same to me."

Since she was definitely on the right trail, she now had to figure out how to stay on it. Without taking his eyes off the gun pointed at him, the big guy handed her the invoice. The name of the shipper was on the lower right side. A confirmation number was below it. If this was a cell phone, it could be traced, and just maybe this would lead her to them. It was time to get the team ready to go in.

"Thanks. I'm going to do you a big favor." She lowered the gun for a moment.

"Really! Like what?"

"I'm going to pay you for the space. It needs to be examined, but not today. I highly suspect it's wired to explode if anyone tries. Since this might tip them off that I'm on their trail, I want to attempt this with some experts, but not for a few weeks."

"Do you really think it's rigged with explosives?"

"The last several places of theirs I located have been, and I don't see them changing now." She dropped a few more hundred on the table. "This will help cover your medical bills. Now, if you hear anything else that might help me find these guys, let me know. I can be generous."

The big guy leaned backwards. "Just who in the hell are you to come in here like you're some kind of female mercenary?"

"A mercenary fights for money. I'm totally

dedicated to my country, and will do whatever is required to keep it safe." She turned to the door. "I hope you don't disappoint me and try to warn someone that I'm after them. I would sure hate to make a trip back here." She stopped long enough to allow him to see the full force of her concentrated smile before she flashed her white gold teeth. As she walked out, she dropped a card on the side table, which simply provided her name as Matt and a phone number where she could be reached.

Chapter 12

Matalina studied the isolated landscape of the western part of Texas, the perfect place to continue testing their drones. The long strings of giant windmills, establishing a wind farm that stretched for endless miles, covered several of the ridges. With small towns hundreds of miles apart, a group could be hidden here forever.

When she made a trace of the cell phone number she had originally received, one signature returned, but it had changed locations rather quickly. Her best guess was that it was being transported by way of a plane or fast vehicle on a road somewhere close to where they were heading. Since it hadn't connected anymore since then, it could mean that they knew they were being traced, or that they were tipped off by the guys at the storage facility.

Matalina yelled at the guy driving the truck behind her. "We have a gas station ahead. This might be the last chance to make sure all vehicles are topped off with fuel before we head off-road."

The driver responded as he offered her a grin. "I agree. We'll try to get in and out as fast as possible. I'll feel much better when we get our caravan hidden in the mountains somewhere."

She knew what he was concerned about. In these wide open spaces they would become sitting targets for any kind of drone attack. "Understood. Although we have two planes in the sky above us, it's good to keep your eyes open. I suspect they know we're after them."

Her men knew the risk they were taking, but also that they had much more protection than they normally did, since they assumed the terrorist group might be laying in ambush for them. The real gas tanks had been repositioned to fortified positions inside the center of the storage part of the trucks, leaving the outside ones as decoys.

She paused as she considered her secret weapon in the truck she drove. Thanks to the Germans, she had the latest in laser defense technology under the tarp. If they had to engage the drones, the knowledge gained in a live exercise would be invaluable in stopping drone attacks later.

Matalina turned to Olaf Joachim, the German designer, who nervously shifted in his seat next to her before she spoke in German to make him more comfortable. "I know it's one thing to build something, and totally different to put total faith in it to save your life."

"This is the best system in the world. I know that. What worries me is that it has to be functional before we're fired upon. This traveling has me scared." Olaf kept glancing at the sky and his cell phone where he had internet connection.

"Tell me again how much time you need to be operational?"

"Normally five minutes, but in a full emergency it can be operational in slightly less than ninety seconds." He swallowed hard before he continued. "We did this test many times, but never in a field operation like this."

"You could've assigned this to many people in your company, but you volunteered, if I remember correctly." She checked the skies above her that were crystal clear and without a hint of a cloud anywhere.

"Yes, I did. I was given little time to think about it. Also, since this is so new, I didn't have time to train someone else into using it, and there are no manuals on how to operate this system."

Minutes later, Matalina saw the small station ahead of them. She slowed as she checked in with the pilot ten thousand feet above her. "We're going to pull into a station to top off our tanks and get any last supplies the men might need. Do you see any activity around us anywhere?"

"A little, but nothing too suspicious. You have a commercial flight fifty miles north of you, some workers from the power company checking some lines in what appears to be a normal maintenance schedule. About eighty miles due east of you are a group of gliders organized by an adventure and outfitters company for tourists."

Matalina realized that while this was in a small controlled area, these gliders could quickly cover a lot of territory while being almost undetectable as they rode the winds funneled along the sides of the mountain ridges. "Keep a close eye on these gliders, they could offer a great cover for this terrorist cell."

"I totally agree. I can have the other pilot make another recon pass in that direction if you wish."

"Not now, but after we refuel that might be a good decision." As soon as they finished making the last stop, they would be heading due north and not too far from this area. "Since the low flyer is much like us, a target, be sure to monitor the area around him. He needs to make a circle around us before we make the stop."

"Agreed. I'll let you know if I see anything."

Matalina turned toward the guy beside her. "I think this will be a quick stop, but I want you to stay with the truck, just in case." She stopped the caravan several hundred yards from the station as she addressed her men over the radio. "Listen up. They only have one major pump there, so we need to take turns pumping and keep the trucks at least fifty yards apart. I also want one man from each truck to stand outside as an observer. I don't want to be blindsided again."

The station had a small cover above the pump, but it allowed enough clearance for her trucks to safely drive under it. Since the parking lot could host about half of the trucks in her ten truck caravan, the others would have to wait as instructed on the side of the road.

The small wood framed office had a one car garage attached on one side, and a small café on the other side. The rusty looking ice house in front of the office had a small neon sign on top advertising Lone Star, a local beer, which was the only indication that the place was operational. The few cars on the side of the garage looked older than the garage and totally worthless.

She lowered the truck into first gear and eased forward. From the rearview mirror she watched a guy step outside the truck behind her to secure his position. Eventually, she made it next to the pump, where she waited for about a minute to see if there was any activity coming from inside the station. She saw nothing, which was unusual, since she had verified earlier that the station was open every day.

She reached for her radio and turned to the guy next to her. "I'm going to check things out. Something doesn't look right." She double checked her PUD before she spoke into the radio. "I think it would be good to have the pilot do a direct flight over us and give some better details of any activity around us."

The pilot quickly responded. "Agreed. Matt, I'm a few miles to the south of you now."

As Matalina stepped to the ground, she felt the intense heat of the sun above her. Even with her sunglasses, the bright sun made it difficult for her to focus above her. She had to rely on those with her to monitor these skies. Why was it so quiet here? Had they been warned to stay away? Was she being set up?

She had almost made it to the office when she heard the warning from the pilot. "I have movement along a ridge to the north of you."

"Identify!"

The pilot spoke fast. "I see what appears to be a small jeep."

Matalina made a sprint back to the truck. She suddenly realized the gas station tanks might be the target instead of her caravan. She saw one of her trucks close to one of them. "Get all trucks away from the station gas tanks now. Move it!"

The pilot's voice alerted her again as she made it to the truck. "I see a man outside the jeep now. He's pulling something out of the back of it. It's hard to see what, but from his movements he appears to be in a hurry."

"Listen to me! I don't want you to get too close to him. If he's about to launch a drone or two, you need to stay out of range. How far is he away from our position?

"I would estimate slightly over one kilometer."

From what she had learned earlier, the drones had

to be less than two hundred meters to retain the penetrating power required to pierce their target. She had, perhaps, a few minutes to move the truck and get the equipment set up.

As she jumped into the truck, she yelled at Olaf. "We may have a problem. I think we're going to be under attack in minutes. I sure hope you know how to use this damn thing."

Olaf reached for the door handle. "I need to get this tarp off fast."

"Not yet, I have to move us first. I think they might be targeting the pumps. I should've thought of this first."

She watched him stare at them. "Shit. I agree it's a permanent target they could've been preprogrammed into a computer chip."

Matalina cranked the motor as she heard the pilot yell, "I see what looks to be a drone in flight, which is headed in your direction. I can attempt to intercept it."

"I know these are small and hard to hit, so for now give us visual for as long as you can."

His responded quickly. "I see another drone in the air. This one appears to be heading in my direction instead."

"Get out of there. We still don't know the full range of their technology. It could be targeting you. We'll try to give you some help in a minute." She raced the truck forward for a full one hundred meters before she stopped.

She yelled at Olaf as she opened her door. "Let's do this now." After they rolled the tarp back, revealing the laser guns underneath, Olaf switched on the system and slipped into a programming mode in front of a small screen.

Matalina surveyed the area to her north which consisted of many small foothills before heading up into one major mountain range. The jeep had to be there somewhere. Still, she saw no sign of the drones.

She yelled back into her radio. "Get several bikes out and have them ready. We'll need to go after this guy in a minute. I want him taken alive."

The pilot broke back in. "We have three drones airborne now."

Matalina glanced over at Olaf to see if he heard. In response he pointed a thumb upward as he switched from German to English. "I have them on radar now. Just give me the order to fire."

While tempting to fire now, she waited for a second. However, she knew she had to fire before the rocket boosters were ignited, which would send them to hypersonic speed. "How close is the drone from our pilot?"

"Not far."

She couldn't take a chance. "Take that one out first. Fire at will."

After his fingers floated over the keys, he slapped the return key hard. A quick blast of light startled her, as she glanced at a line burnt into the sky above her. In the distance she saw a small white puff of smoke. Was that a direct hit?

Olaf turned and winked. "One down." He pointed to his screen. One of the drones had disappeared, and perhaps already under rocket drive. He worked the keys fast as he searched for it. "There . . . it's also going after the plane."

"Can you hit it?"

He didn't answer, but concentrated on making adjustments. Time was running out. Should she tell the pilot to abandon his plane? As she started to yell over the radio, he clicked the final entry and raised his fingers as another pulsating flash streaked northward. She saw no puff of smoke. She yelled into the radio. "Take evasive movement now and be prepared to bail out, we'll come and get you."

Olaf fired again. This time she saw a small flash in the sky and the barely visible image of the small plane not far away. She yelled back into the radio. "Are you alright?"

"Yeah, but that was close. I received some scattered fragments, and it'll take me a minute to see how much damage I've sustained."

"You've done your job for now. Look for a place to land and we'll send a copter after you soon."

"Won't it be dangerous for a copter right now?"

"I think they'll be more interested in clearing out now. Be sure to leave the plane after you get it on the ground and take a radio with you."

"Will do."

She glanced at the last drone, which had quickly closed on their position. They had to destroy it quickly. She knew the guy in the jeep had to be racing away while they were distracted and would soon be hard to track.

Olaf turned toward her, giving her another thumbs up. That was all she needed. "Destroy it now!" Another pulse electrified a stream, followed by a white puff of smoke. Was that all of them? "Stay here and destroy any others you see. I have to go after the guy in the jeep."

"Be sure to have someone find any drone parts. It'll be invaluable for us to study how much damage we inflicted."

155

"I'll send a team in a second." Minutes later, she had organized several teams including one to retrieve the pilot, one to find any parts from the destroyed drones, and one of men on dirt bikes to chase the jeep in the mountains north of them. A base would have to be formed where they were for now, utilizing their new laser defenses. She would see about moving it again shortly.

Since she still didn't know where their base was, she assumed they would be considering moving it soon, just like they had in the past. For some reason, however, she felt like this might be a much better fortress that they might want to defend. She had to hurry to catch this guy in the jeep.

Matalina geared up for the chase as fast as she could. From the steel-toed boots to the bullet proof helmet, nothing was left to chance, since the chances of taking direct fire from a hidden assailant were highly possible. To find his trail and to follow it, they might have to split up, putting all of them at increased risk.

With her PUD snapped to her side as her main weapon of choice, she also had other weapons available, including a short ten gauge shotgun she might need for close encounters, and a rifle to reach across the ridges if it was needed. There were no roads in this area, but a large number of caves and abandoned mines he could hide in.

The trail bike was specifically designed for this kind of mission. It had high clearance, reinforced wind guards to stop bullets, heavy casing to protect the motor, and tires made out of solid reinforced rubber that could handle the sharp and brutal terrain.

After clearing the initial foothills, she looked for an observation position this guy might have used to launch the drones. From such a launching point, he had to have hand launched them. With several locations possible, she rapidly pointed them out to her team, with her taking the one on the far right. "Stay in touch men, and report anything suspicious."

With a quick salute from them, indicating they were ready, she turned her attention to the mountain ahead. There were potential hiding places everywhere. She yelled into her mic attached to her shoulder. "We're heading into the mountains now."

Her team member assigned to giving logistics responded. "The GPS trackers are responding without any problems, but we still have no signs of the jeep anywhere. He must've known somewhere he could quickly hide."

"He had to leave some tracks here somewhere. We know he can't simply vanish without any traces." As expected, thirty minutes later she found tracks, many tracks leading in different directions. She stopped her bike and stood beside them. Could it be this easy? Was this another one of their bases she had located?

Team member one suddenly reported in. "I'm seeing many tracks, and from many different kinds of vehicles. Some of them are old, but I see others that are fairly fresh. We could be highly outnumbered here."

Team member three quickly added, "I'm on the far eastern side and see the same, but most of mine are older tracks."

With all of the tracks on the ground, there had to be vehicles somewhere. "It appears they're underground somewhere. Since I don't think he's making a run for it, we need to find entrances to some of these mines and caves. If these terrorists are who we think they are from Afghanistan, they'll have a lot of expertise in hiding and utilizing caves. We need to establish some perimeters to make sure they don't escape. We might be in for a long standoff here."

After finally admitting it was enough for today, she knew that she needed to coordinate a better base close to this area. Doing battle inside the caves could be very dangerous. She also knew, without a doubt now, that the attacks on them were designed to draw them into a trap. Letting them believe that they were successful could work in her advantage, but she had to be careful.

The next few days proved to be frustrating. This mountain was full of caves and tunnels that many prospectors had used to hunt for gold for a long time. There were also many indications that native Indians had used these many years earlier. She sipped on a crude Turkish coffee she had managed to make herself, while she smoked another cigar, one where she had dipped the butt into the coffee first. As she planned the next move, she knew that each day she spent here also diverted her from other places she needed to be investigating.

Matalina glanced at the drone parts that had been recovered. The basic pieces of plastic showed no real signs of sophistication. The best they could guess was that a small electric motor was used to carry the drone forward. A smaller metallic missile was tucked inside the outer plastic one, and used a rocket propellant to accelerate the armor piercing point into its target. At least that was the general thinking since a tip wasn't located this time.

She glanced at the reports from the night before that indicted no significant heat signatures coming from any of the caves or mines. From the amount of information they had gathered, they had narrowed the possibilities to about eight major places.

The decision to use robots made sense, but it would be a slow go. What she expected to happen was for the men in the caves to flee from it in many directions. If so, she only had so much manpower to follow them.

After the order was given, she walked over to a small copter and talked to the pilot, who acted a little nervous. "Matt, are you sure this is a good idea? They can launch these small mini drones from anywhere, making us a sitting target."

"True, but it would also give away their hiding place, something I don't think they want to do now." While it was a danger in doing so, it would also be perfect for getting a jump on anyone trying to escape. "We also have the laser defense system to protect us. It has been programmed to destroy anything that approaches us."

"It's your call. I'm ready whenever you are." He adjusted his weight in his seat and started checking his reading. "Olaf also added a small laser to the copter. I have no experience in using it, and he plans to operate it remotely from the ground."

"We'll have to trust him, since he's the most

qualified person in the world in using this kind of technology." Matalina stretched her back as she buckled into her seat. She had packed many other weapons she might need behind her.

As soon as she was in position, she needed to have all of her men check in. "Okay, men, communication is going to be the key. We need to take some of these men alive to get answers, but I also don't want any of you unnecessarily placed in harm's way."

Ten minutes later, several robots were sent into three different caves. Some were sent in quietly, and others were sent in to make it sound like a full assault was underway. Images from cameras mounted on the robots were relayed to a monitor she had with her. It was all a waiting game now.

Thirty minutes turned into an hour, and then two. Still nothing. How had the man driving the jeep disappeared? Was there no one else there? If so, what accounted for all of the tire tracks?

Suddenly, images from one of the cameras went blank. She yelled in her mic to the control center. "Which cave is this?"

"It's the one we've named North 1A."

After finding it on her map, she pointed it out to the pilot. "We need to cover this one, now!"

Minutes later the copter hovered in front of the entrance, but far enough away to avoid any direct gunfire should they make a run out of this entrance. Then the unexpected happened. Several white drones floated out of the cave. There was no doubt what they had been programmed to do. She spoke into her mic. "It looks like we have a new wave of drones being released. We're going to make a run for it to get out of range."

As the pilot banked to one side, preparing to disappear down a ravine, Matalina made a change in plans as she pointed to a small ridge along a trail coming out of the cave. "There, drop me off there with one of these hand-held lasers. They'll never expect this."

With the drones already gaining altitude, the pilot acted reluctant, but complied. "You'll need to find cover fast."

"Don't worry about me. You're the one who needs to fly like a bat out of hell." She jumped to the ground and waited for the laser to be tossed to her. "Got it, now move it!"

As the drones floated closer, she watched the copter race out of range. She realized the drones might be too low to be seen by her home base. In minutes, they would be passing over her. Now, would they have video capabilities, or be carrying warheads?

Matalina grabbed a pair of binoculars and focused on the first one. She noticed a small rounded glass covered compartment which could provide video. She yelled into the mic. "I think they have a video on this first drone. I'm going to hold the laser in position, but I need help in locking in the target."

Olaf responded. "That's the best you can do with a handheld laser." Damn, this might prove worthless. She pointed and fired. Nothing. She fired again and still missed. "To hell with this," she yelled as she pulled her ten gauge from her side. With little time left before it would pass over her, she aimed and fired, scoring a direct hit.

As it fell from the sky, she mentally marked where it could be found. The two behind the front one suddenly ignited and rushed across the sky above her. They were being fired, but at what? The copter was too far away to be a target, or was it?

Seconds later, she saw the flash first before she heard a loud explosion. After jumping on a large bolder, she glanced in the direction of the explosions before yelling into her mic. "Was anyone near that blast?"

"Everyone is okay. I think that was wild fire, but it sent everyone into cover."

Matalina glanced at the opening to the mine one more time to see more drones floating out of the entrance. Just how many did they have in there? "Listen up . . . we have more drones coming our way."

After rushing for cover behind the bolder, she glanced back at the other drones as they turned into the wind coming from the west. The heavy winds made them climb almost vertically, much like a kite would, as they began to accelerate out of sight.

At such a height they could present a much more dangerous threat, especially if they had video capabilities attached to them. It was time to take them out. She yelled back into her mic for Olaf to target them immediately. No answer.

Several seconds later she watched a small puff of smoke coming from their direction as the others kept climbing and racing eastwardly. She understood he was much too busy to respond, since the drones were racing out of range.

With the drones disappearing, her attention returned to the entrance to the mine. That had to be attacked before they released even more drones. She needed cover, but couldn't wait for long. "I need backup before they send more of these damn things out. I'm going in closer, but I need anyone close to assist me as soon as they can get into position."

The copter pilot responded first. "I can airlift more men to your position the fastest."

She had to agree, but that would set the pilot up as a potential target if they released more soon. "Okay, but come in low and fast. You need to be out of this area if they send more. I'll try to get to the entrance and provide some cover."

She estimated the distance across the open area in front of the mine to be about three hundred meters, the distance she could run at close to full speed. With the element of surprise on her side, she made sure all of her equipment was firmly attached before she made a dash toward the entrance.

The first fifty yards gave her a feel of the land, which was both rough and loose, making hitting top speed a challenge. Still, she saw no guards at the entrance and pushed on. The next hundred meters left her in the middle of the open area with absolutely no place to hide, and although her lungs began to burn, she ran harder.

From her observation point earlier, she thought the last half of the space would be flat, but it wasn't. The incline quickly taxed her reserve, especially with the loose stones. With about fifty more meters to go, she started looking for a place to take cover. Some small rocks on the right offered her little protection, but it was something until her men could join her. She pushed on.

Before she could make it, three more drones floated out of the mine and in her direction. After dropping to a knee, she grabbed the ten gauge and clicked off the safety. These were much larger than the earlier ones. "Men, we have three more drones coming out of the mine. Get ready for them."

As they passed over her she fired at the first one and hit it, tearing it in half. With little reaction coming from the others, other than their increasing speed, she swung around and fired at another one that was racing away from her, scoring another hit. The loud explosion shocked her as she crouched lower, just in case any fragments would be sent her way.

In doing so, however, she was unable to get a third shot off. She quickly dropped her ten gauge and assembled her rifle. This would be a long shot, but she had to try. Seconds later she fired the entire clip but she knew she had missed. It was all up to Olaf now.

After a full minute, she heard Olaf checking in. "We have a problem. I know I had a direct hit, but nothing happened to the drone."

"Do what?" She yelled, knowing this wasn't good.

"I think they must've switched to a different material, and one that doesn't absorb the laser energy."

"Damn, this is bad."

The pilot responded. "We can try to chase it if you wish, Matt."

It was quick decision time. Should she ask for a quick pick up to see if she could get another shot at it? Matalina snatched two charges from her pack and ran toward the entrance where she threw them inside as far as she could before jumping to one side for cover. The explosion was much more powerful than she had expected. She must have connected with more explosives inside.

She yelled at the pilot. "All is clear, but let's make this fast."

She waited on the copter to land as smoke continued to bellow out of the mine. It wouldn't be long until her men would be there to cover it in case any of the terrorists wanted to surrender.

As the copter rushed in, she ran to jump on before it made land contact. "Let's move it." She quickly prepared every weapon she had, not knowing which one would be the best.

Seconds later, she saw it ahead of them. It was changing direction to face them. Her heart beat fast as she realized she was now coming under attack. Instead of firing any missile at her, however, the drone caught the high winds and soared upward. Could they catch it now?

The amount of speed the drone climbed astonished her. How could it do that? There was no way any drone she knew of could climb that fast and that high. She scrambled for her jet backup. It had no firepower, but could, hopefully, follow the drone to see where it was headed.

With no way to catch the drone, she instructed the pilot to return to the mine. Her men had the entrance covered. With smoke still blowing out of the mine, they had to wait before they could enter, which she knew might take some time.

After recovering all parts of the damaged drones they could find, she rode the copter back to her base. The men would stand guard until tomorrow morning, when they would enter the cave.

As expected, Olaf was standing outside his control center, examining the drone pieces made out of some kind of Styrofoam. "It appears they've leveled the playing field. This has proved to be a good testing field for our laser, but it may have been more

165

productive for them in testing their latest model."

"What can be done?"

"They obviously can't make the entire drone out of Styrofoam, so it does have weaknesses. We'll have to center in on the rocket booster and the payload."

The jet pilot soon reported in. "The drone is nowhere in sight. If it was up here we would see it on radar."

Matalina turned to Olaf who patted the material before he spoke. "I'm not surprised. This material isn't strong. I would guess that it has broken apart and fallen back to earth somewhere along the way."

Matalina glanced at the payload taken from the one she had shot with the ten gauge. "This one was remotely controlled. How were they planning to do this over a wide area?"

"While hacking a communication satellite isn't easy, it's possible. It'll take a while to see what info is left on this chip. I don't know if they had time to erase it or not after you shot it."

"Do your best," Matalina said before she opened the door and headed for her trailer. She felt like all was secure for the night and tomorrow would be an interesting day. Either the terrorists had been killed inside the mine, or they were cornered and ready to fight. In case this was true, she knew the battle she would face then.

The inside of her trailer was nothing special, but it did give her access to her computer which had a direct link to a satellite. It was time for her to check in and let everyone know how her mission was going. Even it was possible that the mastermind behind these planned attacks was cornered, including the remote case of Bjorn being with them, she doubted it. She would have expected much more security and firepower if such was the case. The best she could hope for tomorrow was to capture one of the men alive and make him talk.

After enjoying one of her small cigars to clear her thoughts, she decided to call her mom, who answered on the first ring. "Hello, Matalina. I was hoping you would call me soon."

"I know it's getting late there, but I wanted to check in with you before you go to bed."

"I hope you have good news to report. Your father's getting a lot of pressure to contain this drone crisis, which it's being called now."

"It's amazing that we're in an almost all out war in America and no one else is paying attention."

"I can see the good and the bad in that."

"Well . . . the good news is that I think we've eliminated another cell where they've been testing their drones. We have some people that are either dead or fortified inside a mine. However, we'll not be able to go in until tomorrow morning to verify."

"When are you going to meet again with the CIA there?"

"I'm not sure right now. The best I can hope for is to stop this attack from ever happening, and especially to keep it out of the news. This is one kind of crisis the politicians here would like to get exposed so they can increase their control over this country. It's something many other nations would also love to exploit as well. I still have no direct evidence that any faction of Illuminati is behind this, but I highly suspect they are."

"Many people here are also suspicious of Bjorn being involved."

"Interesting enough, I haven't seen any more

connection to him after Florida. It has occurred to me that he might have a different take on this, and one he could exploit. I know he would love to see the government blamed for the attacks, and as if they were actually behind them. He still believes a more direct approach against any one world order development is the best approach. He's so wrong, but somehow he has managed to convince himself and his followers that he's right, even if it might destroy us in the process."

"I hate to discuss him, but we also know that his zest for doing things his way has led to him becoming power hungry himself. He'll destroy us if we don't destroy him first."

Matalina knew her mother was right. She closed her eyes and remembered the day her sister, Adelaide, died. Bjorn had killed her. Not directly with his own hands, but with his actions that caused her to be in the center of the fighting. Adelaide had been left unprotected. Matalina would never forget this or forgive him. She opened her eyes as she spoke. "Trust me, mom, I'll kill him on sight. He has to die."

Her mother lowered her voice, as if to express concern for her. "Your trainer has also been asking about you and the injury to your head. He's a good guy who cares for you."

Her mother was right. If she only knew that they were also . . . . She stopped as she paused and considered using the word . . . lovers. They were simply sex partners and nothing more. She had to force herself to always remember this. "I understand his concerns, but I'm doing fine. Tell him *thank you* for checking on me."

"I will. We have also located the people who knew Zafar in Afghanistan. It might be good for you to make a trip there to talk to them."

"If I run into a dead end here, it would be my next move. We hope to find out more when we enter the mines tomorrow."

"Take care, Matalina. You know we're all depending on you."

"I know."

As Matalina hung up, she paused for a minute to reflect on her life. So many people were relying on her. While she had willingly accepted this responsibility, she allowed her thoughts to wonder to her past. As far back as she could remember she had been pushed to be the best. Coming in second was never an option. There has never been a challenger who came close, except for Bjorn. Just like her, he had been bred and raised to be the ultimate warrior. She had stayed true to her country and the Maliviziati. He, however, had betrayed it, and thus in her eyes, he had failed.

The nights they had spent together had given her the only nights she can remember of intimacy and a need for sharing any part of her life with another person. She had trusted him–damn it! That would never happen again. Matalina drifted off to sleep as she envisioned their final battle where she would kill him.

Chapter 13

The predawn smells and sounds of someone preparing breakfast for the men alerted Matalina to the fact that she needed to get ready for the assault on the cave. A tasty meal drove her to hurry, but that would be after her first cigar and a cup of Turkish coffee. She smiled, knowing some of her men enjoyed Turkish style as much as she did. They could keep their big fat cigars, she had plenty of the slim ones she enjoyed.

She needed answers and she hoped to get them this morning. As she stood, she started stretching, attempting to ignore the dizzy feeling of standing too quickly. Another doctor would have to be consulted about her growing inner ear problem, which she hid from everyone she could. Vic would know, obviously, but it was one weakness she wanted no one else to know about.

After completing her morning exercises, she walked to the shower, but knowing she would be getting extremely dirty exploring the inside of the mine later today she wondered why. With limited water supply, she would have to do it quickly.

After showering, she knew what might be in front of her today as she selected her gear carefully. Since any power source they had used to light the inside was probably gone, she had to carry her own. A gas mask to filter any poisons that might be inside was essential as well as a temporary oxygen supply.

The weapons she needed were hand to hand combat style and full body armor for any ambushes, which she fully expected. Additionally, she had to be equipped to climb over and under rock facings. When she assembled everything, she estimated she was carrying an extra sixty pounds of gear. So be it.

She greeted her men, who were gathered around a small fire in the center of their small encampment area. They were all dedicated operatives that Vic had trained. This short time of being together was special in helping them bond, but another spot would have to be located later today, and this all depended on what they discovered this morning. She glanced in the direction of the mine, which still had a small amount of smoke filtering into the air. "I assume we saw no activity during the night."

"Nothing at all. We've received some more robots we plan to send into the mine first. That should give us some valuable information on what to expect."

"Great! I was hoping they would be here in time. We'll still need to go in and do a comprehensive search. I think there had to be someone inside manually handling the drones. We also know that one guy using a jeep disappeared somewhere around here."

"Per your instructions, we're going to do our best to take him alive."

As she helped herself to the eggs and sausage she studied her men. These ten men were all seasoned and ones she could count on. "Okay, let's get the copter and plane in the air for coverage. I still think there're other entrances to this we don't know about. If so, we can expect them to make a run for it when we go in."

An hour later, she waited outside the entrance as the robot was directed inside the cave. As expected, it was totally dark inside. The images fed back to the monitor were eerie, but detailed enough to see a road leading back into the mine, but no equipment of any kind was visible.

Abruptly, the road ended. The best she could tell was that a cave-in had happened and blocked the path. It would be impossible to have the robot negotiate around this. They had to go in by foot.

She turned to her men. "I don't know if my explosions made this happen or they did this to hide their getaway. We need to be careful and provide full backup to each other. Stay with your partner and keep the communication lines open. Report anything suspicious."

With the men behind her, she stepped inside and moved to a wall on the right, allowing an armed car to use its lights to give them their first full view of the inside chamber. If they were to receive any gunfire, this might be the moment. After several minutes of waiting, there was none.

When several more men had used the blinding lights to establish positions, she ordered the truck forward. The floor was covered with tire tracks, indicating the cave had been heavily used lately. Still, nothing had been left behind.

Eventually, she saw the spot where the ceiling had collapsed, blocking their path. "Men, make another search to make sure there's no other way out of here." She pointed at two men who were close to her and gave hand signals for them to stay with her to search for a way through the cave-in.

She shifted her flashlight upward. "We have to be careful, since this has to be very weak." Over the next few minutes, the chances of finding a safe way through the blockage weren't worth the risk. The only conclusions she could reach were that either these men were sacrificed, or there was another way out.

Now, she was faced with another decision. With the possibility of more drones being hidden behind this wall, should she permanently seal it, thus killing anyone on the other side?

She opted for one more solution instead. She ordered a camera equipped with motion detectors in addition to an explosive device rigged to permanently seal the cave. If someone tried to climb out later they would be given one warning to surrender. This way the order to destroy everything could be delayed.

As she left the cave, she heard the copter pilot checking in. "I have movement along a ridge three miles north of you."

"What do you have?"

"Three bikes sneaking out of a canyon. I'm not sure where they came from, but they're heading out fast and hard."

"Stay on them, and we'll see if we can intercept them." She turned to the men with her. "Get me a map."

Matalina realized in seconds that the only way of overtaking them, and which had any way of success, required them to mount their own bikes and chase after them. If she had the copter return to pick her up, they would get lost in the rugged mountains somewhere, or make it to a cross road. "Get the bikes ready. We have some hard riding to do."

The trip over the top of the range proved more brutal than she had anticipated and she lost one of her men to a broken cycle, leaving her with just one other man. Descending the other side wouldn't be any easier. From her vantage point she could see out over the prairie stretching in front of her. In the distance she could see a copter, which she assumed was hers.

After she briefly stopped to refer to her map, she saw the shortest route, but could only image how rough it might be. She turned to the man with her. "Do you think you can make this, or would you prefer to try this longer but easier route? We might make the same time, but who knows. Since he was a warrior much like her, she was not surprised when he nodded his head and pointed to the steepest route. "Good! Let's stay close in case we need to help each other."

Minutes later they were sliding sideways but under control. Still, her bike soon slipped under her two different times. Each time, however, she had managed to get it upright and pointed down the hill. After she made it to a small knoll, she knew they had the worst behind them. The guy behind her soon moved in beside her. After nodding her approval of his skills, she twisted the throttle and attacked the next section.

Fifteen minutes later they hit level ground and a trail many bikers and four wheelers had used. She yelled into the mic for the copter pilot. "Do you still have them in sight?"

"Yes, these guys are good and they must be either locals or I would suspect . . . mercenaries. You're going to have to match their speeds to catch them. On your right is a short cut that might help some."

"Can you see us?"

"Yes, the dust storm you're kicking up is highlighting you big time in the sun."

If the pilot could see them, she wondered who else could spot them. Becoming a target or not, she had to push on. She nodded to her only team member with her to follow her lead as she sped along looking for a fork to her right.

The copter pilot soon broke in with a quick command. "The trail's on your right now."

She hit the brakes and looked for it. She saw another rough downhill torture trail. The bikes couldn't take much more. With a quick rake of her teeth over her upper lip, she twisted the throttle again and eased forward.

After making it to the bottom, she turned to see her team member slide sideways and lose his bike. She pushed off her own and rushed to help him. He was favoring his leg as they made it to the bottom. "Are you okay?"

"I'll survive, let's go."

She started to insist he stay, fearing that he may have broken his leg, but she needed him if at all possible. "Stay with me if you can. If not, I understand, and I'll send someone to get you soon. We won't attempt any more hills like that one." After she watched him nod in appreciation, she yelled at the pilot again. "We had a small accident. How far are we behind now?"

"You aren't in bad shape now. You have flat roads ahead of you that will help you gain on them."

Ten minutes later she checked in again. "Give me an update."

"The trail you're on will intercept with theirs in a few minutes. I'll advise which way they head when they get there."

She glanced at her team member who was following her and had managed to stay with her. Good for him. She owed him something special for being such a good soldier.

The pilot shouted back at her again. "Damn,

175

they're splitting up. I'm fairly sure they've spotted me by now!"

"Take the one to the right and I'll send the other bike after him. I'll chase the others on my own. How far ahead will they be?"

"You're perhaps two minutes behind them. You'll see a paved country road ahead of you. Head west on it. We also have a plane scrambling to help, but I'm still not sure how long that will take."

"Good! Let me know." She saw the crossroad ahead. Since she knew that the other guy was monitoring the conversation, she waved at him as they split company, wishing him the best.

The bike she was on was for trails and not racing, but she pushed it to close to one hundred, the top speed she could get out of it. With no eyes in the sky, she had no idea if she was gaining or losing ground. She could see nothing ahead of her.

The pilot broke back in with a report. "This rider's making a stop behind a small sign. I think he's planning an ambush." She hoped her team member got the message as the pilot continued. "I'm swinging to the other side to get a better view now." She couldn't wait for more details, since she had to press on and catch the guy ahead of her. The pilot breaking the silence again, however, made her slow to listen better. "Damn, I think he had recovered a missile launcher of some kind. We have to make a run for it."

"Shit, get out of there now!" As she waited for an update, she saw blue lights behind her in the distance that were gaining on her. Not now! "I have problems also. Are you safe?" Since there was no response, she feared the worst. Even at her top speed, the police cruiser was gaining on her.

She suddenly heard from her team member. "The copter has been hit and is circling, but going down. Shall I assist or continue to chase?"

She quickly made her decision. "Check on the pilot, since he might need your help. Without his eyes in the sky it would be hard to go after the biker. Watch out for this guy also. I doubt it, but he might be still waiting for you as well."

Matalina glanced behind her. How was she going to lose this patrol car? She had no time to explain who she was. Then, she saw a roadblock ahead of her. The other biker must have made it pass them moments before. She had no choice but to stop. This guy had gotten away this time. Whoever he was, he was definitely good on his bike. Who was he?

As she slowed her bike, she checked in with the other member of her team. "Did you find them?"

"Yes, I'm with them now. They crashed, but are alive. We need medical attention as soon as possible."

Another member of her team responded. "We have a medical copter in route to you now."

As Matalina came to a full stop, she issued one last order. "Shut down this operation and clean the area."

"What about the explosives that have been rigged in the mine?"

"Since they have another way out, seal the cave from that side." She raised her hands as two Texas rangers walked toward her with their weapons raised. With a slow motion, she removed her helmet. As expected, they stopped to study her. Yes, her white spiked hair definitely caught their attention. "Relax! I have a diplomatic card in my pocket."

Both men stopped, but acted unconvinced as they

177

slightly separated and waited as she calmly retrieved it and handed it to the first one to step forward. After glancing at it, he handed it to the other ranger. "This is Texas, not Washington. I'll have to check this out, since we just received a call reporting multiple explosions and casualties in the mountains behind you."

Interesting! Who would report such? "As I'm sure you understand, I can't be charged with anything."

After jumping from the car that was chasing her, the next ranger rushed in behind her. "You saw the lights. This is going to get you some serious jail time."

"You need to take a look at this." The other officer waved him over. "She has diplomatic immunity."

Matalina glanced at the road ahead of her. She would love to have their assistance in chasing this guy, but she knew to keep this quiet. She waited for them to complete their mandatory incident report, which she knew would soon be buried back in Washington from everyone but the one guy she maintained some contact with in the CIA. Yes, she knew he would want to talk to her again.

She listened without drawing attention as the guy who appeared to be the highest ranking officer there received a call on his cell phone. It was obvious he was getting a call to investigate the copter crash west of there. Someone must have seen it and called it in. Somehow she needed to stall him and give her team time to clear the scene.

Matalina reached for a note pad. "I think we all know you're all violating the Geneva Convention rules by stopping me today, and I don't have to answer any questions. I do need to make a note of what happened and report it myself, so I'll need to see your ID one more time to record this."

"I would love to accommodate you, but it appears we have a situation I need to attend to." He started to walk toward his vehicle, but he stopped when she stepped in his path. "I see. I'll have to make a call first."

Since she didn't want to overplay her hand she waited for him, knowing any other rangers in the area would be a long way from here and would thus give her team the necessary time to sweep the crash site.

Matalina slowly scribbled the information until the tall ranger answered his phone again. "Yes, sir. She's right here." He extended the phone her. "The CIA wants to talk to you."

That was much faster than she had anticipated. She placed the writing pad back in her pocket and accepted the phone. "I'm listening."

"Matalina, what are you doing there? I thought you had gone back to wherever it is you live."

"Apparently, I'm back to take care of some unfinished business."

"And from what I've heard, you're using my country for your own private war exercises. Do you care to tell me what's going on?"

"You know I don't have to answer that question."

"And you know I can have your diplomatic immunity revoked."

"You can try, but if you want me to make it easier for you I can get the state department on the line for a three way." She waited for him to respond. He didn't. "I have a better solution, if you're willing to do a fair trade of information. I promise I've something you'll want to hear, and to sweeten the pot, I have a special

179

gift for you."

"Really!"

She needed more information on what they knew, and if they had no clue, she needed to discretely inform them. "I'll only make this offer once."

"Where and when do you want to meet?"

"In Houston . . . the day after tomorrow. I'll contact you with an exact address then."

"Shall I say you're on very dangerous ground here?"

"I usually am. See you then."

The rest of the day revealed few clues on what was going on other than this must have been another testing ground for the drones, but why here? Yes, it was isolated and had high winds that might be used to gain altitude for the drones, but that would make them readily visible to radar. Was designing a stealth design the next objective? That's what Olaf had suggested.

Since she didn't know when the rangers might discover them again, she knew this had to be the last day in the area. The decision to split the team was difficult, but she needed the laser defense trailer moved to Houston, where it would secretly be given to the CIA to defend the Houston oil tankers. While she hoped it would never be needed, she felt better knowing it was in place. Still, final delivery required the approval of her father and the German government.

The small team she had remaining were specialists she would need when she got back to the storage facility they had discovered earlier. She expected the place to be rigged with explosives, which is why she had the best explosive expert she knew with her.

"Men, we all know what we have to do. Take your time traveling, and try hard to avoid drawing attention."

Olaf looked at the trucks. "This equipment isn't something I can teach anyone to use quickly. It'll mean I'll have to stay for many weeks, if not permanently to supervise this loan."

She knew he might be right. Although she hoped to see the Germans gift the system to the United States, a loan for right now might be all she had authorization to grant. "I hope to have an answer on this when we get to Houston. Much depends on the CIA and the guarantees I receive from them."

Chapter 14

The two owners of the storage facility, who had beer cans in their hands and many empty ones around them, weren't too happy to see her walk in. "You . . . I thought we would never have to see you again."

"Stay calm, sweetheart, and all will be cool." She waited as her two men walked in behind her. "I'm here to do you a favor."

"What's that?" The smaller guy had a cast on his arm where she had broken it earlier.

"Since I've heard nothing about an explosion here, I'll assume you haven't tried to open the storage unit. We're here to see if we can defuse it."

His eyes widened as he stood. "So, you really do think some foreign terrorist type group has chosen us to store their fucking explosives?"

"There's only one way to find out for sure. Since we don't know what to expect, we'll take every precaution we can. Anything close to this unit that can be moved needs to happen now."

"It'll take a while to notify the other renters."

"I'll leave money to compensate others, but that's not what I mean. You have three hours to move any vehicle and sensitive records you might want to preserve."

"Just how big of an explosion do you think we're facing here?"

"Since this might be stolen military explosives, it could be massive. On the other hand, it could be just rigged to kill us as we go in. We'll know soon."

Several hours later, the owners were persuaded to guard the entrance coming into the property as she and her men went to work. The blast suit felt uncomfortable, but she knew it was imperative that she wore it, even at this range. "Okay, send in the robot and let's get started."

As she watched the small robot roll forward, she double checked the monitor which gave great images. The first step would be cutting a small hole in the door using a laser. After this was accomplished, she held her breath for a second. All was going as planned so far.

She watched the technician extend the video camera through the hole so any motion type sensor wouldn't be activated. The room appeared to be vacant as the camera scanned the room. Then, in the back corner she saw a box, which was perhaps two feet tall and four feet wide. At this angle it was hard to tell how long it was. The grayish green color matched the ones she had seen in the Florida Everglades.

"We need to be careful." She slowly breathed in as she told the expert while pointing to them. "I think that might be the explosives we're looking for."

"I don't see any wires going to the box, but I'll keep doing a scan to see if I see anything else suspicious."

Fifteen minutes later he stopped the scan and pointed to the monitor. "There." She could see what looked like a small box attached to the far right side of the door. A small green light was flashing from the top of it. "I thought we might be faced with this, but since they were apparently coming back for this box, there has to be a way to disarm it remotely."

Eventually, they found wires going to a sensor

above the door, and contacts to the door itself. With another laser mounted on the robotic arm, they would try to cut these, but it was tricky. Before doing so, they would take more photos of the box and any samples they could from the floor. There was writing on the side of the box in Arabic. It would have to be translated better when they had time.

An hour later the laser had worked perfectly in cutting the wires. The moment of truth would come next. Cutting the lock with the laser was easy enough. Prying the forklift arms under the door was the next challenge. It was also all that might be needed to set off the charge.

A whistling sound above her made her glance up. Another missile had been fired. She grabbed the back of the bomb technician and pushed him to the ground. The first explosion was much lower than she had anticipated. Seconds later another explosion rocked the entire area, throwing debris from this unit and others around it everywhere. She felt the force of the explosion racing over the top of her.

She waited several seconds until she glanced up. Debris was still wildly flying around the sky above her. With the chance of this falling on them, she braced herself. Then, she heard her other member who had gone to secure the gate check in. "Matt, are you okay?

"We're fine, but shaken a little. Where did this missile come from?"

"Missile? I never saw it."

"Since we know these things have to be hand launched, someone has to be within a mile or so of here. Let's find him–now!" She quickly stood and started removing her bomb suit, knowing she had to move fast. She yelled at the technician, who wasn't a combat operative, as she prepared to move out. "You stay here and see if you can find anything useful. I'll be back soon."

The guy she had left at the gate checked back in again. "These two guys want to help. Since they know the area and will be more eyes, what do you think, Matt?

"I hate to involve them any further, but we don't have time to argue with them. I want you to head north for one mile and then circle eastwardly. I'll go south and then circle to the west. Report in with anything you see. Let's find this assassin."

As she carried her pack, which was loaded for combat, Matalina jogged to the south, looking for any vantage point she could use. About a mile to her southwest she saw one small hill. She had to suck it up and push forward.

Her hard work paid off when she saw a small van at the base of the hill. This time she had to take a prisoner she could get info out of. While calculating the best way to get there without being seen, she yelled for her backup as she jogged. "I think I might have something. It's a small van parked at the edge of a small hill. Do you have anything?"

"I've a good view from a hill here, but I see nothing. I'm several miles away so it'll take me a while to get there, but I'm on my way."

"I'm not sure how long these guys will stick around, so I might not be able to wait for you. When you get to the last half mile, check back in with me and try to stay hidden as best you can."

"Will do. I'm mobile."

As Matalina crawled to within a few hundred

yards of the van, she saw the two storage owners rushing toward the van. They had spotted it also. Convenient, she thought at first, as she waited to see what would happen next. She checked her watch and calculated her backup was still better than five minutes away.

After dropping to a position behind a small bolder, she assembled her rifle, mounted a scope, and loaded the chamber before she focused the scope on the van. The owners who had too much to drink half ran and half staggered on toward the van.

As they stopped about thirty feet in front of the van, she could hear them yelling, but she couldn't make out the words. Still, she saw no reaction coming from the van. With few seconds left to prepare, she added a silencer to the front of her rifle. She had no clue how many men might be in the van, and she needed any advantage she could obtain.

Moments later, she saw a door open, but no one stepped outside. One of the owners decided to rush toward the van, but fell as a small puff of smoke came from the van that was immediately followed by the sound of the blast. He struggled on the ground as the other guy tried to make a run for it.

Since he needed cover, she focused on the front of the van, hoping to hit the motor and disable it. The three shots had to grab their attention, but not before they shot the guy making a run for it. He had, however, disappeared from sight, making it impossible to see how bad he had been hit.

She yelled into her mic again. "We have the two owners down, and I'm not sure if they're dead or not. The shots came from the van, and I still don't know how many men are inside. Let me know when you're in place."

While she waited, she targeted the tires on her side of the van. Even after hitting them, she saw no more reaction coming from the van. They had to know they were a sitting target. Why didn't they make a run for it?

Shortly, her backup was in position as he reported in. "I see the van."

"There has been no movement since they shot these two guys and I disabled their vehicle. We may have to smoke them out doing something different. I want to take them alive if we can."

"I understand. Just let me know what you want me to do."

"Let's try this. I'm going to fire some more warning shots and see if they get the message." Seconds later, she fired a half round into the front of the van. It worked, as one guy raised his hands when he stepped out of the van. Somehow, however, she assumed there would be more than one since the earlier shot came from the passenger side.

He stepped several feet from the van when another shot broke the silence. Moments later, she saw one of the owners staggering forward with a gun in his hand. No! She needed him alive! She yelled into the mic. "We have no choice, move in now."

When she reached the clearing where the van was parked, several more shots erupted. After the owner fired many rounds, he went down harder this time, indicating he had taken a direct hit. With her backup covering her, she swung open the door and pointed her gun inside, prepared to fire at the slightest of movements if she needed to.

Blood was splattered everywhere. One gunman

inside had taken a bullet to his forehead. There was no one else in the van. She backed out and went to the other guy from the van. He had been hit in the chest and was spitting blood, but alive. At the rate of blood he was losing, she knew he might not live long.

She lifted his head. "What's your name and who do you work for?" He simply spit more blood in response. "Talk to me."

He attempted to speak, but his words were in Arabic, a language she slightly knew. His deep black hair and beard, along with his dark olive skin placed him from somewhere in the Middle East, but it would take some time to have him positively identified.

As she held him, he attempted one more time to say something. He reached for a gold necklace he had on him and said one word she recognized. "Family." She thought she understood. He wanted this returned to his family.

"You have to tell me who and where."

As he groaned one last time, he patted his pocket as he spoke in English. "They forced me here. My family will be killed. Please tell them I love them."

Chapter 15

This wasn't the first time Matalina had visited the Port of Houston to see their complex network of commercial and private shipping facilities. The smell of oil mixed with salty ocean breezes permutated everywhere, including the fish market which competed with it at times. The horns blasting away on some of the larger vessels confirmed just how busy the traffic was in the bay below.

This vacant warehouse she was exploring would be perfect in hiding their operation. It was next to Galveston Bay that adjoined the Gulf of Mexico, one of the busiest ports in all of North America. Since these giant oil tankers were constantly loading and unloading there, they could easily become the target of these drone attacks.

CIA Agent Nelson's car soon arrived, followed by two other officially matching vehicles. He had always been hard to get information out of, but she had a major negotiating chip this time. She retrieved one of her small cigars and lit it as she waited for him to approach her.

"Hello, Matt. I hope you've something good to offer me. My boss is demanding some answers on why you think you can bring in a small army and run rampant all over my great country here." Nelson slowly but steadily spoke, allowing his words to accentuate his slow southern drawl.

Matt waved her cigar around. "I'm always impressed with this place." She grinned to accentuate her white gold teeth. "And . . . your southern hospitality." She twitched the corner of her mouth in a teasing play of wits she knew she had to play.

"This time, I think you've pushed your weight around a little too much. So, don't waste my time and tell me what you have for me, Matt."

Matalina pointed to her cigar again. "As we both know, one small spark is all that's needed to ignite a major fire." She inhaled and blew out a major puff before she continued. "In exchange for a major gift that you desperately need, I also need something."

"Matt, you still haven't said what it is you need, and what gift we're talking about. I don't think you've ever attempted to bribe me before."

"This isn't a bribe, and I'll be honest. What I'm about to give you, or loan you, is something you do . . . *desperately* need. This isn't only for your protection, but for the interest of many countries, including mine."

"I'm still listening."

"You have information on many terrorist groups, and much of which you're not sharing, including certain players that I need to be told the truth about."

"Matt, you have to know that gaining information on our various operatives will never happen."

"Sweetheart, I'm not looking for an open house to satisfy my endless curiosity." She studied him, hoping to detect any giveaway signs. "But since it's in our mutual interest, I need to know more about cases you're working involving drone attacks in America. These terrorist are operating on a worldwide scale, and I'd hate to compromise your men by mistake." That was about as diplomatic as she could present her case. Everyone had agents, who were often known to be double agents.

"This is still too classified to allow you any access. Now if you have a specific name you care to mention, I'm listening, obviously, but you know I can't confirm or deny anything at all." He twisted his head slightly, a small clue she did have his interest. "Just be sure you can backup what you infer."

"I see. Maybe a small glimpse of what I have to offer will encourage you to be a little more cooperative." She motioned for Olaf to walk over from her van. He nervously followed her direction as he apparently knew what the stakes were in this game. "This is Dr. Olaf Joachim."

Nelson glanced at him, but said nothing.

"Dr. Joachim is German. Since you might not know who he is, let me mention something to you that might be of interest. Since we're talking about drones."

"Are we?"

Matt laughed at the comment. "America has concentrated on and is currently dominating the development of drones. No one questions that, if you're talking warfare use that is."

Although Nelson acted like he wasn't studying Olaf, she knew better. "And your point is?"

"The Germans haven't been blindly standing on the side. They see an entirely different use for drones, and they also see the need to develop a defense system to protect their country. Until now, that technology has been top secret."

Nelson yawned before he spoke. "It's no secret that the average American approves of the use of drones in warfare by a large margin, while in Europe it's . . . shall I say . . . highly unpopular."

"At least we can agree on one thing, but this is

also why America isn't having this new technology shared with them." Since this was no surprise to him, she, at least, opened the door for him to proceed.

"Matt, are you here to offer me some kind of new technology that I can't obtain, for some reason, on my own?" He paused for a minute. "Additionally, what makes you think I would want or need this new technology you're hinting at?"

Matalina smiled again, giving him a full view of her white-gold teeth. "Like it or not, you have more of a current threat than you might know or want to admit."

"I assume you're talking about this little commotion you caused in western Texas. If so, I think we have that handled."

Bingo. He had more information, but would he share? "As you know, the development of drone technology requires a lot of testing." She decided to drop the bait in front of him and see if he would bite. "You do know the winds from western Texas blow most of the time directly over Houston."

"That would take a lot of technology that we both know will take a while to develop."

"Nelson, what you don't understand is that one of the top minds in drone technology may be already testing prototypes, oh yes, right here in America." If this didn't get his attention, this meeting was useless.

"In the spirit of cooperation, I'll see what information I can clear to give you, but I can make no promises. Additionally, in the future, you have to leave any more missions in America to us."

He could hope for such, but she knew she would be back soon. "I have to return to my country, and then another part of the world needs me. I would love to know that you have this contained." She turned to Olaf. "This man will stay here and show you how to use this defense system that will hopefully prevent a drone attack on these tankers. It will be your responsibility to see how effective this works out. I also hope we can keep this operation quiet, which will be good for all parties concerned."

For one of the few times she ever remembered, she watched him offer her a smile. "It's good to see you again, Matt. I trust you'll be leaving soon, however."

"I will as soon as this is operational. I'm sure you would expect nothing less."

Chapter 16

After Matalina finished her strong Turkish coffee and the first cigar of the day, she stood to stretch inside the darkened cabin of the small jet she was using to sneak her inside Afghanistan. This would be an unofficial visit. While listening to the gentle hum of the engines, she quickly recognized the dizzy sensation which had started to haunt her more every day. While she blamed it on the concussion she had received a few weeks ago, she worried about how it would affect her future ability to complete missions.

From the last specialist she saw, she had consented to a small medical procedure that might help. He had diagnosed it as perilymph fistula caused by the blow to the back of her head. He mentioned that until she had it repaired she would not only feel off balanced during times of stress, but also when she was subjected to rapid changes in air pressure.

All of this was the result of tears in her inner ear. The surgery wasn't difficult, but would require her to take time to rest and allow it to heal. That wasn't possible now. She had to research this group more when she had a chance. The CIA was either too smug to realize they had a major problem, or were part of it, thus being used as a tool of some new world order group. As expected, the information she received from Nelson was disappointing. They had concentrated on various Al-Qaeda type groups, and they have completely left off any ties to any various splinter groups of the Illuminati. Still, this wasn't too surprising since many remnants of the Illuminati had major influence over the CIA.

She just had a few days available to complete her current mission inside Afghanistan. Since Zafar had disappeared again she had no more leads other than what she might learn from his past. The last terrorist who had died in her arms had given her one clue she wasn't expecting. As such, she felt compelled to honor his last request. Something told her he was, as he inferred, not a willing participant in this terrorist attack in America.

She turned the Christian cross over in her hand again. The number of Christians who openly professed the religion in Afghanistan was extremely rare. As such, how had this man been recruited, or possibly forced, to join Zafar's group?

Since her Arabic was limited, she had taken a translator by the name of Aqil Kassab with her. As the jet descended, she had to find a seat to keep from falling. She could tell no one she had this problem. Only her doctor and Vic knew anything about it, and it would remain that way.

While she thought about using her diplomatic flags to get around, she had changed her mind so she could cautiously approach this guy's wife, and not put her in additional peril. Matalina had no clue if the wife knew her husband had died or not.

Although it would be Aqil, the translator, who would arrange a private meeting, she needed to be active after she arrived. She knew the dangers involved, since she wasn't the kind of woman most of them had ever seen.

She slipped into her cover she had to use while there. Her spiky white hair was covered with a black wig. Just in case she had to remove her veil, which she doubted would ever happen here, the solid white-gold teeth had white veneers covering them. How could anyone permanently live like this?

After clearing through the airport, she rode in the back seat of her rented car with her driver clueless as to who she was. She allowed Aqil to do all of the talking. If anything, they might think that she was his wife. At this point, it didn't matter if she could slip quietly into the countryside and to the small town, where she hoped to find answers.

The one large hotel in the area had been booked for her, and with the amount of money they had paid for discretion, she doubted they would have any problems for a few days. While this was the first of her three tasks, it might be the one that yielded major clues as to how to track down Zafar's terrorist group again.

She had no doubt Zafar was in America somewhere, but with Nelson watching her every move there, she had to wait and come in with surgical skills the next time. Finding out how Zafar was able to recruit others and how he was funded was critical to stopping him. It was obvious he had been able to force some people to work for him against their will.

After checking in, she waited until the front desk was quiet. Then, she sent Aqil to see if the wife of the man who had given her some information before he died would come to visit with her. Zafar had forced him into going to Columbia to work for him and maintain that outpost on the mountain there where the drones would be tested.

Matalina knew how much of a risk this would be for his wife, but one that would be necessary if she was to receive information about her husband. In addition to returning the necklace, Matalina also hoped to provide some support if she was helpful in helping her get to the bottom of this mystery.

After a long wait, she heard a knock on the door. She covered her head, just in case, and walked to the door. "Hello."

"It's me, unlock the door." As she did, she saw Aqil with a small woman and one man. The woman was fully veiled, much as she would have expected. She had no clue who the guy was, but he could have been a relative, realizing that married women were not allowed out of their home without a male escort who was part of their family.

She stepped to one side as she used her limited Arabic. "Please . . . be welcome."

The stranger wore a keffiyeh on his head. His beard was dark black and full length which hung to his chest. His heavy black eyebrows semi framed his deep dark brown eyes that constantly shifted from side to side. Since he hesitated, Matalina stepped back further, giving him more space.

Although this made her mission more complicated, Matalina still intended to give this unexpected widow the necklace the dying man had insisted that she take to her. While it was with a strange sense of compassion, it was also part of a burning curiosity as to how he was recruited. This was something she had noticed several times during this mission. She knew she was missing something.

Aqil motioned to a sitting area in the suite, suggesting that the man have a seat. As soon as everyone was settled in, he began. "This is the brother-in-law to the guy you have information about."

This information helped, but still made her keep

her guard up. Matalina decided to lower her veil to test the situation. "Tell them that my name is Matalina, and that I was recently in America."

Before he could translate, the brother-in-law spoke. "We speak English, if that helps."

"Thanks, my Arabic is limited." She lowered her veil more, hoping to make them at ease.

Thankfully, the women lowered hers also. "I understand you have information for me regarding my husband."

Matalina reached for the small package that contained the necklace. "He insisted that I get this to you," she said, as she waited for the reaction from the widow.

She whimpered softly, as if trying to stay in control. "No, please don't tell me what I've feared would happen to him."

"I'm so sorry." Matalina watched the widow briefly touch the cross before she glanced at her brother.

Her brother spoke as she sobbed. "Thank you for bringing this to us, and for being discrete in doing so. This cross signifies that we're Christian, and this could get us all killed."

The widow grasped the cross in her hand tighter. "How did he die?"

"He was shot during the commission of a terrorist act." The truth couldn't be sugar coated since she had to come to grips with what he did. This might be the only way she could get to the *why*. She could tell he wasn't a willing participant in this.

The brother-in-law stopped her from saying more, as he leaned forward. "Before we say too much, is it alright if I ask you who you are? Do you work for the government?"

"No, not this one."

"Then, what's your part in this?" He looked confused.

"For the sake of conversation, let us assume I work for a special task force that fights terrorism. It might be best if I don't tell you any more than that."

"Fair enough. I hope you'll respect us when we tell you something, something I think you might have already guessed by now." He glanced sideways. "We're Christian, and her husband had been a minister to our small house church for several years. That is, until we were discovered. He was given a chance to escape and go to America. There he was to get himself established, so that the rest of us could follow."

He had been sent to America as a sleeper cell, and one they activated when he was in Texas. She wondered how much more information she could find out on this operation. "If I understand properly, he was forced into this operation, or he and his family would be killed. Is that what I'm hearing?"

"Exactly . . . and now that he has been killed, they'll be back for a replacement." She cried as she moved closer to her brother. "What can we do?"

"If you're willing to tell me everything you know, I might be able to help."

"How can you do that?"

"I have diplomatic immunity and I might be able to get you out of the country, right now."

"And the others?"

"Depending on the number, we can work on it. They'll need to go into hiding for now." She knew this wouldn't be easy, but she would do her best. Just in case she ran into problems, she needed questions answered now. "It would tremendously help me if I knew who recruited him, and for me to find out who he was working for."

She watched both of them shake and close their eyes. "You know this will get many people killed here."

"Many people here and around the world will die if you don't tell me."

"There was a guy here who was part of our group, a good kid at the time. His family was killed in a drone attack. We accepted him in our homes and helped raise him, until he left us."

Could this be a missing part to what had bugged her? She retrieved the photo of Zafar to show them. "Is this that guy?"

They both looked at it before glancing at each other. "It has been many years now, but I think that could be him. How do you know him?"

"I don't know him, but I've been hunting for him. I think he might be the leader of this terrorist group."

"If so, we're in much more danger than you know. He knows everyone here."

"How many people are we talking about in this group of yours?"

"About thirty, which also includes all of the children."

"This is a full bus load. Let me see what I can arrange."

"I don't think we have much time. You know we were probably followed here."

Matalina walked to a window and moved to one side so she could see outside. "I think we might be safe inside here, but I think we can expect an attack as soon as we leave." She quickly considered her options.

A rescue copter could be called in to take her to safety, but it would only have room for a few extra passengers. She needed a bus of some kind to haul the rest to a place of safety.

"Listen, you need you to get a message to the others, but you're not to leave here. Do you think you can do that by phone?"

"Phones aren't safe here." He wiped his face before he continued. "I have a nephew, by the name of Abdul, who works at the hotel. He can get a message to them, but it'll take time for everyone to be contacted."

"Can they all be trusted?"

"Yes, they're all relatives. You'll see." He stood. "How much time do we have?"

"I'm not sure, but they need to be ready to move soon, perhaps even later tonight."

"I'll send word to them. I hope we can trust you and your word."

"Just remember that I said that I would try. This is going to be tricky."

"I understand. We have no weapons. You have to know that."

"My rescue team will be well armed. If they can make it to the hotel without being seen, it would be good."

"I'll work on it. Thank you."

After quickly assembling a team, Matalina concentrated on getting more answers. The best she could determine was that over fifty other men had been sent to America, and all of them could be sleepers like this guy had been. She realized that all of them had been sent against their will. With so many people in Afghanistan who hated America, why were these men chosen?

The answer surprised her, but she should've seen it earlier. While it might be hard for a Muslim to be active and undetected inside a Christian church, these men would easily assimilate, and they could do so for years.

She accepted an incoming call. "Matt, we'll be arriving at close to three in the morning. In whisper mode we'll be hard to detect, but not impossible. It'll take three trips to airlift everyone. We have a team of six who will establish a base in the hotel and they will be the last ones out. How's everything on your end?"

"We have about one half of the group already safely inside. The others are waiting until later to sneak in."

"As requested, we'll make contact with NATO just prior to entering Afghanistan airspace. We might need their help if this doesn't go as planned."

"Good. I'll let you know when all is ready here." She ended the call and removed her local clothing, revealing the battle fatigue underneath. The brother-in-law stared at her. Yes, she had to be a total shock to him.

Several hours later they were still waiting for one family of six when a loud blast shook the hotel. Matalina rushed to a window and peeked outside to see a car burning below her. She had little doubt that was carrying the last family.

After alerting the incoming copter, she studied the people who had placed their lives in her hands. Would it be safe to have the copter land on top of the hotel now? Not hardly, as she yelled instructions to the pilot. "We need backup, but it's too dangerous to land long enough to make a pick up."

"Understood, I'll find a place to drop some of the men and make it back to a hillside not far away where I'll wait further orders."

Matalina turned to the brother-in-law. "I have help coming, but I'm not sure what we're facing when we try to make a run for it."

Abdul rushed over to her. "We have a couple of shuttles we use to go back and forth to the airport. I can get the keys."

Matalina reconnected with the pilot. "We're working on a plan, and we'll need a combination of diversion and cover. We're going to use the shuttles at the hotel to make a run for it. How far away are you?"

"Ten minutes. What kind of diversion do you need?"

"Come out of whisper mode and draw some attention to the west of here. Don't take unnecessary chances, since we'll need the copter after we get out of the city. After we clear the hotel, we'll be heading east toward Pakistan. Please see if you can drop some of the men to ride on the shuttles with us. This . . . will have to be played by ear."

"Understood. Will ten minutes give you enough time to get prepared?"

"We're heading for them now. I'll let you know when we're all aboard." She turned to Abdul and waved at the small group. "We have to leave fast. Let's move it!"

Abdul led the way down a back stairway to the main floor. He hesitated as he prepared to open the door. "We'll be in the open for a minute as we walk to the garage."

Matalina breathed in deeply, wishing she had the pleasure of waiting for the copter, but she knew the longer they waited, the more time they had to plan an ambush for her. She motioned for everyone to stay behind so she could check it out. The door creaked as it opened.

At first she saw nothing, so she opened it wider to see in the other direction. Almost a dozen men turned to study her from across the open lot. When she saw several rifles swinging in her direction, she raised her Glock eighteen and pulled the trigger, releasing all thirty two rounds in seconds. She saw the men drop, with some hit full force, and with others scrambling to avoid her fully automatic weapon.

She pulled the clip and slammed in another one. There was no turning back now. Several were frantically firing while attempting to regroup. The next round she fired silenced the group. She reloaded and glanced around. With all looking clear for now, she swung the door open and yelled at the frightened crowd she was responsible for. "Let's move it now. We should have the copter distracting them any minute."

The shuttles weren't nearly as big as she had hoped for, but they would have to do. Abdul grabbed the keys and tossed one set to his uncle. As the crowd scrambled to pack the shuttles, she heard more gunshots with bullets hitting the side of one of the shuttles. She used her instincts and turned to fire in the direction she anticipated the shots were coming from.

While this stopped the shooting for now, she knew it would only be temporary. She yelled into her mic. "We need that diversion now!"

"I see flashes coming from gunfire ahead. We'll be able to fire upon them in seconds."

She rushed onto the shuttle and yelled for Abdul to make a run for it. Since the windows were worthless in stopping anything, she smashed out the side window with the butt of her gun, giving her a much better view of the entrance to the hotel where more men were running in her direction.

Then, she heard the machine gun fire from above. Her men had arrived. As the shuttle made the turn onto the main street, she unloaded the Glock eighteen one more time by firing back at the men chasing them.

After making it a block away, all looked good. Still, she expected them to continue chasing them as she yelled at Abdul. "We need to push it and find a place for the copter to drop off some more firepower for us."

"I know a place about a mile ahead that's near a small bridge. There'll be room for the copter, but it'll mean being in the open again for a minute."

"So be it. I'll contact the pilot." For several minutes she attempted to hail the copter without receiving any response. Had they been hit?

After another block, she glanced behind them where she still saw no one chasing after them. Then, she received a weak call from another copter located in Turkey stating they had received a mayday call. They had the location of the downed copter and were scrambling, but it would take some time to get there.

Matalina yelled for them to stop the transporters. Should she jeopardize this rescue attempt and help her men, or ask them to dig in and wait for the backup? As the minutes ticked off she knew she had to make a decision soon.

Finally, she heard from one of them. "We received a direct hit and the copter is gone."

"I need a location. We don't have much room, but we'll have to work it out."

"We're near a river, where we plan to make it to as soon as we rig more explosives to this copter. We know it wouldn't be good to have it identified."

Abdul pushed forward. "They have to be just north of us on the river I mentioned to you earlier."

After convincing herself the extra manpower would be worth the chance in looking for them, she yelled back into the receiver. These were, also, her men, ones dedicated to her. "We're in two transporters from the hotel. Look for us! We're heading your way."

"Are you sure, we have a rescue team on the way."

"I had a weak message from them earlier. We'll still need them, but as cover for now."

"Understood. You'll see a large explosion in about five minutes. We'll be somewhere just south of it on the river bank."

Matalina pointed to road ahead. "Let's go get them, but we'll have to move fast and make some more room somehow. I want them posted on the front and rear of the transporters. I think we're going to see many more people after us soon."

True to her operative's words, another loud explosion rocked the early morning tranquility less than a half kilometer north of them. They had to be close by. She saw a small warehouse to her left. "Pull over close to it and look for somewhere to get out of sight until we find my men."

Abdul pointed to the right. "The river's two blocks that way."

Matalina attempted to make contact again. "Listen up! We're about a couple blocks west of you and next to a small warehouse. Do you copy?"

No response. Since she didn't hear anymore gunfire, she assumed they were safe but on foot somewhere along the bank. "Stay here. Make room for six men, and get these transporters ready for a wild run. We have to get to the desert and find an extraction point fast."

"You need to hurry, since this place will be crawling with people any minute."

"No shit!" She tossed him a gun. "You might need this." She had a general idea where the river was, even if the few scattered lights didn't help much. Finding them wasn't going to be easy. Luckily, she saw no one walking around. With the explosion loud enough to wake everyone for miles, she knew that wouldn't last for long.

She ran hard, hoping to hit nothing in the dark. The river had a small road running next to it, but left her more exposed than she had wanted. Now, were they slightly north or south of her? She tried the radio again–nothing.

She decided to head north for a few hundred meters. If she saw nothing, she would retract double time and attempt to overtake them. A block away, a spotlight shattered the darkness, blinding her before she could locate a place to hide.

While the words yelled at her were in Arabic, she had no doubt someone wanted her to halt and stand still. Like hell she would! Since she remembered the river bank offered very little cover, she bolted to her left and tried to find anything she could use.

As expected, she heard gunfire and saw the bullets

hitting the ground in front of her. She had to stop and hit the ground before they locked in on her location. With the Glock set for fully automatic, she unloaded all thirty two rounds at the light.

At least one of them found its mark as the light vanished, but leaving her night blinded. She hoped it was the same for them, as she staggered toward a building she had seen earlier.

She replaced the clip in her Glock and located her combat knife as she edged along a wall. Surely, if her men were close by they would come to help her. The eerie quiet, a strange calmness along the darkened street, surprised her. She expected much more attention to the gunfire.

Without warning, she heard a voice on her radio. "We hear gunshots ahead of us. Please advice."

"I had company, and I'm not sure if it was neutralized or not. Investigating now."

"Understood. We're running hot, and should be there shortly."

"Hurry!"

She heard a noise, a sound of someone running in front of her. Had they heard the radio? She backed against the wall and waited. The best she could tell was that she had two or three men heading in her direction. They could be her men, but she doubted it.

Two blocks north of her, she watched a small vehicle make a turn toward her. While it could be a military jeep of some kind, she wasn't sure from this distance. One thing was sure–she would be in the spotlights again soon.

One guy rushed at her from her right, slamming her against the rock siding of the building she had been edging along. Her hand found the back of his head, where she twisted to her side and in turn smashed his head into the wall. Since he acted slightly stunned, she repeated with much more force. This time he crumbled to the ground like a deflating balloon.

Even in the dark she could tell he was wearing military fatigues. With little time to waste, she hunted for anything on him that might be of use. As she concentrated on any movement around her, she relieved him of his radio and a flashlight. With the approaching vehicle closing, she activated her plan by sending out a quick Morse code signal using the flashlight, but using it to locate the approaching men at the same time. Before these men could react, she tossed the light to one side and ran in the other direction toward the river.

Seconds later, she heard the gunfire coming from the men who sprayed the area around the flashlight. None made a direct hit. However, by giving away their own position, she fired at them. As she raced away, she saw the vehicle speeding toward her.

As she prepared to fire at it, she heard more gunfire coming from behind it. From the way the vehicle veered to the right and stopped, she had no doubt that at least the driver had been hit. She edged forward to investigate as she heard one of her men yell out. "Matt!"

"Yes, it's me."

She watched five men race forward with one of them immediately checking out the jeep. Their commander rushed over to her. "Matt, we lost all communications and I'm not sure what caused that. It's like the satellite has been destroyed."

"Understood, but I just obtained a backup. How are the men?"

"We lost one guy who took a direct hit to his head."

Another brave man had sacrificed his life for the benefit of mankind everywhere, and no one but her and her select group would ever know that. She raked her teeth over her lip. "We'll retrieve his body soon."

"Matt, you can count on us doing that." He glanced to the north. "Where are those transporters you mentioned?"

"Just a couple of blocks that way." She glanced at the man who got the jeep restarted. "We'll need this. After we connect with the two transporters, I want three men using this as an advance scout. I want one man each on both of the transporters. We need to move it."

Chapter 17

With Abdul's help in locating some deserted back roads out of town that edged along deathly quiet neighborhoods of run down older buildings, they soon left the sleepy confines far behind them. Still, she knew the lights from the three vehicles would be an easy target to locate in the desert. Occasionally, they were able to kill the lights on the transporters and closely follow behind the lead jeep.

Matalina made another call to the rescue copter. "Stay alert. I don't think we made any friends here."

"We're about fifteen miles out. Have you set up a retraction point yet?"

"We're looking for a good spot now, and should be able to send you the coordinates soon. I know this is going to take two trips. We need to find somewhere we can establish a base while we wait for you to return."

"As I mentioned, we have the base in Turkey secure. We just need to get in and out of Afghanistan before they know we were here. I don't think we can count on NATO for any support. As such, we're moving in fast and low."

Matalina turned to one of the men from her team. "We need to find a place soon and get these transporters out of sight. The sun will be rising soon and perhaps before they return. This is going to be close."

Matalina kept monitoring the radio she had lifted from the guy she had knocked out earlier. At this point it looked like they were looking for the transporters, which had been reported as stolen. The conflicting details of the thief told her just how confused they were, and how unorganized their search would be. This advantage wouldn't last long.

The copter was five minutes away when her luck changed. She saw a line of vehicles racing in her direction. Somehow, they had located their position. "Okay, everyone out of the transporters. I'm sure they'll be targeted any minute."

As they all rushed for the cover of a nearby hillside filled with small boulders, her men positioned all of the firepower they had hauled with them, including one small handheld rocket launcher. It was nice to have, but it had a limited range.

After finding a better observation point, she grabbed her binoculars and focused on the chase which consisted of three land vehicles and a small copter following them. Being in Afghanistan this group could be anyone, including the newly formed government, local tribal lords, or perhaps the good old USA who started this war. The chances of this being NATO remained doubtful.

About a mile away, the chasing caravan slowed and allowed the copter to zoom over the top and gain attitude. With the lights on, however, it would soon be an easy target for her men to take out. At least she hoped so, since the three land vehicles had now split and started to circle their location. Somehow, they had a fix on her location. Could they have been able to trace her from the radio she had taken from the one guy? If so, she had made one bad decision in taking it.

A plan developed, however, as she patted her right hand man on the shoulder. She pointed to a ridge above her on the right. "Get the men over there. I think I know how to lure them into the valley below."

"What about the copter?"

"It will also come in closer for a look. Take your best shot. Hit or miss, the pilot will not like knowing we have a rocket launcher available." She pointed to the jeep. "I'll need this to draw their fire."

He stepped forward. "That's too dangerous. Please allow me to try that."

Although she appreciated the chivalry, she paused before she lifted the radio. "This is what they're looking for. I'm simply going to make it easier for them to find it."

He nodded as he agreed. "We'll cover you."

"Good!" She glanced at the hill. "That's a big hill, you need to hurry."

As the men started moving everyone, she jumped into the jeep and looked for the copter. The running lights on it had disappeared. It had to be in attack mode now. Since she didn't know how much time she had, she floored the gas pedal and turned the lights on.

The baited area wasn't far away, but she had to make sure they concentrated on her and not the people she was trying to rescue. The dust she threw into the air lit her up. She had little doubt the three chasing vehicles could see it now. There were no roads to follow, just an endless sea of dust. When she saw scattered boulders ahead, she knew she was getting close.

Seconds later she stopped long enough to tie the steering wheel in place and drop a small tool kit on the accelerator, sending the jeep on its final mission. She thought she had made the perfect escape until a spotlight focused on her from above–the copter had found her. She dropped to her knee and fired. While she wasn't sure if she was in range or not, she definitely caught their attention as they veered off to one side, but soon turned to face her again.

As she made a run for it, a missile lit up the sky as it raced from the copter, heading directly at her. She dove behind the tall boulders, hoping to get out of the way before it struck. Surprisingly, the missile changed course and veered to the right.

She glanced up, as she understood. It had been programmed to hit the signature coming from the radio. The explosion soon shattered the sky like a large lightning bolt, but she had no way of knowing if it had hit the jeep or not. Even if she couldn't see the attack copter any more, she could hear it. She knew it had to be closer to the boulder where her men were setting up. Could they see it?

Moments later, she received her answer with another fireball piercing the early dawn. Her men's rocket had found its target. After scoring a direct hit, the copter burned as it fell. Seconds after it landed, the copters fuel tank also exploded.

Now, she needed to somehow rejoin her men on top. The men chasing them still had three vehicles on the ground somewhere and perhaps still centered on the last known address of the jeep. As she climbed one boulder, she saw one set of lights coming across the sands she was on earlier. The other two vehicles that had split off to the sides were nowhere to be seen.

She wasn't worried about this smaller vehicle heading her way. The men in it would have to abandon it soon and climb the same rocks she was on. This was something she assumed they would have to think about, knowing her men would be fortified on the top of it.

Before she started to climb again, she checked in with her men. "Good shooting, men."

"Thanks to you, it was an easy target. How are you?"

"I'm coming back to you, but I'm having to climb in the dark."

"Understood. Any light will give you away. I see the vehicle at the bottom of the hill. Shall we engage them now or later?"

"For now, keep them in sight and advise me. Our rescue copter should be here soon."

"From what I can tell, this may be a problem, since they're right in the middle of the flight path."

That changed everything since the copter would be arriving anytime. "Lock in on it and wait my orders." With little time left, she had to climb an open face. While it was dark, her silhouette might be very visible. She had no choice.

Half way up, and in the proverbial no man's land, she heard the ricochet of a bullet off the boulder she was climbing. Before she could react, several more shots bounced off the rocks above her. It wouldn't be long until they adjusted their range for her distance above them.

She started to call in for support when she realized that wouldn't be necessary. Another rocket streaked across the sky as it flew past her toward the vehicle below. Her men scored another direct hit. In the flickering light from the resulting fires, she could see several men running away from it. With this place becoming a war zone, she knew they would have much more attention soon. They had to get out of there now!

From her far right she saw another burst of light entering the sky. Their other vehicles had full firepower as well, as she helplessly watched a rocket fly above her toward their base on top of the ridge. The commander soon gave her the news. They had been hit!

She checked back in with her rescue copter. "We need you here now. We're under rocket fire."

"We saw the flash ahead, and will be there in a few seconds. Can you light the target?"

"I have one way that might work. Let me know when you're in place." She looked for a round of tracer bullets. These would give her away, but also give the copter a perfect target. She tried to climb harder with her muscles burning. Then it hit her. She felt dizzy. Her inner ear had to be causing this. *Not now!* She shook her head, but she was still unable to focus on the rocks she was climbing.

The pilot checked back in. "We're directly above and need to see the target. Everything is dark."

The commander responded as she fought with her dizziness. "Keep your eyes open, we'll draw their fire from here."

No, he didn't need to do that. They had already received causalities there. They had information she needed, and more importantly, they had placed all faith in her to keep them safe.

Was it the height, the fatigue, the darkness? Her world began to spin again as she pushed from the side of the cliff. If she could just make it to the top of this one, it had to get easier. Several meters later she slipped, but she luckily relocated a footing. She had to be more careful.

Before she got to the top, she heard the gunfire

coming from above her. Seconds later, it came to a stop. Would the group chasing them return the fire now, giving away their position? She hoped the men were dug in well and had the people protected somewhere.

Seconds later she saw another missile streaking across the sky from the truck below them. Whoever they were, they were well funded with good armaments. The missile struck just above her. Had anyone else been killed? She assumed her men had planned for this, but she didn't know for sure.

The pilot responded. "I have a lock on their position."

"Good, take it now!" She glanced above her to see the rocket flash through the sky toward the truck below. This explosion was much more than the previous ones. It must have been carrying a big supply of arms.

That left one more truck to worry about now. She assumed they must be on the far side of their hilltop position. "Does anyone have a fix on that last vehicle?"

The pilot responded first. "I can make a circle if you wish before I land."

"No, that might just make you a target. Let's get these people out of here."

The commander added. "We received a direct hit earlier and have about half of the number we had earlier. Some of these are also critical."

That's what she was afraid of. She hated to ask one question, but felt like she needed an answer now. "What about our men?"

"I was hit with some of the rocks thrown from the blast, and I might have a broken arm, but I'll be fine.

All of the others are going to be okay."

"Can we get all of the survivors onboard in one trip?"

"It'll be close."

"Get a place ready for the copter to land. I'll provide cover from here, just in case we have any more surprises."

"We can cover you from here until we can get everyone loaded and take off. Matt, you need to spend your time getting here."

"It's not necessary. I need to stay and find out who these men that were chasing us work for."

"Matt, I'm not sure we can get back in to get you any time soon."

"Thank you for your concern, but I also have one more thing to do while I'm here. I just need some transportation to get there."

"Where?"

"I need to go to the village where Zafar went to grow poppy to see if anyone remembers him from there. Since this is where he was recruited, it might be the best way to find out who that was."

"In such a case, I want to go with you."

"With a broken arm, that's not a good idea and you know it." As she waited for his response, Matalina checked the nearby hillsides. That other truck had to be close.

"I'll send one of the other guys to be with you. As soon as all is cleared and my arm is patched we'll join you there."

After realizing how it might work for her advantage on some check points, she changed her mind. "In this country it might be good to have a male escort get me through some check points, therefore, send me Aqil."

"Matt, are you sure that's the best choice? You have a lot of hostiles around you."

"In that case, make sure he's packing a lot of new supplies for me. I'm almost out of ammunition. And get me a satellite phone that cannot be traced by these people."

"I'll put together the best of what we have."

She heard the copter in the background as she yelled one more time. "Get those people out of here and to safety. I'll be fine!"

Without any more incidents, the copter soon lifted off and headed west. How long did she have before reinforcements would be sent to find these men who had chased them? With the sunrise casting reddish streaks across the sky, she knew it would be hard to hide for long.

Aqil soon used the radio. "Are you here?"

"Yes, I'm right below you. Stay out of sight until I get to you."

The breather helped a lot as she managed to make the rest of the climb without any more dizzy feelings. As she walked over to the blackened area where the rocket had exploded, she saw Aqil walk out from behind a clump of rocks. He definitely didn't look happy. "We moved all of the bodies to this area here. It's not very pretty."

She had seen many dead bodies in her life, but the loss of innocent victims always affected her differently than men of war who were killed in battle. Since she hadn't had time to discuss with her men which ones were killed, she needed to know if the ones she came after were now dead or alive.

She followed him behind the rocks where these victims were partially covered. The dust had caked with their blood into a red casting that made them look like they had been there for days, and not just a few hours.

Three of those killed were young children, but none matched the people she had talked to, with the exception of Abdul. Of all of those killed, he's the one who should be considered the real hero, since he had sacrificed himself to save the others. Without him, the ones who made it to safety never would have.

Matalina glanced at the bags he had with him. "Let me see what they left for us. I'm glad you agreed to go with me."

"I wasn't given a choice, was I?" He acted combative, something she didn't need to deal with. It could get both of them killed.

"I think we both can agree these people deserved much better than they received. Someone had to have tipped off those chasing us that we were leaving the country."

"And you think that was me?" He acted even more combative.

"That might be hard to prove, but you're one of the few people who might have had a chance to get a message to others. However, I'll give you the benefit of doubt for the moment."

"What do you want from me?"

Matalina paused for a moment until she had carefully selected the right words. "I'm going to the place Zafar went to grow poppy. I think we can find answers there as to who recruited him. I'll need an interpreter there. One that knows he'll instantly be killed if he betrays me."

"I heard you offering to take these people to a place of safety. If I do this for you, I'll need to flee this country also."

"If you handle this right, we might have a place for you. Your translation skill will make you very valuable, especially if you can do so under pressure."

"Again, it appears that I have no choice." He glanced at the bodies. "Do we have any time to cover them better? The wolves will make a meal out of them tonight."

"If my plan goes as planned, they'll be well taken care of." She searched the bags to see what they had left her. "There's one more thing."

"What?"

"You'll have to pretend to be my husband as we travel." She watched him smile. "I think you know why. It's the best way to avoid any problems along the way."

"How do you plan to get there?"

"There's still one truck here that's operative. We need to take it."

"And what about the men who own it?"

"The name of the real owner is what I need, but as far as these men driving it, they'll be busy burying these bodies properly." Matalina glanced at the cliffs again, realizing that it would be much safer for them to come to her than for her to go after them. Still, she had no time to wait for them to send additional reinforcements. She needed a trap to lure these men to them.

"How do you plan on doing this?"

"If they think another airlift was coming, they

might want to rush the location now."

He nervously glanced around him. "I thought we might be able to disappear and flee before we're caught. This sounds like a stupid idea to me."

"I thought you might think this." She found a small cigar and lit it. "You're going to love this. How loud can you yell for help?"

"What?"

"Don't worry. I'll have you well covered. Since I think they're monitoring the calls, we can also send a message that will slow any backup they might expect. There will be no reason for backup if the first group gives an indication they have everything under control."

"Who in the hell are you? I've met some of the best freedom fighters in the world here, but none compare to you."

The truck was soon lured into a ravine below them. With a short blast from her Glock hitting the sand in front of them, however, they quickly surrendered. Good! She felt like she might get some answers, but still, she knew she didn't have much time to get away.

She imagined the thoughts coming from these men who had no respect for women, but now faced one with a fully loaded Glock eighteen. Her spiked white hair, glowing white-gold capped teeth, and muscular body had to be the worst nightmare they could have ever imagined.

When she got within ten feet of them, one guy yelled and rushed toward her. She kicked head high, popping his neck backwards. As he attempted to recover, she reached for his throat and dug in with her reinforced nails, which immediately severed the veins in his neck. She didn't need the others to break and try the same thing.

As he dropped to the ground, she faced the rest of the men before she waved for the translator to join her. Since this man had attempted to kill her first, she felt no remorse for him. If he wanted to die a martyr, then so be it.

"Tell these men they have but one chance to live. If they don't do exactly as I ask, I'll make sure their dead bodies are fed to the swine." She knew this was pushing it to the limits, but she wanted answers.

She waited for the translator to relay her message. She had no clue how accurate it was given, but she assumed it was close from their frozen stares. They all stood at perfect attention as he finished.

The translator turned to her. "What do you want from them?"

Since the men attacking them had little choice in answering her questions, she soon learned who was behind the chase, but not the initial attack back in town. The local militia had been alerted. While none of them could identify their leader who always operated through others, she did receive one . . . somewhat surprise.

When she showed a photo of the guy who worked as a double agent for the CIA, they identified him as one of the connections they worked for. This guy seemed to be everywhere. Although she considered

223

calling the CIA and alerting them, she altered her decision, knowing they might have him in that position as a spy. Still, it remained to be seen who his real alliance was with.

The one thing that disturbed her the most was the fact that if he was a spy for the CIA, he was doing a lousy job of providing them with information. She still wondered if he had tried to stage his death to make the CIA think he had died.

These men she had captured had been drawn into a war zone and a life they had little control over. They were the perfect men to be recruited and manipulated as low rate mercenaries or suicide bombers. In this world of theirs they had few options available to them. She felt extremely sorry for them. Some of them acted as if they could care less if they lived or died.

They had accepted her alternative to immediate death, something her father would be proud of. Their death would be staged, using the people she had lost as cover. This way they would be given a proper burial, and these men would be able to flee to another country.

The jeep she had driven earlier was soon located. It hadn't taken a direct hit, but had crashed into a large sand dome which had flipped it over on its side. After some small repairs and refueling, she was ready to push on using it instead of the larger truck.

After she headed out to the east, as if she was making a run for Pakistan, she turned northward toward poppy country. While the one person, the double agent, was the one person she expected to be active there, she needed other names. She knew that the CIA definitely had a presence there, but there had to be others, like the AL-Qaeda, or some Illuminati faction involved. There was also a high expectation that Bjorn or one of his friends might have a part in it. She knew only one way to find out.

The road was rough and unmarked for the most part. At this speed it would take all day to get there and somewhere along the way they had to take on more fuel. On the map she saw one small settlement ahead. She had little choice but to chance it.

As soon as she stopped the jeep, she dug out a wrap she could use to hide her combat fatigues underneath. The least suspicious they looked, the better. Aqil had to do all of the talking, passing them off as a married couple who were, trying to find a dead relative and return the body to where they lived.

As she assumed the role of a submissive wife, she kept her hand on her Glock, just in case, as they entered the village. A few villagers walking the side of the road stopped to study them out of curiosity. The village, composed of elderly women for the most part, filled her mind with the tragedies of war. With so many of the men killed in the military conflicts, many women had little choice but to escape to these lonely outposts and try to live out their lives.

Finally, she spotted a small supply store with a few old trucks parked around it. At first she felt disappointed at not seeing a pump, but relaxed when she spotted it half hidden behind one truck that was also taking on fuel. She whispered to him to drive on the other side. "Do whatever you have to do to top off all of the tanks. I don't know how much longer we'll have to use this jeep to get around."

His hands began to shake. "This might look like a quiet little outpost, but I can assure you the drug lords around here run it and know everything that goes on around here."

"I'll be here to cover your back. If we don't get fuel, we'll have to relieve them of one of their trucks."

His eyes widened, giving an indication that he knew she meant business. "I'll do my best without drawing attention. You need to stay completely covered. Your white skin is a dead giveaway."

As he walked toward a small door, she knew she had to trust him. Without her being able to see him, he could easily give her away, but she doubted that he would. She felt sure he knew she never hesitated in eliminating all threats.

After the time crawled along for about fifteen minutes, she had second thoughts. Was she being sold out? The intense heat coming from the late afternoon sun caused her clothing to soon smother her like she was in an oven. She needed relief.

The driver of the truck that was fueling glanced at her before he climbed inside and pulled away from the pump. She noticed several holes in the side of his truck which were apparently from gunfire, but rather than looking like a trained fighter, he looked more like a farmer.

Eventually, she saw the translator walking back toward the jeep, but being closely followed by two dark bearded men. With their assertive nature alerting her to trouble, along with the translator standing directly in the path of fire, she hesitated as she switched the safety to off on her Glock. They would soon be close enough to see her partially unhidden face.

Aqil stopped short, and yelled at her in Arabic, as if she could understand him. His hand motion, however, indicated she needed to get out of the jeep.

As she stood, the tallest man grinned with what remained of his teeth before he pushed Aqil to one side. Should she take him now?

The man said something else in Arabic and waved for her to follow them inside the store. It became obvious what they wanted in exchange for the fuel. She glanced inside the door to make sure there was no one else inside. As she walked inside her hand released the Glock and located her combat knife.

As soon as all were inside, the first man reached back and prepared to backhand her. She reacted by catching his hand in midair, surprising him with the sharpness of her nails that dug into the back of his hand. He yelled what she knew to be obscenities at her while stepping back and preparing to strike at her again. Matalina struck first, using the palm of her hand to smash into his nose, breaking it instantly. The blood splattered on his white outfit, a desert robe of some kind.

As he yelled louder and backed away to regroup, the other man pulled a long knife from a sheath on his side. With the reaper bend in it, she knew how deadly this weapon was, especially in the hands of a man who must have used it many times.

After ripping her robe to one side and sliding the veil off her head, she prepared for battle. The man briefly stopped to study her. Again, his Arabic was beyond her. She waved her combat knife which was much shorter than his weapon, anticipating his attack any second.

The longer she waited, the more time she gave the other man to recover. Should she pull her Glock, thus giving away their position and inviting others to come after them? She watched the translator back toward the door.

The knife-wielding man lashed out at her, missing her by inches, before he swung backwards at her. Without giving her a moment to rest, he repeated the two slash approach. At the moment he finished the last swing, she stepped forward and traced his knife with her own, connecting with his hand. Her razor sharp knife cut into his hand like slicing cheese, making him drop his blade.

As he leaned over, the first guy produced his own knife and rushed toward her, swinging it wildly. While she avoided any direct cuts, his large body slammed her against a back wall, knocking several pictures from it.

She grabbed his hand before he could take another swing at her with it. With his arm in front to her, she reached out and used her metallic teeth to bite a large plug from his arm. His scream had to be heard for miles.

When he retreated from her, the other man rushed at her, holding a knife in his left hand. She shoved her knife deep inside his chest before he had the chance to use his. His eyes rolled backward as she added a final twist to open the wound in his chest.

As she started to push him backward, she saw the other man reaching for another weapon, and what looked to be a small pistol of some kind. Unable to remove the knife in time, she used her palm again to smash his nose, this time sending the broken parts deep into his brain. He stumbled for a few seconds until he fell across a small table.

As she stepped over the dead men, she glanced at the translator. "Thanks for the help."

"Don't mention it." His whole body shook. "You

know who this is you just killed, don't you?"

"Other than a rapist, not really." She waited for a response, but wasn't really in a good mood. "I assume they work for the local tribal lord."

"I know you want answers here, but this just made it impossible. No one will talk to us now. Word of this will spread fast."

"I can order an emergency extraction at any time, but I've come too far to stop now. Let's get our fuel and get out of here quickly." She studied these men one more time, and wondered if they had any information on them that might prove useful. She soon found a small bag full of paperwork on one man. It would have to be analyzed later. The small amount of paper money he had on him wasn't much, but it might come in handy later that night. "Here, help me move these guys to a corner where we can try to hide them under something."

As they walked back to the door on the way out, two women attempted to enter. Both had veils on, but their large brown eyes expressed an immediate fear when they saw the lumps hiding the men in the corner. The horror in their eyes escalated even more when they switched their attention to Matalina.

Surprisingly, one of them spoke in broken English. "Are they dead?" Matalina allowed her silence to answer her question as the woman walked over to where they had been covered. She quickly spat at them.

Matalina turned to the translator as she yelled, "Get us fueled now, and we need to make room for two more to go with us." As he shook his head on the way out the door, Matalina turned to the women. "You're welcome to come with us. I don't think it'll be safe for you here."

"We have nowhere to go." She watched the two women snuggle closer together, acting much like sisters.

"I have others that I'm helping to relocate."

"Why would you want to help us?" the woman asked as her eyes darted around with a growing fear flowing from them.

"I need information I'm fairly sure you might have. I'm willing to take that chance."

The silent women started to cry, but the other one acted braver. "All men are the same."

"Not all . . . and you'll be in a different country." Matalina tried to be patient with them, hoping they wouldn't spook and run away or scream.

"It will not take long for the others to find out what happened." The more this woman talked, the better her English became. This couldn't be a local. Where did she come from?

"You have to trust me, and we have to leave now."

She looked out the door. "If you're heading north, we'll need more supplies. I can have them ready in five minutes." When Matalina smiled, the woman immediately grimaced as she studied her teeth. "Who are you?"

"My name is Matt. That will have to do for now." She patted her on the shoulder. "We need to hurry, and we don't have much room to pack many things. How much time do you think we have until these men are discovered?"

"Because of the heat, many men travel late at night. Some of them spend the night when they get here. We'll be lucky to have a few hours, but who knows for sure."

###

Three hours later, Matalina thought they had pushed it as far as she could. It would be dark soon, and she needed to find a place to stay hidden until in the morning, when she knew they would be looking for them.

After making a small camp, she used a small flashlight to study a map. There were many small farms scattered around the area north of them, including many more small villages. The best she could determine was that Zafar had lived there for several years, making the money he would need to go to school and learn aerodynamics.

In a way, she understood the pain he must have felt, and the need for revenge. Striking out directly against the United States government was one thing, but killing innocent third parties was different. She could see where he would be a great recruit for many people. Her job was to find out who that was.

After making a meal on some old bread and dried meat, she settled in next to the two women on a blanket. She glanced at the one who spoke English earlier, but pointed at the other woman. "Does she speak English also?"

This girl answered for herself as she lowered her veil, revealing her light brown hair. "I still remember some English."

With little doubt, Matalina knew they had been kidnapped earlier and sold as slaves there. "How long have they held you here?"

"We were kidnapped when we were twelve and

231

sold to these two men. They're brothers of one of the ruling drug lords here. He's going to be very mad when he hears what happened."

"I'm sure he will be, but we'll not be here for long." She pulled some photos from her jacket pocket. "I'm going to show you several photos, and I want you to tell me if you've ever seen any of these men."

After glances of apprehension passed between the two women, Matalina showed them the first one, and then the next. The responses were disappointing. She had hoped they had seen some of these men. However, she saved the most important ones until the last.

This woman pointed to the CIA double agent immediately. She gave him an Arabic name she hadn't heard before. This guy really got around. Finding him would be extremely valuable.

With trembling hands, the women pointed to his photo. Matalina knew to take this slow. "What can you tell me about him?"

"Many people are scared of him. Even the tribal lords here stay clear of him. It's said that he has killed many men. He has many enemies, but none strong enough to stop him."

That would account for why he wanted to stage his death. It also left many questions as to who he really worked for, which could very well be himself. "Do you know who he works for?"

"That's a question many people would like an answer to. I heard our kidnappers talk about this many times." She glanced at the photo again. "Many times when he was here, people vanished."

"Do you mean like kidnapped or killed?"

"Who knows for sure, but he also hired people to spy for him. This is well known. He has an endless supply of money." She pointed to the photo again. "How do you know of this man?"

This was a dangerous question for her to answer. She didn't want to compromise a CIA agent, if that's what he was. It was better to stick to her cover for now. "I'm here as part of a mission to see how and where people are being recruited for terrorist activities."

"Who do you work for?"

That, of course, was the one question she couldn't answer. "The best I can tell you is that I work privately. It's best that way."

"I see. Since you seem to know many of the men in control here, what is it you want to know now?"

"I've reason to believe that men are being recruited from here to go to America as future terrorists. I need to know who is behind this and where to find them."

The women tapped on the photo again. "Nothing like that happens around here without this man's approval."

"I agree it looks that way, but he has to have other contacts, and that's what I'm after." Matalina started to place the photos in her bag, but she decided to show a few more of them, the friends of Bjorn. She had to know if they were connected to this. "I just have a few more."

She waved her head no on all of them until she saw the Italian. She leaned closer to study it. "I think I recognize him, but he hasn't been here for a long time."

"Have you ever spoken with him in the past?"

"No, he was here before the others showed up."

Was this another dead end trip? Finally, she

showed them the photo of the guy she had the most interest in–Zafar. Did she ever see or meet the guy who she assumed was the mastermind in all of the drone attacks. Since she was young when he was here, Matalina doubted it, but she had to know if he had every returned to his hometown.

"No, who is he?"

"I think he lived here at one time. Tomorrow, we need to find anyone that might have known him then."

"What did he do here?"

"I understand he grew poppy for the cocaine traffic."

She began to shake again. "You've no idea how dangerous this is. We need to get out of here. You promised!"

Matalina felt sorry for these two women. "Be brave for me. We'll be out of this country by tomorrow night. It'll take a little time to coordinate the rescue copter. With your knowledge of this area, I need your help in knowing where would be the best places to ask questions. Remember, the faster I get answers, the sooner we can leave."

Just before dawn Matalina was on her phone planning their extraction from this northern village in Afghanistan. With no one in the air looking for them, she wondered if the two men she had killed the day before had been discovered yet.

Today, she would have to pull off the next to impossible. She had to find where Zafar had grown his poppy and any friends he might've left behind. There had to be some way to find his trail again. With the local drug lords diligent over their fields, she knew they would soon be after them. She had to be ready for them. Even if the chances of making direct contact with them were slim, they were the ones who would have the best answers. If she could isolate a couple, that would be her best chance in getting honest answers.

As they finished clearing their overnight camp, Matalina signed off with her rescue team, assuring them she would keep her phone with her that would send her GPS location. They could be on location in less than an hour from her call.

She quickly covered her head and face, just like the two other women. While trying not to attract attention would be vital in finding his old home place, she needed to be ready to spring into action at a moment's notice.

Aqil turned to her. "You know this is crazy. No one is going to talk to us." He cranked the jeep and left the safety of their hiding place behind the rocks as the sun peeped above the horizon.

"This guy I'm looking to get more information on had to have help. If I can determine who that is, my job will be much easier."

Thirty minutes later, she saw the first village. Several small boys stopped to watch the jeep's tires kick dust into the early morning light. A truck with a large open bed carrying several men rambled along in front of them, who she guessed were farmers being sent out into the fields.

"Those are the kind of people I need to talk to." Matalina studied the area around them. "We need to see if we can approach them somewhere where it's not so obvious. Follow them for now."

As they followed them out of town, she constantly scanned the sky. "Okay, this is far enough. Pull in front of them and tell them we wish them no harm."

As soon as he did as ordered, the driver jumped from the cab and raised a pistol. Matalina remained still as she told the translator to raise his hands and tell him they had money for information.

After a heated exchange Aqil spoke loud enough for Matalina to hear, but kept his face directed toward the driver. "They want to know how much."

"A year's wages for the right answers."

The driver wasn't impressed as he walked to one side of the jeep and motioned for the women to get out. As soon as he approached Matalina, his eyes squinted. She knew it was time to react. Her arm thrust forward, hitting his arm, knocking the gun from it. When he bent over attempting to recover it, she kicked him in the face, sending him over on his back.

Before he could recover, she raised the pistol and pointed it at him. The men in the back of the truck scrambled to stand, but didn't rush her. Obviously, the gun in her hand acted as a sufficient deterrent.

She yelled at Aqil again. "Tell them the offer of money for information still stands."

After he made the offer again, no one said a word. "They're all too scared to say anything. I can see it in their eyes. They all work for the tribal lord here."

Matalina pulled the stack of photos from her bag. "Tell them I will pay for any information on any one they recognize." The first guy she offered the photos to attempted to ignore her until she pointed the gun between his eyes. She yelled back over her shoulder at the Aqil. "How do you count to three in Arabic?"

"Please, these are just farmers. You can't kill

them."

Matalina turned toward him again. "One . . . ."

The man yelled something in Arabic as he accepted the first photo. Seconds later she distributed the rest of the photos. One of the men pointed to a photo of Mario and yelled at the interpreter in Arabic. The discussion became heated as a few others attempted to enter the conversation. Whatever they knew, she understood that it would be very important to have it properly translated. As long as they were talking she was gathering information. It would be Aqil's responsibility to translate everything to her later. She wished she knew Arabic better. They spoke too fast.

Finally, Aqil paused for a minute and handed her Mario's photo. "You're going to find this interesting. This is an old photo of this guy, and before he grew a beard. This is what he looks like now." He handed her the photo of Carlos.

No way! She studied the photos. This would have to be verified later, but it might be possible the two photos were of the same guy. Both had dark black hair, olive skin, and heavy eyebrows. How could he have worked his way into working for the CIA?

She decided to walk over and talk to the two women again, and get their opinion. On the way around the jeep, she saw a movement in the sky. They were being targeted. She knew it!

She yelled to everyone around her and pointed to the sky. "Run! Find cover now." She saw a small ditch next to a group of rocks about ten meters away. She saw a missile streaking toward them as she leaped the last few meters toward the ditch. The blast that hit the truck was massive, throwing bits and pieces of it everywhere and knocking the jeep over on its side.

The blast caught her feet which hadn't made it into the ditch, flipping her like a rag doll behind the rocks. She felt a burning sensation pass over her next as she dug in deeper. She held her position several seconds until she felt like all falling debris had settled.

She dreaded looking up, knowing it wouldn't be pretty. The first thing she saw was a severed arm, then several mutilated bodies which had to be some of the men who couldn't make it off the truck in time. She rubbed her feet, attempting to assess how much injury she had sustained. There was a good chance she had a broken ankle, maybe more.

Another image in the sky caught her attention. Another missile was making a circle about one kilometer away. It wouldn't take long before it made it to her side of the small boulders. She guessed who ever fired the first one wanted confirmation of the kill.

Although she considered playing dead, she decided not to chance it and grabbed her backpack, hunting for the extension to her Glock. The drone like missile was at the limit of her range, but she would do her best. She had four clips, giving her over one hundred and twenty rounds.

As the drone, which was much larger than she had anticipated, circled to her side, it drifted closer to her. She fired one clip after another, hoping to hit it. It appeared to be a frugal effort, until she watched the drone fall from the sky. Had she hit it, or was it preparing a new attack?

She made the call for backup, hoping the rescue copter would get there before they had new attacks. It would be armed for combat, but how would it handle a drone attack itself? She couldn't tell them how many survivors, if any, they would have to make room for.

As Matalina struggled to walk, but mainly hopped on one leg, she saw the full devastation caused by the blast. It didn't take long for her to realize all of them must have been killed. Still she searched through the bodies. She especially felt sorry for Aqil who was forced into helping her.

On the far side of the jeep she saw movement. One of the women was still alive. She was bleeding and missing a hand, but other than that, she was alive. The other woman was under the side of the jeep. She had no pulse.

Somehow, she had to find them better coverage. After ripping off part of the women's shawl, Matalina made a tourniquet and stopped the bleeding as best she could. This woman needed immediate care if she was to survive. "Hang in there, help is coming."

After telling the pilot they had one survivor, she glanced around for anywhere they could find a better cover. Another drone could return any moment. The best cover was over fifty meters away. With her bad ankle and her injuries, it might as well be several hundred kilometers away. With no choice, they struggled toward it, as the pilot relayed that they were at maximum speed and would be there soon.

Like a mirage from a bad horror movie, she saw the drone drifting above the horizon. This was too sophisticated to be anything but the CIA. There was no way they could out run it. At this range they had to be visible in the camera monitors. Were they being targeted?

During the standoff, she could hear a copter racing toward them. Would they arrive soon enough?

Chapter 18

Matalina blinked her eyes as she attempted to gain her bearings in the quietness of her bedroom. Even in the dim lights, she made out the images of her Italian marble bedpost she had always loved. The surgery! How did it go? Her head felt dizzy, obviously the lingering effect of the drugs used to sedate her during her operation. A lingering taste of bad breath mixed with a dry mouth made her wish for a small glass of water.

She concentrated on her feet, her toes and then her ankles. Other than feeling like she had been tied down and her feet immobilized, she felt nothing. As a feeling of helplessness swept over her, she forced herself to fight the numbing feelings of the drugs she had been given.

When a side light suddenly broke the darkness, Matalina saw a nurse and her mom walk to the side of her bed. The pleasant smile coming from her mom indicated that all had been successful. She would have loved to hold her mom's hand, but she realized that her hands had been tied to her side. With one IV still in her arm and a monitoring cup wrapped around her arm. She felt like she had been asleep for a long time. What time was it?

The nurse spoke first. "How are you?" After Matalina said nothing, she continued. "Your surgery went well, and the surgeon is happy with it. He said you should make a full recovery."

"I can't feel my feet."

"I'm sure it's from the local anesthetic used during the surgery, but the doctor will be here soon to make sure no other complications have occurred."

"How much recovery time are they expecting I'll need?"

"It's too early to tell. You had torn tendons in one ankle, but multiple bones were fractured in the other one. Admittedly, these weren't major bones, but they're ones that can be painful. You were very lucky." The nurse glanced at the queen, Matalina's mother. "She needs to rest, but I know you have some things that have to be discussed. I'll be waiting outside."

After the door was closed, her mom started. "Matalina, that was close. I don't want to lose you." For one of the few times she could ever remember, she noticed tears in her mother's eyes. That wasn't the sign of a warrior.

"As soon as I get better, I'll get some answers on what happened." Matalina closed her eyes for a moment, but forced them open as she felt her mind floating. "How are the others?"

"The girl you rescued has lost a hand, but she's expected to recover from a massive blood loss. It'll take some time to see how that has affected her mind. We had no choice but to bring her here for the surgery. The others you rescued earlier appear to be in much better shape, and they were taken on to a place in Italy that we own there. We have several people there interviewing them and gathering information."

"Good." Matalina hated to admit it, but she needed rest as the world slowly faded away.

###

Several days later Matalina used one of her crutches to push open the door to the conference room. After seeing all chairs occupied, she realized that they must have been waiting for her. The information they had obtained from the last woman rescued was minimal since she was still recuperating, but the others had given them much more than she had hoped for.

She glanced at her father as she walked in. He looked aggravated, with his face flushed, something he rarely projected. He paused talking to the man next to him as he turned in her direction. "How's your ankle?"

Matalina glanced at the cast on her ankle, a clean white torture chamber. "I won't be winning any races soon." She wondered what the men around the table were told about her injury.

One man quickly assumed the chivalrous role of helping her into her chair. She didn't need this help, but she also had to play the part of a princess during this meeting. "Thank you."

After a short briefing of world affairs, her father turned to her and bit his lip before he started. Perhaps that's where she got this habit. "I received the final report a few minutes ago. There's no doubt that Mario and the mystery CIA guy might be one and the same. The question now is what to do with this information. From the CIA file we were able to access, it appears that they wanted him to stay in deep cover. They know he's working as a double agent, but they believe he has his main alliance with the States. As best we can tell, however, they have no knowledge of him being part of us earlier."

Matalina had a hard time in stopping her fist from slamming the table in front of her, but it didn't stop her from interrupting. "We all know he's a traitor, not just to us here in Baltonia, but his own country, Italy, and not to mention to the Maliviziati."

"I don't think you'll find anyone to disagree with you. Still, we're not sure why or how he aligned himself with Bjorn."

Matalina knew Bjorn had major skills in influencing people, and was perhaps why Mario and his three other friends joined Bjorn on his attempted coup of Baltonia. "Speaking of Bjorn, when is the last time we know these two met? Also, can we assume Bjorn is also behind this, or can we assume that Mario went off on his own?"

"Since we can now place both Bjorn and Mario in Florida at the same time, the chances of them coordinating on this are high."

Matalina cleared her throat. "Perhaps, but there is one more possibility. What if Bjorn was there to warn Mario, or maybe to stop him instead? This isn't the way Bjorn likes to do things."

Her father spoke next. "The last we heard, Bjorn was in the San Francisco area. He appears to have taken a big interest in boating."

Matalina would like nothing better than to get back on his trail, but she knew this drone problem had to take precedence for now. "What about Mario? Do we have any word on where he is now?"

"Since I think we'll all agree that finding him will answer many questions, we've focused all resources on locating him. We're attempting to keep our inquiries away from the Americans, who either seem to have no clue who they have working for them, or have a hidden agenda which puzzles us at this time." Her father said, as he pointed to a screen behind him.

243

"These are all of the photos of Mario we could find. I thought it would be good to see this, along with the time frame they were taken."

Matalina studied them, which started with a much younger Mario taken when he was a student. He had all black hair and a clean shaven face, making him the perfect bronze god that gave Italy such a reputation for great, sexy men. This had to be taken before his parents died. It was their great wealth and friends that lead him into being accepted inside the Maliviziati.

As the photos faded one into another, she saw the transformation into longer, unkempt hair, the addition of facial hairs and clothes that were no longer designer brands, but more like street people.

Eventually, she saw photos of him with Bjorn, as they became good friends. After Mario had reached the age of maturity and acquired access to his parent's funds, he had moved back to Italy. Since he had a great personality, like Bjorn, he was eventually used to recruit others that the Maliviziati would need to use as assets outside their country.

As he worked with Bjorn, she noticed where he had gone through many changes, consisting of going from a long black beard to a clean shaven Italian with a flair for sophistication. "Stop a minute and go back through those dates."

She watched her father smile. "I thought you would notice this." With the time dates disclosed, she knew that no one could grow hair that fast. He either had a double, or had become a master at disguises.

"Since he worked for us, why don't we have more information on him?"

"It appears that many of his records have been destroyed." Her father motioned for more information to be displayed on the screen. "We know he's a computer expert, trained by some of the best. We also know he has a special hatred for certain members of an Illuminati branch that he feels were instrumental in his parent's deaths."

"Which ones?"

"Those involved in the oil industry."

Matalina understood the connection to Houston and who that might be. "Bjorn had made it clear he thought Baltonia should take a more direct approach to hurting anyone connected to the Illuminati factions by attacking their wealth. It appears that Mario was a good student."

Her father's voice became loud and forceful. "A direct fight with the Illuminati would bring both of us to the center of attention worldwide, making both of our worlds impossible to remain hidden. No one would win."

"Bjorn was convinced he could win, but only under his leadership."

"And if he failed, our way of life for thousands of years would be gone. He had no respect for the traditions that have held us together all of this time."

"I understand, but I know how much he has studied the way the Illuminati split a few hundred years ago. And we have also had a few of our own in the past. We're just lucky that no one has connected the dots of us to the Sicilian mafia."

"It sounds like you're supporting Bjorn."

"No, not at all! I'm just trying to understand him so that I can anticipate his next move. When I find him, I will kill him." Matalina hoped the brash statement would clear any doubt in her resolve.

The door opened and another man on the security

force entered. "I hate interrupting, but I have just received information I know you would want to see." He handed a small flash drive to another guy at the table. "This is the latest on Zafar."

Good! They must've discovered some leads on where he was. Matalina examined an e-mail concerning the CIA commander who was in charge of the Houston defense system. He had been reassigned. "Oh, hell no!" Carlos, who they knew was really Mario, had been directed to come to Houston to assist in a new project involving some new laser technology.

Her father turned to the guy who had discovered the e-mail. "Do we know when he'll be there?"

"It's hard to say since we don't know where he is, but I'd assume he would be there within a few days at the most."

Matalina rose, shoving her chair behind her. "I think I've seen enough. I need to leave as soon as possible if I have any chance in intercepting him. He doesn't need to get his hands on this new technology."

The man who had delivered the flash drive interrupted everyone by raising a hand. "Should we alert the CIA with what we know?"

Her father quickly responded. "I think that would be the wrong thing to do. I'm sure they would tip our hand. This is something we need to handle on our own."

"I agree." Matalina prepared to turn, but stopped as her father also stood.

"Matalina, please stay for a minute. I know you want to take this mission on, but you're still recovering. Additionally, you're on the CIA radar and they'll be alerted to your arrival in minutes."

"This time I don't plan on knocking on the front

door as I enter the States. That would take too long for one thing. I heal fast as you know, and I'll not let such a small problem stop me." She raked her teeth over her upper lip. "I need to put together an assault team, and get more security in place there until we arrive. We may have little time."

"I agree we don't have much time, but you'll need a special strike team." He looked amused. "Just how do you plan on entering the States undetected this time?"

"I've been studying aerodynamics the last few weeks, and I need to check out something I fear they're also working on. Let's just say I plan to float into their country."

Her father glanced around. "Matalina will need the help of all of us, and we all know our level of expertise. I suggest we move on this immediately." He paused for a second. "Matalina, I need to see you about one other matter before you leave, so please stay for one minute."

A minute she had, but not much more. "As you wish."

After the doors were closed, he walked over to her. "Matalina, as important as this mission is to all of us, it's also important that you remember you have to stay alive to take your place as Queen in a few years."

Okay, that again! "We both know that I'm much better doing what I'm doing."

"Yes, you're doing what you were destined to do, but this isn't all you were born to do. When you become queen, you'll have to have someone to take over for you, you know, like hopefully a son."

Matalina remained quiet. She had no time to enter into a full fight with her father. Hopefully, this would blow past her, just like it had many times before. "I have no one as a mate. So, what are you proposing?"

"We have several men being discussed. As soon as you produce an heir to the crown, you can return to you missions. To make sure that an heir exists, we're also thinking you need to produce three heirs."

Too much. She had no time for this. "You know how much time this will take me out of the field where I belong."

"We fully understand. You'll be able to direct men in the field for as long as you can. As soon as you deliver, you'll have the babies raised for you. I know this sounds callous, but you know the way it is."

Yes, she knew all too well. It was the way she had been raised. There had been very little time she had privately enjoyed with her father or her mother. "As usual, I see I've no choice in this."

"Not much. I hate this as much as you do, but it's necessary if we keep our way of life going. You have many people around the world depending upon you."

"So, father, why are you telling me all of this?"

"I said we had several men under consideration. One of them might surprise you."

Chapter 19

Matalina sipped her Turkish coffee while enjoying another cigar she often dipped the butt into. The large pleasure boat they had acquired out of Cancun roared across the salty smelling Gulf of Mexico and beneath a clear blue sky that blinded Matalina even with her dark shades. With little chop in the water, they were making great time. This would be a perfect way for her to sneak back inside the States. She just hoped she would make it soon enough to rescue Olaf and move the equipment somewhere safer.

Still, she also realized by moving it that the Houston Bay area would be vulnerable to a new attack during the relocation. If word got back to Zafar, then she felt sure he would wait to launch such an attack to when the system was disabled. A coded message had been sent to those in Houston to be on high alert. It was the best she could do and not disclose everything she knew, which might be intercepted.

As the boat sped across the Gulf of Mexico, she had a few more minutes to prepare for her flight. This would be the ultimate test for what she assumed they planned to do with the drones. The glider they had prepared for her on short notice would act like a large drone. By controlling the elevators and ailerons, she could have the glider ride on the wind currents and float quietly in place, much like one of the sea gulls she had watched many times on the various coasts around the world.

Even if she could make manual changes to control

her flight, she knew a computer could do much better. The only energy needed to launch and fly these silent attackers would be for the electronics and the small electrical motors controlling the aerials, etc.

Of course, she planned to keep this glider barely above the waves as she approached the Houston coast line. The ones they were planning were meant to climb into the upper atmosphere and ride the jet stream. These winds could be extremely violent and tear any flimsily designed drone to pieces. Were they now that good in designing these drones?

Several hours later, she read the weather reports, looking for any problems. Once she got airborne she would have limited communicating ability. The specialized boot around her ankle helped, but still didn't stop the agonizing pain.

She glanced at the captain. "It looks good. If all goes well, I'll be on dry land within an hour. I'll give you the all clear when our assets make contact there."

The captain removed his sunglasses. "We'll head back toward Cancun, but I'll be looking for a much better boat to use in case we need to come and get you."

"Perfect. I'll be in touch." She double checked her pack, and all of the attached gear. She hoped she wouldn't need the small raft, but she felt like it was worth taking with her. "Let's do this."

The bright sun above her would help to some extent, since it added a blinding effect to all of the other sparkles coming from the breaking waves. She knew the boat couldn't stay for long, since the coast guard might arrive at any time, thinking they were drug smugglers.

A cable was connected to the front of the glider,

allowing her to be lifted upwards in a controlled manner. This would be the only time she would be able to get a feel of the controls. They were much more sensitive than she had assumed. When they cut her loose, she would have to fly higher for a while in order to master their movements.

Eventually, she lifted her thumb. It was time to soar. The initial rush into the heavens surprised her. The winds became much stronger as she climbed. She soon managed, however, to slow the climb and turn into the winds. It took an hour for her to master the feathering effect of floating like a seagull, but she thought she had a rough idea of how to do it.

While she had the chance, Matalina attempted several more movements. It was much harder than she had anticipated, almost sending her spiraling many times. Since she didn't need to attract too much attention, she eventually abandoned her testing of her theories and headed north.

As the traffic in the gulf grew, she changed direction, looking for the scheduled pick up point just south of the harbor. This had to be executed quickly. The island had a small cove like entrance which was perfect for her to hide in, assuming no one was fishing around it.

She saw one boat, a small sailboat that matched the description of what she would connect with. After seeing several men wave at her, she knew all was safe. She hadn't been detected, or had she? She watched a small powerboat veer in her direction.

After pointing to it for the crew below, she landed the glider on its belly and next to the sailboat. It floated just like it was designed to do. The men rushed her aboard and went to disassembling the glider.

As they stored the pieces, the powerboat made the corner and headed in their direction. She saw no governmental markings or blue lights. However, her three men shifted to high alert as they assumed various positions on the small sailboat.

She breathed easier as the boat cut power and started to glide over to them. A young guy was at the stern with two girls behind him. Even it was now obviously a pleasure boat, she knew it could still be problems for her. No one needed to know she had entered the country like this.

Seconds later he stopped his boat next to them. "Hey, did you see the hang glider crash near here? I think they must be in the middle of the island somewhere." The guy yelled as the young girls, who were in their late teens, walked to the front of the boat in their skimpy bikinis.

The last thing she wanted was them reporting this or mentioning it on Twitter or Facebook. Matalina spoke for her group. "Yes, that was our play toy." She might as well admit the truth since they saw it. Also, she had to make it sound like it was no big deal.

"Really!" He stretched taller, actively trying to find it. "Where is it?"

"It went that way after skimming the surface. I'm surprised you didn't see it." She watched them turn in the direction she pointed. One of the girls stumbled as she walked around the front of the boat. Good, she had been drinking. "You have to be careful around here. We saw the police checking out several boats a few minutes ago."

The guy looked nervous. "No shit!" He motioned for the girls to take a seat. "Which way did they go?"

Matalina motioned to her left, and then watched

him retreat in the other direction. She laughed, knowing she had cut his day of fun short. Still, his rich dad would be glad to see he was doing his best to avoid a ticket. American kids weren't much different than kids from other rich parents around the world.

After docking the boat and switching to two black sedans, which Matalina hoped would be somewhat hidden in the maze of vehicle parked around the building housing the laser, she left the driver inside and went outside to study the surrounding area to the north. A quick call to the other vehicle separated the men there as well. She needed all four corners covered.

After insuring all was in place, Matalina checked with her guards she had posted inside earlier. All was calm for now. This expected attack could happen any minute, but it could also be days away. Additional command centers had to be discretely established in a short period of time.

Over the next four hours she had over fifteen additional men stationed around the outside of the building, monitoring everyone who came or went. Although she doubted Mario would storm the building, she didn't put it past him. While she wanted to make sure he didn't destroy the system or harm the men operating it, she wanted to take Mario alive. She laughed, knowing how happy that would make the CIA.

After all became operational, Matalina felt tired from the lack of sleep. The back of the command center had a small room made for resting during the long shifts. A few hours there would definitely be time well spent. Hopefully, her intelligence people would have a better idea where Mario was and when he might be arriving when she woke.

Sleep didn't come easy, since Matalina had some major decisions coming up. It sounded like her father was going to give her a choice between three different men to be her mate. Well maybe not a final choice, but at least a word in the decision. That was a start. Kids! She had no time to have children, not in this ever changing world where it was getting harder and harder to stay on top of new developments.

The thoughts of having sex with someone new intrigued her. There would be no doubt the guy selected would be a superb athlete, with qualities of a warrior. He would also be selected for intelligence. As much as she hoped her father would disclose who these three men were, he had given her no indication. Perhaps he gave her this small enticement to encourage her to accept the fact that duty called and she was expected to fulfill her destiny.

As she attempted to drift off to sleep, she envisioned making love to an unknown man. During her life she had only had two men. When Bjorn had been selected for her earlier and they were forging a relationship, she had made love to him many times. Just like her, he was extremely passionate in bed, aggressively taking her and ravaging her for hours, pushing her to incredible heights.

Then, there was Vic. His body was much more massive than Bjorn. He shared much of the intense lovemaking qualities with Bjorn, but he offered something much different. Bjorn was more forceful and dictating, much like a born leader would be. Vic acted much more caring and considerate of her needs. While she never considered him to be weak, he lacked the internal drive that would make him a king one day. Perhaps she thought she was being a little too harsh on him. After all, he was still a subject under her. Again, it could just be that it was his way of showing respect.

Her mind wondered back to her bedroom where she invited him to come see her earlier. He had walked in without saying a word, slipping silently in her bed after removing all of his clothes. Their engagement in sex was almost immediate. Damn! It was too bad he couldn't be with her now. Still, what set him apart from Bjorn was the cuddling he offered afterwards. Bjorn always left as soon as he was finished with her.

As her world drifted into a restful place where all was at peace, her deepest desire was that the rest of the world could be as such one day.

A few hours later, thunderous bangs on her door shattered her dreams. "Matt. They're here!"

Matalina glanced at her watch. Local time was three in the morning. She should have known they would pick as quiet a time as possible to make their move. She jumped from the bed and prepared for almost certain confrontation ahead of her.

After making it to the front of the command trailer, she studied the video cameras that had been placed at critical points of entry into the building hosting the laser. She counted four black suburban trucks parked on the two front corners. "What do we have here?"

The Russian guy she had running the command

center communication room spoke swiftly. "These four vehicles arrived all at once. I counted ten men coming out of them. We've no idea how many are still inside, if any. However, I think we can assume some are there. Also . . . look at this close up."

"That looks like Mario to me."

"We're trying to get a match on the computer, but the light is low, making the image too low quality."

"I wasn't expecting such a large confrontation. It appears the CIA is behind this after all. This is going to make taking Mario complicated."

"I've already alerted the guards inside the building, but since they're all Americans they'll have to stand down when the CIA shows their badges. The men we have operating the laser will be totally unprotected. What do you want us to do, Matt?"

"These men have full diplomatic immunity, but we'll see how that works out." A full assault on the CIA to prevent this would be disastrous for everyone. Still, she couldn't idly sit by, watching this happen. "I need to get Agent Nelson on the phone."

"Matt, you know it's three in the morning?"

"Exactly!" With this kind of operation going down, she knew he wouldn't be asleep.

As they finally got him on the phone, she realized he was, however, deeply asleep when they called him. "What is it, Matt?"

She had no time to make small talk. "You have about a dozen of your men headed by the guy you refer to as Carlos making an assault on the building hosting the laser I talked Germany into letting you use."

"What are you talking about? Carlos isn't even in the country."

"Really, I just saw his face on a video. Are you telling me you know nothing of this?"

Rather than answering he attempted to turn the tables. "Matt, how do you know this?"

"I've been alerted to the situation." That much was true. "Then, we're to assume this isn't a CIA operation."

She waited for an answer but received none, a typical response of not confirming or denying any action. "Let me make some calls. Can I reach you at this number?"

"No, this is a pass through number, I'll have to call you back." She lied, knowing he would soon have her placed at the building. She had to move fast. "Bye."

"Have the guards stall them for as long as they can. We're on the way." She pointed to two men. "Okay, we need to get to the top before they do. Suggestions?"

"I can get a grappling hook over the back of the building. By using a pulley we can hoist each other to the top."

"Let's try it, we don't have much time. If this fails we'll have to scale the backside on our own." She watched him grab a shotgun-looking device which had the grab hook extending out the barrel as she waited.

They got lucky and the first shot found something to tie to. As soon as the pulley was attached, the three ascended one after another to the top of the building. She saw the laser in the middle of the roof, protected behind a small wall that had been built around it. With a radar saucer spinning behind the wall, all appeared to be operational for now.

She checked back in with the command center.

"Bring me up to date, we're on the roof."

"The guard captain said the lead man flashed a CIA badge and they had no choice but to step aside. They should be on the top floor any second. Olaf and his crew have been informed of what's going on and to show their diplomatic cards."

One of her men pointed to a dog house looking cover to a door that must be the way down. It was locked. She started to kick it open, but stopped as she tested her ankle. So much for being subtle. She pulled her Glock eighteen and motioned for her men to move behind her. The blasts ripped the door around the lock to pieces. With no lock to contend with, she replaced her clip, pushed the door open and rushed down the stairs.

After finding a door to the top floor, she stepped to the side this time as the guy behind her threw his weight into it. He dashed to the right after passing into the hallway, with the other man moving to the far left. She covered the center.

They all froze in their steps as they came face to face with five dark suited men. No one wanted to speak first, as they all had pistols pointed at each other. She studied each one and saw none she recognized. The man in the center spoke slowly. "Whoever you are, you're interfering with a federal operation. Drop your guns now."

Matt knew that counting the other two Glocks that backed her up, she had almost one hundred rounds that could be delivered in less than six seconds. "I don't think so. I, and all the men on this floor, have full diplomatic immunity. However, I'll need to see your identification."

The men, who were supposedly CIA, stood their

ground, but they were obviously stalling for some reason. Yes, she remembered that about half of the ones entering the building were accounted for in front of her. Where were the others?

Matalina hated depending on her bullet proof vest in saving her life, but she knew she couldn't play along with this stalling game much longer. "I'm going to count to three. That is all the warning I'm going to give you." She knew her men understood that countdown to be really only to a count of two.

The CIA men twisted in a nervous stand off until a sound of scuffling came from the door behind them. When the door opened, Olaf stepped forward, being pushed by a dark haired man. She knew it was Mario. There was no way she was going to let him leave there alive. Since no one was behind Mario, that left four more men unaccounted for.

Matalina watched Mario smile, with whitened teeth that contrasted with his dark olive skin and black hair. Her first instinct was to fire now, but he held Olaf in front of him with a pistol pointed at his head.

Still, no one said a word. It was going to get bloody any second. She hated it for Olaf, but her first shots would be at Mario. He couldn't be left alive.

"Matt, you shouldn't have gotten involved with this. You've no idea what you're involved in." Mario announced as he stayed hidden behind Olaf.

"Well, I fully intend for you to fill me in." While any second might be the one that all would explode in a full gun fight, she wanted any information he might let slip away. "To start with, how did you work your way inside the CIA?"

"Thanks to my so-called earlier friends in Baltonia, I did receive some valuable skills. And . . .

259

what makes you think I work for the CIA?"

"Sorry, my fault. I should've known you're one guy who can never be loyal to anyone."

"Are you sure about that, Matt?"

"I'll admit you have me somewhat confused. Would you like to enlighten me?"

"I think that would be an impossible task." He laughed briefly. "I know you think I turned my back on my country. One day you'll see that it was just the opposite."

Bjorn. He was the only one who could convince someone like this to join him and think like this. If anyone knew how to find Bjorn, this was the guy. "Is that you talking, or is that Bjorn?"

"Listen, I know you two have some major issues. You both are headstrong, and have a similar goal, just different ways of getting there. If you weren't so blinded by your parents and your sense of loyalty to such old thinking, you would see that we're right in our approach."

"Really? Your attempt of overtaking us cost the lives of many people, including my sister."

"I don't know why Bjorn allows you to live. He has had many chances to kill you. I guess I might have to do his work for him."

"You can try, but you know that will not be easy." She kept her pistol pointed directly at his left eye, which was only inches to the side of Olaf. She just needed a few inches at this range. "We both know you're not going to shoot Olaf. You want him alive, or you wouldn't be here attempting to kidnap him."

Matalina knew she wouldn't get any more from him, and she had pushed the limit on time. She kept her pistol in her right hand and moved it to her far right, making it slightly move out of his vision. Would he take the bait?

When she saw him stretch to his right, she made her move and uncoiled at him with all of her strength, knocking two of his men to the side. Without a clear shot on either side they couldn't fire without hitting their own men. Her left hand grabbed Mario's hand, where she used her thumb nail to drive under his trigger finger that extended pass the trigger guard, effectively making it impossible for him to fire his weapon.

As Olaf struggled to get free, he moved just enough out of her way to allow her to smash her Glock into Mario's face, sending him staggering back against a wall. Her metallic coated finger tips dug into his hand as the shots rang out from the others.

She shoved Olaf to the floor before she backhanded one of Mario's men in the back of the head with her Glock. When Mario gained his senses, he struck out with his clear hand, hitting Matalina across the face, but she held on to the gun he had in his hand.

A new barrage of bullets shattered the room, with blood splattering everywhere. Not sure who was left standing, she smashed her hand into Mario's nose, stopping him from fighting back with any more vigor. As she snatched the gun from his hand, she moved behind him, using him as a shield.

The walls around the hallway were full of bullet holes. All of her men and his were on the floor, presumed to be dead. More deaths she would have to live with. Olaf was shaken, but unharmed. She needed more backup since Mario's other men had to be close by.

She had the chance to kill Mario. He deserved it, but he also had more answers she needed. She hesitated for several seconds too long as several men rushed around the corner of the hallway and rapidly fired automatic weapons at her. Several bullets hit her in the chest, knocking her backward. Even with the bullet proof vest on, they hurt like hell. She fired her Glock as she fell, taking out several, but probably not all of them. Her world went black.

As her head cleared, she struggled to her feet, ready to continue the fight. "Matt, it's over, their gone." One of her men attempted to restrain her. How long had she been out? Damn! Her chest hurt. She felt of her ribs, wondering if she had broken one or two. The pain grew as she explored her body.

She scanned the dead bodies scattered all over the place. Blood pooled all over the floor. This would require some major work. The two main bodies she tried to identify weren't there. "Where are they?"

"They had apparently planned for contingencies and had a copter waiting to take them off the roof. They got away, but we're tracing them."

"Good, we need to get after them."

"Matt, you're not in any shape to chase anyone." The voice came from down the hall and was one she had heard before. "Also, you have a lot of explaining to do here."

"Nelson. I'm glad to see you could make it." Exactly how long had she been passed out on the floor? Even with a fast copter he had to have covered a lot of territory fast.

"What are you doing here? There's no record of you entering the country."

"To tell the truth, Nelson. I'm here doing your job for you." She knew that was harsh words he wouldn't appreciate, but to hell with it. "I came to stop your man Carlos from destroying the laser. We'll have to check it since I don't know if he had time to do that or not. He kidnapped Olaf."

"What are you talking about? Carlos is still out of the country."

"You think so? Well this is his skin under my nails." She tried to stand. "If you want to stop a major attack on Houston, I'll need your help. Like it or not, I need you to tell me some things." She stumbled as she rose, her broken rib sent flashes of pain that pushed her limits.

Nelson looked concerned as he stepped forward. "For right now we need to get you to a hospital. A broken rib could puncture your lungs. Please, let us help you."

She lowered her body back to the ground. "We'll see." She knew he was right, but that would mean Mario had gotten away.

The rib had been cracked, not broken as feared. Still, it would dramatically hinder her abilities when she needed to be a full speed. The laser had received minor damage, but it was still functional for now. Several of the crew being trained to operate it had hidden in time to escape being killed, unlike a few who weren't so lucky.

With no clues as to where Olaf had been taken,

his fate was still unknown. Since he had designed the laser, there was a major fear that he could remotely disable it under force. The Germans were extremely upset with the failure to provide adequate security. She had to do some major damage control. It was time to get out of the hospital, but first she needed to wait for Nelson. He owed her the truth.

As she struggled into her clothes, she called for her security guard. Her door opened as she was finishing and in walked Nelson with a sour look on his face. "Where do you think you're going?"

"Since I'm not in a life or death situation, I think it's time to get back to work."

"I have information for you, but as you can imagine, this conversation never happened." She watched two of his men walk out and cover the entrance to her room. "We ran background checks to make better identification on the men you thought were CIA agents. They're all hired mercenaries supplied from a group based out of Columbia."

Was this more of the Columbian connection from earlier? If so, it made sense. "What about Carlos? When am I going to get the truth about him?"

"I promise I have some information on him I intend to give you, but first, if I may, what's your connection to him?"

She decided a little information might sweeten the pot to make sure she got what she wanted. "He's a wanted terrorist in my country."

She watched the shock register on his face, one that in spite of all of his training, he couldn't hide. "With the amount of background checks we do, it's hard to believe we missed something."

She decided to reveal something else. "We know

he's being used as a double agent by you, but what I think you don't know is that he has many more than two connections."

"Interesting. I'm listening." He walked to the side of the bed and stopped, waiting.

"He's associated with one main group I've been tracking for several years now."

"I see. Here's the problem, the guy you call Carlos, isn't the same as the guy we identify as Carlos. Our man was still verified in Turkey this morning."

Her first thoughts, a double. It had to be. "I think the only way to get to the bottom of this is to arrange a meeting. In the interim, I suggest you recheck your information on this guy first. For now, the guy I tangled with in Houston was no doubt the man I'm after."

"Now, exactly how do you plan to track this guy?"

"With your help. I think you owe me that much." She waited for his response.

"Really, and why would you think that?"

"The laser is still operational. But . . . if you don't help me, that shield will come down, and there will be a drone attack." She knew she had him.

"What . . . exactly is it you want from me, Matt?"

"You're not going to like this, but I need the complete file on your guy Carlos, and where you tracked the copter that Mario, the guy I know of as Mario, went to after they left."

"If we knew exactly where this guy went, don't you think we would have already done so?"

"Probably so, but this is where I can help. For now, you'll have to trust me. I don't think we have long until the drones will be launched."

"I can have his files here in a few minutes, but we have to have an understanding. All information stays here. I can't have his mission compromised."

Whatever it was that he was working on had to be the missing part of the equation. Could it really be this easy?

Chapter 20

The copter had been discovered dropping off several men in Knoxville, Tennessee near an abandoned warehouse, before it disappeared again. This had to have been a preplanned stop with a car waiting for them. If they thought they were undiscovered, their new base had to be somewhere close, perhaps in the Blue Ridge Mountain area that was isolated in places.

The remnants of her team were spreading out over the area. It was still a lot of territory to cover, but she had her computer searching for any clues that could help. A message from her father helped. One of the men planted in America from Afghanistan against his will had gotten a message to the ones she had rescued. He was working at a small farm just northeast of Cherokee, North Carolina, and on the south side of the Smokey Mountains.

She knew his farm would be an ideal place for Zafar and Mario to hide for a while. With no other prime places to concentrate on, she decided to assemble her men. She had to hurry.

There had been no reported movement coming from the farmhouse, but a number of late model vehicles had been discovered near a barn to the far north of the farm. While this was still considered to be a prime location, they had obtained nothing conclusive that Mario was there.

A call to the owner, the Afghanistan man planted there, would be the only way. She knew this was going to be a major challenge in reading coded words. Her team was in place, just in case, and while the CIA had agreed to do other searches, she knew they might be around somewhere.

She motioned to her communication expert to make the connection to the farm phone line. She waited.

"Hello." The accent was definitely one from the Middle East, a good start.

She shifted to a southern American accent. "Excuse me, but I'm with Southern Realty, and I was just wondering if you would like be interested in selling your farm?"

"No, it not for sale."

Matalina checked the voice recording for stress. "I understand, but I have an interested buyer from Europe."

"Sorry, I not interested. Not for sale."

"Listen, honey, this guy is very interested and willing to pay all cash. I think you might be able to name your own price. I'm sure you would love to do the best, you know, for your family." She waited.

"It bad time."

She could only imagine. "We'll not take long, honey. You just tell me when would be a good time?"

"Maybe in a few days. I have guests here now."

Matalina nodded at her communication guy. "My buyer, a Mr. Luden, will only be here for a couple of days. His family will be relocated from Italy. He would love to move them to America." This had to be a name he would recognize, and no one else.

She waited for a response as the tension mounted. "This is great farm, and I sure he find what he wants here, but I sorry. Nothing I can do to help him now. Please . . . you call me later."

"In that case, thank you so much for your time." She ended the call as she turned to other members of the team. "We have to go in now before they have time to prepare for us."

"This has been hasty, but we'll hit them from many sides." He glanced at Matalina. "How are you? Since we don't know how many men he has inside, we don't know for sure just how bloody this will get."

"I've been *bruised* a little, but with all of the gear on me I'll be fine. It's time to get a little payback today." She watched the communication guy study her. "Don't worry, I'm still able to function at close to one hundred percent, and I know the objectives of this raid."

"Good. I still think it's best if you send in the other teams first. The copter will drop you off at the point near the action after we access where that is. They have several barns they could be using as strongholds."

While it wasn't like her to avoid being part of the front line attack, this time she agreed for one reason, she needed Olaf alive, and she needed the flexibility to select a target at the last moment. For some reason she thought he might be in the main farmhouse, but he could also be in a barn that was used to hide a radar and communication station.

"Let's do one last thing before we come in. Can we scan the top of these barns one more time? If they use it for the communication hub, they have to have some kind of antenna or radar device on top of one of the buildings." After seeing nothing for several minutes, she suddenly stopped and focused on a weather vane on top of one barn. "Can we zoom in on this closer?"

"The satellite above can only do so much, but we'll see." They both studied the improved image. A clear radar cup was clearly circulating at the bottom. "Okay, there's no doubt now that they're here, and might be in the main building which we need to take quickly."

"We still need to get the men in so that they can provide cover from any auxiliary positions."

Matalina turned to her men. "We need to make this quick and clean. We've lost enough men lately. I don't want to lose any more. Got it?"

There was one single road leading into the farm from the main public highway, but it was wide and open. The main complex was about a mile inside the property. A detail of five men had already been dropped on the rear of the property, awaiting orders to move in. From her copter high above she felt like she could coordinate the attack, but she wanted to get on the ground as soon as possible. Damn! This had to happen fast. While she thought for sure that Zafar would be there, she also hoped to catch Mario.

One of the men covering the rear of the barn broke the silence. "I have a clear view of two vehicles on the rear of the barn. They appear to be unoccupied, and we have missiles locked on their position."

"Good. Hold your shot until I give the order, but let me know if anyone approaches them." She cleared her throat, it was time to go in. "Okay, let's crash the front gate now." She pointed to the farm from the copter. "Get us in position and be prepared to get me on the ground."

High above the action, Matalina watched the trucks race toward the farmhouse, kicking dust high into the air. She was still too high to see any details when she heard the guy manning the missiles report in. "Matt, I see movement near the back of the barn."

"If you have a clear shot before they get there take it now." She strained to see the action below as two large explosions rocked the back of one barn. "That's where I need to be now. The trucks will be in front of the house as we come in."

"Hang on, we'll be there in less than a minute."

Matalina glanced at the two men going in with her. "Make sure your weapons are loaded and locked. We'll be in the middle of it any second." All three soon jumped to the ground as the copter retreated and flew to the other side of the farm compound. So far, there had been no gunfire.

Heavy smoke was coming from the two destroyed cars, but they offered the quickest and best cover until they worked inside the barn. "Spread out and cover me." Matalina ran for the cover as her ankle decided to betray her. She ignored the pain and pushed on.

Since her point man had seen movement, she first looked for bodies on the ground, but she saw none. Then, she heard the first sounds of gunshots coming from the main house. She yelled into her mic attached to her shoulder. "Take your shots with care. We still need to take Mario alive, if at all possible."

With little time left to capitalize on the surprise attack, she ran toward the opening in the back of the barn before darting to the far right and behind a small tractor. As her men followed her inside, she hurried to cover them, but she saw no one. Still, the dim light made focusing hard.

Eventually, she could see a metal door ahead of her that was closed. Without a doubt, this was a separate room they had hidden inside the barn. They had to be inside there. As she got closer, she examined the cinder block walls. She needed to decide what would be the best way in before they could react.

She moved to one side to try the door handle. It was locked as expected. A machine gun blast ripping through the door startled her, but she had expected such and had moved to one side. She waited until they emptied their guns of bullets.

One of her men attached plastic explosives to several sides of the door before inserting a remotely controlled blasting cap. "Find cover."

Seconds later they were all on the far side of the barn behind a small feeding trough used for the farm animals. It would have to do. The explosion blew open the door and knocked a hole in the roof above them. Matalina rushed forward and tossed in a tear gas canister. They would have to come out quickly.

As they waited, several more of Matalina's men joined them. She hoped the men inside would surrender. With the smoke filled vapors quickly drifted out of the room, they had to know they had no chance after being driven out of their lair.

She heard the sound of equipment being smashed. They were attempting to destroy anything inside, which probably included the computers, but it was still too risky to go in. Then, several gun shots quickly changed things.

"To hell with this," Matalina yelled, as she secured her mask and rushed forward. The smoke blinded her as she entered the room. She saw movement inside the fog with the vague image of an object she assumed to be a weapon of some kind. She fired out of instinct and heard a loud scream. Then the guy's image vanished like a ghost in a haunted house. The room was much larger than she had anticipated.

Matalina ventured ahead with several of her men following her inside. She motioned for them to spread out since she still didn't know how many men were inside, waiting for them with weapons. A few flashing lights indicated that some of the equipment was still working.

A few steps further and she saw a body on the floor. She had little doubt it was Olaf. As she moved closer to see if he was still alive, she saw movement to her left. Yes, she had been set up. She dove behind a small desk as bullets ripped the air around her, ricocheting everywhere.

While she was unable to return the fire, her men had a clearer shot and took it. Then, it was all quiet again. How could anyone withstand the tear gas filling this room? Her men moved forward, still on high alert and with split second synchronization in covering each other. None of her men had taken a hit yet–good!

As they advanced, she saw three men on the floor covered in blood. How many more were there, if any? She inched forward with her Glock pointing the way. When she saw a small hallway, she knew that there were additional offices ahead she had not counted on. They would have to be cleared one at a time. She soon counted two on both sides of the hallway. At the end of the hallway she saw a solid wall.

Her men stepped forward, coordinating a room by room search. They found no one. The fog began to clear as she backed toward the main entrance. That's when she felt someone slam into her back, and attempt to get her in a bear hug while also fighting for control of her Glock.

As they plunged over a small desk she struggled to face her attacker who had one hand on the gun and was using the other to smack the back of her head. She dug into his arm, searching for a place to dig in her nails. His heavy clothing stopped her from doing any damage.

He grabbed at her mask, dislodging it enough for the tear gas to burn her eyes. Her gun became free for a second, allowing her to drop it to her side and fire several shots into her attacker's knee. She could have fired more, but that should have been enough to stop any man.

Instead, he reached for her gun again while butting his head into the back of hers, dazing her slightly. Again, she found herself fighting for control of her pistol. In the struggle she managed to shift out of his grasp long enough to face him. Mario.

Again, he ripped at her mask which wasn't protecting her eyes, and was, in fact, hindering her limited vision. When he tightened his grasp around her throat, she matched his movement and dug her nails into his. It was all down to a battle of strength. She dug harder and felt her nails penetrating his skin. As her world began to fade, she ripped back all that she had a hold of with all of her remaining strength. His hand went limp as he fell toward her.

As she started to fall, she felt a hand grab her. "Matt, I've got you." She felt him reattaching her mask before he lifted her off the floor and carry her out of the room.

It took several minutes for her to regain full use of her senses. Although one of her major adversaries had been eliminated, she felt no victory, only a loss. While Mario had information she would never have now, Olaf certainly didn't ask for this.

Another one of her men rushed into where she was resting. "Matt, I've good news! Olaf is alive, but he has been shot and needs immediate care."

"Get the copter to land now." Matalina ordered as she forced herself to breath in fresh air.

"We're not sure we have the entire area secure, Matt."

"Then, let's make it so." She attempted to stand. She felt dizzy, but had to push on. "We need to get these men identified this time before the CIA does so. Also, we need to find Zafar, since he might be here. If not, we need something to lead us to where he is."

"We had some shots fired from the farmhouse, but I think it has been a standoff since then." The man next to her stayed close, as if he might need her to stand. "Please allow me to check the outside before we venture out. I've a strange feeling about this place."

As much as she hated to admit it, she knew he would be much more effective than she would be right now. "Okay, I'll stay with Olaf, and help get him ready to be transported. Contact the pilot and have him come in as fast as possible, and contact the nearest hospital to let them know what we have."

"Will do," he said, as he turned and motioned for two other men to follow him out.

She moved over to Olaf and checked his pulse again. He had blood coming from the side of his head,

275

but it looked like it was a glancing wound and not a puncture into his brain. Still, he could have a major concussion and other neurological problems from the gunshot. She had to stop the flow of blood. With the help of the other man left to help her, they used cloths they found to apply pressure and hope for the best.

Eventually, she heard the copter outside. Minutes later she saw two men rushing in with a stretcher. "Matt, we have him now. Let's get him onboard."

Matalina stood, but she felt dizzy again as she worked with them to get him on the stretcher. He had to make it. "Tell the hospital that whatever it takes to keep him alive, do it!"

The pilot waved at her. "Yes, we'll do our best to get him there quickly, but you know this will cause some serious breaks in our cover here."

"I know, but we'll get him out of the country as soon as he can travel. One man is to stay with him for security who will have full diplomatic immunity until it's safe to leave. Answer no questions, and don't allow him to be interviewed by anyone but us."

"Understood, we have to lift off now."

She raised a thumb to indicate an all clear. As they lifted into the air, she turned to her other men. "Okay, where are we on the farmhouse?"

"It's surrounded and secured for now. We still don't know how many are inside. We assume the guy you talked to, the owner, is in there also. We still don't know who he's loyal to, or how much to count on him for help."

"I'm sure he's confused, since we don't know how much information has been fed to him on what's going on with his family. I want him taken alive." She glanced in the direction of the farmhouse. "We don't have a lot of time to wait them out, since I'm sure the authorities here have heard us in action."

Matalina soon decided to take one of the armored vehicles to approach the farmhouse, hoping to talk those inside into surrendering. While not too optimistic, she wanted to give it a try.

When she was preparing to stop at about fifty meters away, she heard the warning. "Matt, we have a small copter bearing in on us." She scanned the sky around her and spotted a small black copter over the horizon to her south. Since she didn't see it resurface, she assumed it might have landed.

She motioned for the driver to position the armored vehicle between the farm house and where the black copter had disappeared. Were they letting men off to stage a counter attack?

A response came in seconds as she watched a missile streaking toward them. With a quick glance back along the flight path, she saw other drones veer off to one side. "Brace yourself!" she yelled at the others in the truck.

While expecting the blast any second, she breathed easier as it overflew her, but only far enough to strike the farmhouse, which immediately burst into flames.

With her fully expecting other missiles to be coming in shortly, she ordered the truck to attack the position of the copter that had disappeared. Her best defense at this point would be stopping any more from being launched. In spite of the rough terrain, she yelled for the driver to keep the truck in full throttle.

After climbing a small rise, she saw the copter on the far side of a clearing. Two men who were standing beside it quickly rushed inside when they were

277

spotted. "We have to stop them from taking off." She grabbed her Glock. "Get us in range now!"

However, by the time the driver had reached a smooth area where he could accelerate, the strangely designed copter had lifted into the air. Matalina stretched out the window, taking her best shots at the fleeing copter. While she hoped she might hit something critical, the copter kept gaining attitude and speed. She had missed her small window of opportunity for now.

She yelled into her mic. "I want this copter tracked. Do whatever it takes to follow it, and find us some air transport now!"

The communication commander responded. "I'm on it now. The copter's heading north, but has disappeared from radar from both ours and the local tower."

When she heard gunfire coming from the farmhouse, she patted the driver on the shoulder and pointed back from where they had come. "It sounds like they need our help."

As they raced to the farmhouse which burned like a summer bonfire, she saw two men on the ground who appeared to be dead. No one else could have survived inside. After she climbed out of the truck, one of her other men joined her. "Sorry, Matt, but they came out firing. We had no choice."

"Understood. See if you can find any information on them that might be useful. We also need to see if we can identify them. Did you see any signs of the Afghan farmer they had planted here?"

"We still don't know how many were inside. It'll be awhile until this fire is put out and we can check, and I'm not sure how much time we have until the

American authorities arrive."

The response came much quicker than she had anticipated when two silver copters circled overhead later. At first, she wasn't sure who this was. She braced herself and her men for the worst until she heard the voice of the FBI.

She retrieved her smart phone and dialed for Nelson. He wouldn't like this, but she was doing his job for him. Seconds later, she knew that he definitely didn't like what he heard, making it clear for her to stay where she was until he arrived.

A few minutes later, she saw a man emerging from an underground shelter, one which may have been designed as a tornado bunker. His hands were raised in the air as he yelled something in Arabic. Like it or not, she had to get to him before the FBI did. She pushed away from the truck and raced at top speed toward him with the silver copter hovering in close behind her, yelling for her to stop.

As she reached this guy, he had dropped to his knees and had his hands in front of him, praying for his life. She knew this had to be the guy forced into service by Zafar. She was going to save him at all cost. She yelled at him in Arabic. "Stay where you are. We're here to rescue you!"

The man dropped to his elbows as he surrendered to her. With men from the silver copter chasing behind her, she quickly placed a hand on the man's back before she turned to the men with the FBI. "This man is now under my protection."

The FBI stood their ground, but they didn't speak for a while, obviously getting instructions over their earpieces. "We've been asked to give you protective services until the CIA arrives, please make it easy for us to do so." She smiled at the diplomatic wording they used. Still, she had what she wanted.

As she waited for Nelson, this guy she was protecting spoke in English. "Thank you. I got word you were coming. However, you got here too late."

"What do you mean too late?"

"The trucks carrying the drones left a few hours ago."

"Which trucks?"

"They had several, all solid black, but only one of them was carrying the drones. They have a new base somewhere else. It's the one they will use to launch their big attack."

Yes, this guy had many answers she needed. She had to get him somewhere safe, and soon.

As soon as he landed, Nelson quickly stormed off his much larger copter and headed for Matalina. "This time, Matt, you went too far, I'll see to it your diplomatic card is revoked and you never come back here."

Matalina acted amused. "We both know that will never happen. Remember you told me that *your guy* Carlos was out of the country. I hate to tell you this, but he tried to kill me, but lost his life instead. You'll find him in the barn over there."

"Whoever is over there, it's not Carlos . . . that I can assure you." He motioned for his men to check out the barn. "What in the hell are you doing here?"

"Doing my best to stop a massive drone attack on America."

Nelson looked frustrated. "Isn't that something

you think we should do on our own here?"

"I would think so, but in doing so you need to be more forthcoming. We need to work together on this."

"I'm always willing to listen, but so far you're content to act on your own. This is making our job impossible."

"First, I assume you can clean this scene so we can keep it quiet. This time, I want information on who these people are. It would also be nice if you could positively determine if that is, in fact, Mario or Carlos in the barn. When you see that it's him, a better explanation of how he's involved in this would be good in us building trust between each other." She used an Italian gesture of moving her fingers back and forth between their lips to emphasize the point.

"It sounds like you're good at giving orders, but what makes you think I would agree to this?"

"Information! I assume you would like to know where the drones are and where they might be headed."

"You still think these people are going to release a drone attack on us somewhere?"

"I'm positive of it." She reached for one of her small cigars she kept in a special waterproof side pocket. "But . . . if you keep stalling, they'll get away . . . again!"

"What do you need from me?"

"There are about six or seven all black semi trucks racing away from here, but only one of them is loaded with the drones. I need your eyes on the road to spot them and your copters to intercept them. My men will ride with yours."

"What if I don't agree to this?"

"Then you'll have a lot of explaining to do in a

few days."

He hesitated for a second. "Since this might be the only way for me to actually keep an eye on you, we'll be glad to escort you, but you have to stay under our direction. I make the calls for now. Agreed?"

Matalina pointed to the guy beside her on the ground. "One more condition, this guy doesn't leave my sight. No questions asked as to why."

Within thirty minutes, a few hundred black trucks had been identified. The process of clearing them was time consuming, and this was why she needed the help of the FBI. The longer this sidetracked her, the more of a chance they had of getting away. Since Kazim, the guy she had rescued at the farm, had seen these trucks, she wanted him with her. She also needed time to gather more information from him, and that would not be possible until she lost her FBI tail that was placed on her copter.

One of the strongest possibilities was soon spotted on Interstate 10 heading west. Another copter was sent to intercept. She had decided to head north, the direction the mysterious black copter had disappeared, something she didn't disclose to Nelson.

By the time the truck heading west had been stopped, more valuable time had disappeared. This shuttle game had proven to be successful by Zafar, who she was convinced was now on that small black copter. He was one ruthless bastard for sure.

She answered her phone when she saw Nelson's name. "Tell me something good."

"This truck we intercepted going west on

Interstate10 was empty, but it was dispatched from the farm. The driver says he saw six other trucks just like his. I'm convinced he knew nothing about what he was involved in and was just a driver looking for an easy load. However, we did see some communication equipment in the cab. I'm sure this was relayed to whoever is behind this."

"That makes sense. It also means the real truck will take extra precautions now."

"We now have about twenty other trucks left that are under suspicion. If this doesn't work, I need to talk to you, Matt. I'm sure you know much more than you've told me."

"That all depends on what you can tell me about your man Carlos." She waited, knowing she had a major bargaining chip. While she had no doubt this was one of Bjorn's men, she wanted to know what else he was involved with, and how this tied in with Bjorn himself.

"We'll talk soon." He ended the call abruptly, apparently he had a distraction. While she wondered what had distracted him, she had to focus on any trucks heading north in front of her.

Over the next few hours, several more trucks had been stopped, but no drones had been found. With the elaborate system they had used to hide this shipment, she knew this had to be the final step in launching their attacks. With the size of these trucks, they could be carrying hundreds of drones. How long would it take to assemble them and launch their attack?

Since she was heading north, and she really didn't want to answer any more questions from the CIA or the FBI until she had a chance to talk to Olaf, she told the pilot to keep flying north and above the Canadian line. Their escort from the FBI started to object, but soon changed his mind as she flashed her nails on her left, while holding her Glock in her right. "Don't worry. We'll drop you somewhere nice on this side of the border."

Chapter 21

Hidden away in a remote part of central Canada, Matalina relaxed with her morning cup of Turkish coffee for a while, since only a few people knew of this quiet little outpost in the middle of nowhere. The taste of the coffee coating her cigar butt tasted good this morning. The dark grey clouds and steady mist added to the desolated surroundings where she had stationed her team. However, this would also be the best place to launch her attack when they located where the drones had been transferred to, one she suspected to be near there, but perhaps back in the States.

She needed to talk to Kazim and gain his full trust. With his assistance, she could also help him. Why had he and many like him been planted in America? What had been the future plans for them?

Several days had lapsed with no more breaks. Matalina still didn't know the target Zafar was after, or what he hoped to accomplish with these drones. She only knew this would play directly into the hands of any Illuminati faction that would love to use it as an excuse for world leaders to consider a one world power to control such threats.

While Mario had funds that could have financed such a mission, she doubted if he had used what would have been required. She also knew he hated everyone connected to the original Illuminati, so any direct alliance with them would appear to be out of the question. Like it or not, the double who shadowed

285

Mario, this Carlos guy, held many answers, and talking to the CIA was the only way she could obtain them.

She watched Kazim saunter into the small room where a large window pane was now being peppered with rain from the outside. Although he had given her much information she could use already, he still had much more. "Hello, Kazim. How are you today?"

"Good, thanks to you, but I still confused on who you are and why you help me." With his broken English, he lowered his shoulders and twisted to one side, obviously fighting to control his nerves.

Matalina leaned forward and patted him on the shoulder. "My name is Matt, but that's about as far as I can go, since any more will be dangerous for you to know. I helped you for several reasons–long story. But we have a common enemy, one that's pure evil."

He nodded his head in agreement. "I've told you everything I know. What else can I do for you?"

"As soon as we handle this immediate threat, I'll need your help in finding others like you who have been planted here against their will."

"That will be my honor." His eyes sparked with a deep black tunnel to his inner soul. She knew he had been through a lot and would like to see revenge for what had ruined his life and his family's future.

"First, I need to know more about how he managed to recruit men like you."

"Where we lived, everyone is under the control of the drug lords. The chances of escaping and living a life somewhere else is impossible. Mario knew by offering us the impossible that it would be hard for us to turn him down. He also had the blessing of the drug lords who operated around our town."

"I can see how the drug lords aren't too happy about the Americans messing in their business. That would only make sense. I'm sure you also know about the drone attack there that killed Zafar's family and which caused him to hate America so much."

"Yes, this well known." He nervously drew away from her as the questions centered on why he had agreed to be in this operation. She knew he would and how she had to move slowly, waiting on him to continue. "We not told where we would be sent, but that if we did as told our families could join us in a few years. We were told that we would be farmers." He closed his eyes for a moment. "I love farm . . . I work on. It dream for me. I wish my family join me there."

"As I told you, you're family has escaped, and many others as well. I know we still have some that are still not so lucky, but we will work on it." She paused before she pushed on and handed him a photo. "There was another guy involved in this operation. What else can you tell me about this man?"

"Everyone knows him as *the Italian*. He . . . strange. Even drug lords scared of him."

"Why is that?"

"People go missing, or found dead, when he around. And these often powerful people. It is said . . . he a hired assassin with others who work for him."

Yes, that was partially true, since she had taught Mario the trade. While she hated this part of her job, she knew the world wasn't a perfect place, and as such, tough decisions had to be made at times. "Kazim, what I need to know is how these two men became friends."

A puzzling expression flowed across his face, as

287

he responded with a surprise, she wasn't prepared for. "What make you think they friends?"

"Weren't they? They were obvious working together."

"They often fight each other. Bad words."

Okay, now she might be getting somewhere. "About what?"

"The Italian talk about wealthy people he need to kill, while Zafar talk about governmental people. They both want to use drones. They had weird friendship . . . both need the other. Zafar . . . expert at building drones, but no money. Mario had money."

"I know it would appear that way, but Mario has limited funds, and had to be getting more from another source."

"That . . . I not know." She watched him sink back into his seat. "Maybe he paid as assassin from different government."

Foreign government! She felt stupid. Now she understood how some of the pieces were fitting together. "Thank you, Kazim, you've been a big help."

For the rest of the night, Matalina researched all she could about CIA led drone attacks. She had called in every resource she could. This was digging into the most sensitive data she could obtain. Nelson wouldn't like her searching through his files this deeply.

Could it really be that while the CIA was the undisputed master of drone warfare, they were secretly operating on a much wider scale than originally thought? Were they doing the dirty work for other governments? Had they been operating as killers for hire for other governments or for anyone wealthy enough to pay for their services?

With these disturbing facts haunting her, she had to stop and control her rage that built in her like a volcano ready to explode. She was now convinced Mario had a double. Whether he knew about it or not, she wasn't sure. One thing was for sure, she needed to find this double. As a total unknown, and one with major knowledge of drones, he could be a serious threat to everyone. Perhaps he was the one working for some splinter group of the Illuminati? Since it could be possible, this changed everything.

She retrieved her phone and called Nelson, who immediately answered in his slow Texas draw. "Hello, Matt, sweetheart. I was wondering when I would hear from you again."

She studied the farce in his voice. "You know me, always doing research."

"Since you left the other day without so much as a goodbye, what do I owe this pleasure?" She knew he would be trying to trace her call, but she was way ahead of him on that. He would think she was back home.

"The truth. It's obvious that Mario, the guy I killed in the barn, had a double. I need information on who he is."

"You know there's certain information I cannot confirm or deny." He wanted to stall her again.

"Let me see how close I am. The Mario I know was used to take a fall for your guy, giving him a chance to quietly disappear again. But my bigger question to you is this; do you think you really know this guy?" She waited for a response. This had to get their attention. Nothing. "I thought you would like to hear more about him, but since you're not in the mood to work on good faith, I guess I'm simply wasting time."

Her bluff worked. "Sometimes, as you know, we have to have our operatives work in deep cover."

"Can I assume that sometimes the cover is so deep that even the shepherd doesn't know where his sheep have wondered?" She knew this might be a direct insult to his ability as a handler, but so be it.

"I never heard it . . . exactly put that way." Again, he paused without acting offended at all. His control was well developed, as she knew it would be–openly. "You said you had information you could share."

She ignored him as she continued. "I assume you haven't found a few drones *floating* around have you?"

"We have a few ideas where they are, but I can assure you we have many assets looking for them. I do have one piece of information for you. Olaf, the guy you rescued, is doing better, and he is expected to be brought out of a medically-induced coma tomorrow."

"I'm glad to hear it. You know he has full diplomatic immunity and you can't talk to him, right?"

"So, I've been told. But . . . it appears that we can help each other. You know I can block you from coming back into the country for a while. I would hate to do that, but if you really want to cooperate, I think I can ease the way."

Blackmail. Still, he could make it hard for her, and she had no time to clear it through channels. "What time tomorrow shall I be there?"

Chapter 22

Matalina glanced at the blue haze around the mountains as she heard the pilot lower the flaps to descend into Knoxville. As expected, she felt the dizzy sensation caused by her inner ear condition. It would pass. It usually did. She dipped her cigar back into her great smelling Turkish coffee before she deeply inhaled, hoping to fight off the feeling of being out of control.

 With Olaf's condition still critical, the doctors had induced a coma so his brain could rest and heal for a while. The short amount of time he had been awake earlier hadn't been too promising, since he had reacted badly to such pain. This time, the doctors thought they had his medication regulated much better.

Matalina planned to fly him out of the country just as soon as she could, and hopefully that would be in a few more days. Those few days, however, could well be the days Zafar would launch his much anticipated attack.

As the door to the jet opened and a ramp was lowered, Matalina saw a black sedan waiting for her. Since Nelson was leading this welcoming party she knew he wanted to be in control of this situation.

He tilted his head as she stepped on the ground. "Hello, Matt, it's good to see you again."

Sure, she thought, knowing she was probably the last person he wanted to see. She turned to the pilot. "Get it refueled and ready for a fast departure. I'm not sure how long this meeting will last, or exactly where we might have to go. Everything depends on this meeting."

"Agreed. All will be ready." Not only was the guy a topnotch fighter pilot, but a well trained elite commander. This time she wasn't taking any chances. She had assembled the best team she could, and she fully expected an all-out war over the next few days.

Matalina pointed to the sedan. "Nelson. Since we have little time, I hope we can do some serious talking on the way to the hospital."

He looked smug, as if he was in control. "I hope so. We need you to cooperate with us."

Seconds later they were in the car, speeding toward the hospital. "Nelson, I hope this can be a two way street. The best I can tell you is that there will be an attack in a few days."

"Do you still think they'll try to hit Houston?"

"I think that's a strong possibility. We know they have made plans to do so. From where, I don't know. That's one question Olaf might be able to help us with." She paused. "Were you able to get the defense laser back up and working properly?"

"We hope so. It's a complicated system as you can imagine." He twisted toward her. "I still want to know why you're so involved in this. This isn't your country that's coming under attack."

"My *country* has extensive interests around the world, as you know, and any disruption in the world economy affects us."

"I see. It's always about the money."

"No, you don't see. You only see what you want to see." This might be the best time to ask deeper questions. "I also need answers. First, thank you for clearing the scene at the farm house. It was impressive how you could do that so quickly. What can you share about the dead men you were left with? Could you identify them?"

"You know this is . . . strictly off the record."

"Of course." Good, Matalina knew she had him talking.

"As you have already encountered, most of the men were from Columbia, hired as mercenaries."

"Agreed. This is definitely a way to keep blame away from Afghanistan, but if the leader of this terrorist group wants to claim revenge for his country, why would he do that?"

"That . . . you'll have to ask him." He pulled a photo of Mario out of his pocket. "I think we need to talk about this guy."

"Yes, we do. Let me ask you straight out. How did he manage to come to work for you?"

"He didn't work for us." He tossed his head to the side. "But, from what I've learned, he did work for you."

"As you also know, that's something I can't confirm or deny either."

"I see, but it does confuse me as to why you killed him, Matt."

Matalina decided to open up. "Let me ask you a question. What would you do if one of your most trusted men became a traitor?"

"Since you seem to think this guy works for us, let me clarify the situation for you. He attempted to pass himself off as one of our operatives, hoping to gain some connections. What he actually was going to do with this . . . well I guess that died with him, and we'll never know for sure."

"I see." Hum . . . she has assumed wrong. It was

293

just the opposite. The CIA hadn't created a double for him as cover, but had to contend with him acting as a double. This would take a minute to analyze. Why? "Then, can you tell me more about this guy who actually works for you? From what I can tell, you don't have good control over him."

"From time to time, we have to use assets that have information we need, often at great risk, but can be worth the rewards. Many arms dealers, you know, will snitch on their own if they're paid enough, or the right situation presents itself."

"I'm listening."

"This immediate threat we're dealing with isn't the worst one that will come up. There're many factions around the world that would love to get drone attack technology." He looked forward to avoid her stare. "The world's changing, Matt. Maintaining control over drones will soon be much more important than controlling nuclear stockpiles."

Regretfully, he was right. "So, where is this mystery guy now?"

"I wish I knew for sure. It appears he disappeared back to wherever he came from. As you know there're many secret societies and factions around the world."

Okay, she understood! The Illuminati was still alive in many different groups! Now, everything made sense to her. To survive, they would have to be in control of drone development to some extent. "Nelson, I hate to say it, but I think you were the one used as an asset this time."

"Well, you know how it is; sometimes it's all about damage control."

The sedan dashed into a garage at the hospital. "I'll need to talk to Olaf alone. I hope you don't try to eavesdrop on the conversation, not when we need to trust each other."

Since Matalina knew he would, and she knew how to block it, the game was on. "Matt, for all of our sakes, I hope you get some answers."

Matalina reached out to shake Dr. Kim's hand as she walked into his office. "Thank you for seeing me."

He motioned toward a chair in front of his desk, offering her a seat. "As I mentioned on the phone, I induced this coma to give him time to heal. The good news is that I think with the proper rehab, he'll make a full recovery, but it'll take some time."

"Thank you for everything you've done so far. You can count on him receiving the best medical service money can provide. When do you think he'll be able to travel?"

"Perhaps in a week. Where are you thinking of taking him?"

"To a place in Europe."

"I see. In that case, it might be a little longer. The changes in air pressure wouldn't be good for him." Dr. Kim turned to a side wall where he had an x-ray viewer. "I want to show you what we're facing."

For the next thirty minutes she heard Dr. Kim outline what needed to be done for Olaf. The more Dr. Kim talked, the more she felt sorry for Olaf. She would make sure he was well taken care of. He didn't ask for this.

Finally, Dr. Kim pointed to the door. "It's important to us that we wake him to check his progress. I understand you want to privately ask him some questions."

"Yes, and I'm sorry, but he has information concerning national security, both here and in my country."

"With all of the security here, I understand. Still, if he shows any signs of shock, distress, or really any kind of trauma, I'll have no choice but to put him back to sleep."

"Since I also have his best interests in mind, I'll be as delicate as I can."

"Good! I think we understand each other."

As expected, Olaf's head was covered in white bandages, and he had many lines going to him. Several pieces of equipment had flashing buttons of various colors. She examined his eyes, which were closed, his nose with a tube taped in place, and a mouth that looked dry and parched.

After Dr. Kim moved next to Olaf and directed a nurse working behind him to adjust one of the machines, Matalina clicked on a device in her purse as she studied the equipment. While the electromagnetic signal would disrupt any listening bugs planted by the CIA, she hoped it wouldn't interfere with Olaf's monitoring equipment. So far, so good.

She watched Dr. Kim inject the contents of a needle into a line going into Olaf's vein. She had no clue how long this would take, as he shifted back in his seat.

Eventually, she saw Olaf's eyes flutter. Dr. Kim leaned forward and opened one physically as he studied the size of the retina. "It will not be much longer. Please let him rest for a minute as he gains his bearings. He'll be disoriented for a while, and I'll need to do some minor tests to see how he's doing."

"Do what you have to do, but please let me know when I can ask him a few questions–alone."

Dr. Kim didn't look pleased with the reminder that she needed to talk to him alone, but he steadily continued to monitor Olaf's progress. He motioned to the nurse to dim the lights before he turned to Matalina. "It might be good if you're in the background when he wakes up. I need to keep him as calm as possible until he gains full consciousness."

Matalina agreed as she walked over to a side chair, which would be in the shadows when he came to. She checked her watch. The morning was disappearing and she had other items to attend to.

Surprisingly, Olaf soon gained some strength and smiled when he was allowed to see Matalina. "I'm alive."

"Yes, and they say you'll make a full recovery. How do you feel?"

"Druggy, headache, and mad."

"And with good reason. Just so you know, the man who shot you is dead."

He pursed his lips in appreciation. "What about the others?"

"Listen carefully. This is why I needed to talk to you. Zafar is still alive. We don't know where he is, or what he plans to do next."

"I watched him load many drones into a large black truck."

"Yes, we know. However we lost it. Do you know where he was heading?"

"The one thing I overheard was something about a Mountain close to Canada."

"Thanks, you did good. Is there anything else you can tell me?"

297

"He has some of the codes to the laser. It will only be a matter of time until he can download the main operating program for the laser. You need to shut the laser down."

"Okay, will do, but won't this make Houston vulnerable to his attack?"

"I think they have a new target."

"Where?"

"I don't know, but a much bigger one." Olaf started to breathe in a labored motion as his monitoring equipment started flashing. Something was wrong.

Matalina called out loud, knowing the doctor was just outside. No one responded. She yelled again–nothing.

Her instincts kicked in, something was wrong with the equipment. She grabbed one of the lines and felt a surge of electricity as her nails dug into the wire. Someone was trying to electrocute Olaf. She ripped the wire in two and watched Olaf settle back down moments later. She checked his pulse. All was good.

Where were the doctor and the guards? She looked for a way to secure the room as she tried to use her phone. Then she remembered her device in her purse. She turned it off and tried her phone again. Nelson responded immediately. "What is it?"

"Secure the hospital. We have an assassin inside." She tipped to the door to look outside as she waited for a response. The doctor and two guards were on the floor. Since she saw no blood, they had to have been knocked out and not shot.

Still, she saw no signs of anyone else. She stepped back inside. With the wires cut, he kept recovering. Suddenly, she heard the code call. About time. The disconnected wires had to have set off alarms in the central nursing station.

The door burst open, with a heavy set nurse wildly trying to access what was going on. "Who are you?"

"Long story. I'm here to protect him, do you understand? He's in danger and needs to be moved, like now."

With her eyes widened to take in Matalina, she simply nodded her head. From the doorway Matalina saw more nurses leaning over those on the floor. "Are they going to be okay?"

The nurses acted stunned at the situation, but one responded. "They all have massive blows to their head. We need to get them to the emergency room. What is going on here?" They listened to another code that was being broadcast before she continued. "They just shut down the hospital!"

Seconds later, a CIA agent she recognized from earlier ran toward her. "About time." She pointed inside. "Stay with him."

"Where do you think you're going?"

"To stop someone from getting away." She pulled her Glock and ran out of the room, looking for a stairway to the roof. Each step hurt as she bounded several at a time. She knew she had minutes at the most to get to the helicopter landing on top.

Finally, she opened the top door. The light was blinding as she reached for her shades. Since she saw no one there, she wondered if she had misjudged. She scanned the perimeters but stopped for a second when her phone rang.

As she reached for her phone, the slight distraction made her lose concentration until she felt an attack coming from behind her. The scuffling of a shoe on the concrete was her only warning. She ducked as a metal bat swirled over her head.

She kicked directly behind her, making contact with the knee of the man behind her. After diving to the ground in front of her and flipping to one side, she pointed her Glock at the attacker. The bat knocked it from her hands before she could fire.

Before he could take another swing, she kicked out again at his knee, this time stopping him as he stumbled. After arching on her back she flung herself forward, landing on both feet to face him. The attempt to hit her with a backhand swing failed, allowing her to grab the bat with her bare hand in mid-swing.

For a fleeting second, she focused on her attacker. He had the looks of a Columbian, much like the others who had attacked her earlier. Since she hadn't been able to take one alive earlier, she changed the blow she delivered to his face. She could have killed him.

As he stumbled, however, he reached for a gun. Her knife was faster. With his knee cap broken and his arm sliced open, however, he still defiantly fought on. He threw his best jab at her face, one which she grabbed in her open hand. After wrapping her hand around until her nails dug in to the back of his hand, he yelled in pain for the first time.

"Listen to me! I don't want to kill you. Who do you work for?"

She watched him shift his attention to the right to focus on something behind her. The first sign of fear he ever showed suddenly filled his eyes. "Him! M–" His body jerked backwards from a gunshot, spurting blood from behind his back before he could finish the word. As he fell, she saw the blood oozing from the front of his shirt. Matalina twisted around, attempting to locate where shot had came from. About a block away she saw a black copter, one she knew well now, turned sideways, with a man focusing a rifle on her. She hit the floor as five to six shots ricocheted off the wall behind her.

Before the shooter could adjust, she dove behind a small wall, it would have to do. She saw her Glock on the ground to her far left. She grabbed it and ducked back behind the wall as more shots hit the wall. She waited.

Ten seconds later she edged over the top and aimed for the copter, unloading the entire clip. The copter bobbed a little but showed no signs of being hit. She dropped behind the wall and reloaded. When she popped back over the edge, the copter had disappeared. Were they trying to get a better view of her position? She heard nothing, indicating the copter had entered whisper mode, or had vanished.

Matalina ran for the edge of the landing hub. It had disappeared entirely. A voice called behind her. "Matt! Drop your gun."

She lowered it as she turned and walked toward Nelson, who was standing next to the body on the floor. "I didn't shoot him. You can check the bullet if you want. He was shot from a copter over there."

"There–where?"

"It was in whisper mode. You know what that means. We're talking military type, not a private model. They should be in the air if you want to make yourself useful." She dropped to the floor to rest.

He grabbed his phone and yelled in commands as other CIA types gathered around him and checked on the dead man. She felt exhausted, but reached for a cigar. "His boss was on that copter, and he apparently didn't like him being left behind alive."

"Any idea who that would be?"

"Best guess–your rogue agent."

He must've agreed as he started shouting new commands. She could imagine the massive manhunt that was going to be launched right now. As she caught her breath, she wandered over to the dead man, wondering who he was and who he really worked for. "Did he have any identification on him?"

The agent acted like he didn't hear her, his effort in avoiding her question. She turned to face Nelson. "You wouldn't have this guy if I hadn't chased him." She watched Nelson nod an approval to the other man to give her what she needed.

They handed her a wallet. "This is all we found. There's not much."

She opened it to see photos of his apparent family. He had several hundred dollar bills neatly folded in one pocket. He also had an electronic ticket for a return flight to Columbia. Interesting. "Did he have a passport on him?"

"No, this was it."

Okay, how was he going to get home without one? He must have stashed it somewhere else. She knew the chances of finding it would be next to impossible. Since she knew she had to return this to the agent, she memorized all of the details on the ticket, including his name, the confirmation e-mail and phone number.

As Nelson took a momentary break, she asked, "How about Olaf?"

"He's fine, I'm sure, but the doctor and the others probably all have concussions from being hit with this bat."

"I need to check on them."

"Fine, just don't disappear on me again, we need to talk."

As Matalina made it back to Olaf's room, she saw several more agents or officers, maybe hired guards, but none of which she had seen before. At this point, she trusted no one. The one closest to the door acted like he was going to block her from entering. Really?

Her hand touched her Glock. "I promise you I'm much faster than you are."

He paused. "I'll have to clear you."

"No, what you're going to do is clear this area now."

He spoke into a mic anyway. She couldn't hear the returned message given to him in his earphone, but he smiled and nodded to the others. "As you wish."

Matalina pushed the nurse button as she walked in. "I need the chief of staff here asap . . . understood?" She studied the one CIA agent she recognized from earlier and the two nurses attending to Olaf. "I sent the other agents posted outside away. Did you know any of them?"

"No, but I didn't venture out of the room since I was ordered directly by Nelson to stay with Olaf."

She next called Nelson. "I just sent the men outside Olaf's room away."

"And why would you do that?"

"I didn't recognize any of them, and I assumed that it would be impossible for you to get back-up here this quickly. The agent who was in the car with us on the way over to the hospital is with me."

"I see. I'll be there shortly. Can I talk to my guy there?"

Matalina smirked as she handed him the phone.

"Nelson."

As they talked, Matalina walked over to Olaf, who was still fully awake. "I would've thought they had given you something to sleep by now."

A nurse spoke up. "We have another doctor on the way. We can't do anything until he shows up."

Matalina leaned forward to examine Olaf's eyes. "How do you feel?" He shrugged an okay. "I need to know if you feel good enough to travel."

Before Olaf could answer the nurse spoke again. "That'll be a decision his doctor will have to make."

"As of right now he doesn't have one and this isn't a good place to provide protection for him. My jet's ready to take him to safety, but we have to get him to the airport first."

Nelson briefly knocked before he walked in. "There's no one outside."

"Whoever they were, I'm sure they won't stay gone for long. I need to get him ready to travel."

"If security is what you're worried about, I can have many men here in a few minutes."

"I'm sure you can, but I need to get him somewhere I can do that myself."

"You mean out of the country."

"Exactly, and if you help me I'll be willing to share more information later."

"Since he's a material witness in a terrorist attack, you know I might be able to stall this."

Another doctor walked in. "Hello, I'm Dr. Johnson, the head of staff here. Can anyone tell me what's going on here?"

Nelson stepped forward and flashed his CIA badge. "We have a critical situation here, and a matter of national importance. Several men have been seriously injured, and one is dead on the roof above. All of this has to be kept quiet, and I'll need your help in doing so."

Matalina watched him purse his lips as he collected his thoughts. "I heard we had several trauma cases heading to the emergency room."

Nelson spoke quickly. "Yes, two of them are mine, and one of them is one of your doctors, a Dr. Kim."

A tone of anger overrode his response. "If you knew this might happen, you should've provided better protection."

"I've many more people on the way here now, but we do have a question for you. Can this patient be prepared to travel quickly?"

"Why?"

"Let's just say it might be safer for you and him."

"I'll have to review his file and examine him before I can give any kind of opinion."

Matalina stepped forward. "Since he's leaving here, you need to do whatever is necessary to make it as safe as you can for him."

He looked at her with defiance as he studied her appearance. "Who are you?"

"Not important. I also don't want him sedated again." She turned to the two nurses. "He'll need some care on the way. If you want to come, you'll be well compensated."

"Come where?" the heavy set one asked.

"I can't say, but I don't have time to ask twice."

"Sounds like the most excitement I'll ever have in my life."

Chapter 23

After flying Olaf to Baltonia, where he recovered much faster than anyone had expected, Matalina quickly returned to the outpost in Canada. The smell of her early morning Turkish coffee encouraged her to study the weather that had changed to partially covered skies with high winds whipping the tall firs around the valleys below them. While listening to the sound of the winds, she lit her cigar and stretched.

If the information Olaf had overheard was accurate, the massive attack Matalina feared would be released from somewhere near Eagle Mountain in Minnesota. She had poured over the analysis of the area for hours. The jet stream often blew over them on the way south. The remote location would make it easy to get the drones into the jet stream. Still, had they mastered the technology to keep these drones together in such a wind?

Olaf seemed to think they had. She knew he was in pain, but she had him working on the computer. He might be the one person who could not only track them, but stop them from gaining full access to the technology of the laser defense system. She had assembled the best computer minds in the world to work with him after they arrived back in Baltonia.

The base back in Canada she had left a few days ago was turning into a major command center. She knew she had little time to locate their terrorist base, since she expected the attack to come when the jet stream repositioned over that base.

Several team commanders walked into the meeting room as she stood. "Men, I'm not sure how much time we have to get ready. The latest report says the stream will reposition tomorrow sometime in the afternoon. If our intelligence is correct, this will be the window they'll use."

The team leader on her right spoke first. "There are many mines and caves in the area, as well as many abandoned structures. All could be used, but so far no one has located anything definitive. Could it be that this info is false and we're looking in the wrong area?"

"Yes, very possible, but this is the best data we currently have." She walked to a map. "The information obtained from the assassin that was killed at the hospital has given us some more information which is disturbing. The account used to buy his ticket was also used to buy another fifty tickets. There may be a small army waiting for us."

"That's a lot of people to hide in these mountains and remain hidden this long."

"I would tend to agree. It appears that every mercenary who had connections in Columbia was offered a job. The cost of such an operation had to be massive."

"So you think the Illuminati's new world order has resurfaced and is behind this?"

"The rogue agent holds the keys to many questions. While it's easy to see that Zafar wants revenge for the death of his family, it's not totally clear if that's the main reason anymore. I still think Nelson knows much more than he's disclosing."

"I take it you also think he has leaks in the CIA that he's not aware of."

"Possibly, and at this time I'm not willing to

chance it."

"What about the interception of the drones if Zafar is able to make a massive launch?"

She turned to the guy across from her. "I know you're going to have an extremely difficult task, but if these get airborne you'll have to track them and destroy what you can."

"We're prepared to do our best, considering we'll be operating over a foreign country's airspace and engaging a very small target."

Another man who was in charge of communication spoke next. "How's Olaf holding up?"

"I know he's pushing himself through a lot of pain, but it's the best way for him to focus on the problem of breaking into their computer. When they attempted to break into ours, they left the door open for a counterattack."

The door opened and another man walked in. "Matt, I think we have something."

Chapter 24

While the black eighteen wheeler had been well hidden, a hunter had located it and reported it to the police. The interception of the call was almost a miracle. There was just enough information in the photo to tie it to those fleeing Knoxville several days ago. Their base had to be close to there.

This remote area had many hiding places, but only one with a large enough field to serve as a small runway they would need to get the drones launched. There was also a large barn there, one with a small radar dish on top of it. Still, there was no room for a small army of mercenaries. With little time left, she knew that whatever they found there, it might provide leads to them.

With the fastest way in being from the air, she decided to lead the assault team that would parachute directly into the area. She had to hit them fast and hard, since she knew they had the air monitored and might be expecting such. "Okay, let's do it." She turned and jumped first from the plane. The cold air immediately hit her face as she tucked and dove to reach maximum velocity.

Matalina checked her gauge, she had to cut it close to get on the ground as fast as possible. It would be her responsibility to provide cover for the others in case they were spotted. She ripped her cord and felt the parachute catch the wind. First a small tug, then a massive jerk as it inflated.

While she could've floated, looking for a better

landing, she had to force her way to make a landing fast. She spotted one clearing and headed for it. She landed harder than she thought and felt her ankle give. Damn!

As soon as she released the parachute and had it secured, she hunted for a place to hide. The pain ran all of the way along her leg. As soon as this mission was over, she needed to take time to properly heal. She blinked her eyes and forced her mind to ignore the stinging sensation attempting to paralyze her.

She saw a small knoll about twenty yards away. That would have to do. With a quick glance, she saw the others coming in behind her. As soon as she cleared the twenty yards, she saw the first movement. Three or maybe four men were on a small ridge above her. The range was maybe two hundred meters.

She attached the extension and scope to her assault rifle as fast as she could while she adjusted her position on the knoll. Her men would be landing any minute. After scanning the ridge again, she found no sight of them. Where had they gone?

Suddenly, several bullets shredded the knoll around her as she dug in as deep as she could. With her pinned below the small embankment, she could offer little support to her men. Considering anything was better than nothing, she raised quick enough to throw scattered fire at the hillside.

When her clip emptied, she looked for better cover. An outcrop of small boulders about forty yards away was her best hope. It would at least draw their attention while her men found their own cover. She struggled to her feet and attempted to run. Damn! It hurt and she felt so slow. Several shots hit the ground around her as she dove behind the rocks.

"Matt, are you okay?" she heard the first team member ask as he checked in."

"I'm fine, but my ankle's problematic again. They also have me pinned behind some rocks. How's the rest of the team?"

"One man has been hit in the leg. Not life threatening, but he needs attention."

"Damn!" She glanced behind her to see if she could get a bearing on where her men were. She saw none of them. "Someone stay with him and take care of him until help arrives." She glanced back at the ridge above her and refocused her scope on the ridge. "Does anyone know where those shots came from?"

Suddenly, she saw one man fall off the ridge. Then, another one fell not far from the last one. At least one of her men must've zeroed in on them, but still, no one reported in. Above the last one that fell she spotted movement. While it wasn't a clear kill, she took the shot anyway.

"Come on guys, check in." While she still couldn't confirm she had hit the last guy, all remained quiet on the ridge.

As the men reported in, none admitted to taking the shots. While she assumed they all landed further down the hill from her, they couldn't be too far behind her since one of them had shot they guy on the ridge ahead of her

Her cell phone rang–Nelson. "Matt, get out of there, we can't cover you forever."

"What?"

"You didn't think we would let you do this on your own, do you?"

"Where are you? And we need to talk."

"Just above you," he replied until the transmission

became garbled. "Change of plans. Matt, you have a lot of men heading your way. Dig in."

Dig in where? See saw bigger rocks above the embankment. With little choice she had to make them, but that would get her much closer to the terrorist group. "Okay, but cover me."

She jumped to her feet and started her half run, half hobble trench up the small rise. As she dropped behind a much bigger boulder, she also realized that her visibility was much less also. Not good! Before she could consider another spot she heard the gunfight break open. While she was in the middle she could offer little help. She checked back in with her team. "The CIA is somewhere by us, can anyone spot them?"

"Matt, I see no one around us, but we're trying to push forward to where you are now. The wind current changed and landed us behind you. We hear gunfire."

"I'm being fired upon, but I think I'm hidden well for a minute. Nelson said he saw many men heading in my direction, however."

"If the CIA is here, we need to be able to coordinate, or we might be shooting at each other."

"Exactly." Matalina retrieved her cell phone again, dialing Nelson using the speed dial. "My men don't see you. This can be dangerous."

"Don't worry, we have them in sight and we will make contact soon. Please alert them to that. Right now, we're engaging with many on the hillside above you."

For some almost magical sense, Matalina looked above her. Several drones floated over her head. The launch had begun! After grabbing her Glock, she fired at several and managed to stop two of them. She reloaded in seconds, but she was fired upon before she could take any more out of the sky.

Maybe her men could stop some of them as they floated over them. "They're launching the drones, fire at will. We need to stop all that we can."

Seconds later, a small war broke out behind her. Still, she glanced above her to again see many more being launched. Where was air support when she needed it? She checked in with her own pilot. "The drones have been released, see what you can do."

"Understood, Matt, I'm strapped in and will be airborne in less than a minute."

"We're taking out as many as we can, but they seem to have hundreds of them. Also, I'm sure the CIA has airpower coming in, so be on the outlook for them."

"Will do."

The CIA response came quicker than she had anticipated as she heard a large explosion above her. They must've fired a missile at the terrorist group. The gunfire from the ridge stopped. This was exactly what she needed to be able to push on toward their stronghold. Now, if only her ankle would cooperate.

In the open she saw no more drones. Perhaps, the strike was effective enough to halt their operation. She had to make sure. With no more gunfire coming from the ridge, she made good time. She checked several dead bodies along the way, with all of them showing the possibility of belonging to the same group of Columbian mercenaries.

Then, she saw about a half dozen men rushing from a small opening, all holding additional drones. She stepped forward and yelled in Spanish, "Drop them now!" At first they remained still, and then one after another, they reached for a weapon. She released another full round of bullets from her Glock eighteen. Thirty two rounds fired within six seconds sent most of the men over backwards with blood spurting everywhere.

She dropped to a knee and reloaded. The smoke and glare from the sun above her hindered her vision. Had she gotten all of them? Apparently not, as she heard bullets whisk by her head. She dove to her right and fired again in their direction before replacing another clip.

She yelled into the mic attached to her shoulder. "I'm at the entrance to a small opening in the mountain. I think this is where the drones are stored. I have it covered but I need backup."

Matalina rushed forward to make sure nothing else would escape the entrance. As she stepped closer she heard a command in German from behind her. "Drop it now!"

One of the men she thought she had killed had survived. The German surprised her, but answered one question. This double agent was connected to some form of the Illuminati remnants. She would like to know which, but there were so many of them now. She lowered her weapon as she turned, hoping to get some answers.

He looked almost like a ghost from her past, the near perfect image of Mario. "It's going to be my pleasure to be the one to kill the great Princess Matalina."

"Do you really think you're going to get away with this? Look around. You're surrounded."

"Oh, I'll assure you I have transportation." He pointed toward the opening. Just inside she saw the black copter, close enough this time to see the small wings and thrusters. "This is a work of art, almost completely indestructible, and sheathed to any radar detection. There's nothing else like it in the world. Stealing it was the best break we have ever had."

She remembered seeing it in action before. "You know, I'm confused. Why is the Illuminati involved in this?"

"Is it really that hard to understand? With the proliferation of drones worldwide, the masses will be clamoring for a one governmental body to control this. The information you managed to help deliver to us on the drone defense system will help us tremendously."

"I understand that, but I also know that some families from the old Illuminati group have massive holdings in the oil business. Isn't this kind of like burning your own money?"

She waited for an answer that would tell her which group he belonged to. Instead, he laughed. "Who said we're going to hit Houston?" He pointed behind the copter and deeper inside the cave. "It was the CIA that killed Zafar's family. That's all he's really after. I think he's due what he has worked a life time to achieve."

"So, you're telling me that Zafar's willing to die right here for his cause?"

"I know, pathetic, isn't it?" He looked over his shoulder. "I wish I could talk more with you, but it appears I need to simply vanish for a while." He raised the gun, preparing to fire until he suddenly stopped. He threw his hand to his chest as blood darkened his shirt. Then, he jerked again before he attempted to fire at her. She rushed forward and grabbed the gun as he spitted out his last words, "Fuck you, Princess."

She watched him fall as she turned toward the opening. Someone had shot him, but who? No one came forward. She quickly turned to the abandoned mine. Zafar still had to be stopped. She edged along a wall, walking deeper and deeper inside the mine.

Eventually, she heard the sound of the copter cranking. Someone had gotten behind her and was escaping. She rushed back toward the entrance, where she watched the copter vanishing along a ridge below her.

Then she felt a rumble beneath her feet. She knew. The mine was caving in. She ran away from the entrance as she heard the sound of a major explosion coming from deep inside the mine. She had to make it to safety. She hobbled on her left ankle as fast as she could. The blast pushed past her, but it was still strong enough to knock her to the ground.

It took a while for her to recover, and she couldn't even offer a smile as Nelson ran over to her. She fell back onto the ground as she attempted to stand.

He pointed to the mine. "You're handiwork?"

"No, someone wanted to seal the cave. My being in it must have been a bonus." She breathed in deep as she fought back the pain in her ankle. "Thanks for saving my life a few minutes ago. You know that was your agent you shot."

"Matt . . . what are you talking about?"

She pointed to the mine that was now completely sealed. "When I was over there." Since he looked confused, she realized that he wasn't the one who made the shot. "Never mind." She knew with the ton of rocks that had caved in, this now unnamed agent's body would never be recovered.

Several of her commanders joined them minutes

later. "Matt, you need that ankle taken care of."

She knew she did, and she would soon. "We're not done yet. What about the drones? Were we able to stop all of them?"

"Most, but I don't think all of them. The pilot has several on radar."

Nelson spoke up. "We have the defense system in Houston on high alert."

"Nelson . . . that isn't the target. Think Langley."

"What?"

"Zafar has a grudge with the CIA for killing his family with a drone. Houston was only a diversion."

"But how will these get to Virginia?"

She tried to smile. "By just following the jet stream which weaves back north after passing the end of the Appalachian Mountains near Knoxville. That was the real reason for the Knoxville connection."

"We took out the command center there."

"Did we, or were we simply led to believe that we did?"

"Assuming that I believe you, where is Zafar so that he can control this?"

"Deep inside and where no one can get to him." She pointed to the sealed mine. "He never intended to make it out alive."

"You really think he survived the cave in?"

"Yes, I do. I think he planned this all alone. You have to remember when it comes from learning how to live in caves, he had the best people in the world to teach him how."

Nelson yelled at one of his men. "Get me some plans and details on these mines. We need to see if there are any more entrances that connect to this one." He nodded his head. "Just in case."

"Now, as far as these drones are concerned, I think we'll agree on one of two things. They're either preprogrammed to complete their mission, or they're being remotely controlled. I would venture it's both." Matt rubbed her eyes. "I need to talk to Olaf and see if he had been able to break into their computer system."

"While you're doing that, I need to scramble the air force and see what we can find out."

"I hope you can contain this. If this gets out to the media, they have accomplished what they really wanted." She clicked on another speed number in her smart phone. "This is Matt, I need to talk to Olaf, but first, how's he doing?"

"I know he's pushing it to the limits, but he's doing his best. Here, I'll put him on."

"Dr. Joachim, listen to me. They've just launched many drones. Some we've stopped, and others I feel like got through. What do you have for me?"

"Some, but not much. I see plans for preprogramming the drones, but it's not advanced enough to work yet. Have you been able to find their control center yet?"

"Not exactly, but I think Zafar may be barricaded inside a mountain with a remote control somewhere. How he's doing this, I'm not sure at this point." She paused as she thought of what else might help him. "I also think the target has been changed from Houston to Langley. Just trust me for now."

"No, that makes sense. It would account for so much effort put into testing in Knoxville. Let me check on something and I'll get back with you in a little while."

"Hurry!"

As she ended the call, she had one more question

for Nelson. "Did you see the black copter leaving here?"

"Another copter?"

"The same one that I saw in Knoxville." His blank stare answered her question. "Well . . . kind of. He was either totally in the dark, or he was hiding a very advanced weapon they had recovered."

Moments later, her phone rang again as Olaf called back. "I'm in!"

"And . . . ."

"I have the choice of trying to make them self-destruct or return to base. I think the first choice would be better, the other will be tricky if the other operator sees what we're doing."

"Agreed. I'll stand by as you try."

She held her breath and waited. Nelson held his phone near his ear as he joined her. Then, Olaf returned. "I assume it worked, all signatures have disappeared. Can you confirm?"

She checked in with her pilot. "We think the drones have been destroyed, what are you seeing from where you are?"

"I had something on radar, but it's gone now. I hope you're right."

"Dr. Fritz, it appears you've destroyed them, but it's still too early to confirm, stay on it."

Matalina turned to Nelson. "No pun intended, but it's up to you to pick up the pieces."

Chapter 25

Matalina stretched as she enjoyed the fresh clean smell of soft luxurious satin sheets pressed against her naked skin. The heavy comforter kept her body temperature warm and cozy, while a dim hazy light filtered through her full length window which faced the mountains. While she had never been one to sleep late, she allowed her body to be pampered, just this once, in order for it to heal faster.

She focused on her ankle which had been operated on two days ago, resulting in more metal holding her body together. She knew that this time she would be forced to take time off. With all of the information obtained during this last mission, however, it would take a while to analyze it anyway.

The quietness of the morning was broken by a soft knock on her door. A maid ventured around the door as she opened it. "How are you this morning?"

"Apparently, I'm getting very lazy. What time is it?"

"It's almost eleven. I hope you don't mind me disturbing you, but you're supposed to meet with your father for lunch."

Oh yes, how could she forget this? Matalina rubbed her eyes, forcing her mind to clear. "I guess I need to get ready then. Do you have a list of who else will be there?"

The maid pointed to Matalina's desk on the far side of the room. "Everything you need will be on your computer."

Matalina pulled the covers to one side and examined her cast. "I'll be so glad when this is off."

"I know you will." The maid paused for a minute. "I'm so glad you're home safely. By the way, you received a special delivery earlier." She pointed toward a small table across from her bed.

Matalina attempted to focus in the still dim light as she reached for a light switch on the side of her bed. A large single red rose in a beautifully decorated ornate vase brought back memories she wished she could forget. "Who delivered this?"

"All I know is that the guard at the gate brought it to us. There was no card."

Matalina raked her teeth over her upper lip. "Help me get ready. My father and no one else needs to see this as soon as possible." She strolled over to it, fighting the urge to crush it in her hands. No, she would do that later. "Get a word to my father that I need to see him earlier and alone."

The maid looked nervous as she glanced at the rose. "Why, what is it?"

"A message!"

Matalina wore an elaborate red dress designed by her favorite designer in Milano who had also created the fine Italian jewelry that was, of course, all white gold. While it was fitting for her title as Princess, it left her feeling totally naked and vulnerable. However, she knew the battle today would be won by words and not by her physical ability to fight.

As she approached her father's quarters, two guards directed her to a side room, a small, more private hideaway where they could be alone for a minute. He rose and personally held her chair for her as she hobbled over with her crutches. "Thank you."

"You look much better today. I trust the ankle's healing well."

"Yes it is." She glanced at it briefly. "I know we don't have much time. What can you tell me off the record before the meeting?"

"Oh . . . where to start." He shifted in his seat at the head of the conference table. "We've been able to collect a lot of intelligence since you returned. Off the record, you were extremely successful. Drone defense systems are being implemented worldwide and they will soon counter this threat. Many groups could've exploited this very much in pushing their one world order cause."

"You said off the record."

"Yes, I did. Unfortunately, many people died during this mission, and some on the council aren't too happy about that."

Matalina knew exactly who these were. As a princess, she wouldn't be able to defend her actions in front of them. Many of these men would be highly surprised at her covert role in the Maliviziati. "I'll never complain."

"And . . . one day that inner control you have will make you a great queen." Her father gave her an approving smile, one of the few she could remember. "I'm sure you read the memo on the meeting today, so what's different that you needed to see me about privately today?"

"I've something to show you in a minute. First, tell me one thing. With the terrorist assumed to be killed in the cave-in, one of the top assassins of some group of the new world order killed, and the drone threat eliminated, what is it that the council's really scared of?"

Her father stared at her. "You missed several other accomplishments during your mission, but still, they're focused on one major threat. While you also managed to eliminate Mario, his leader, Bjorn, and his other friends are still at large. They consider this mission a mere diversion from a mission that's of the ultimate importance."

"I truly understand their concerns, and it's mine as well. The part that still confuses me is the part the Illuminati had in this."

"As you know, the council's concerned about Bjorn mounting another attack on us, or revealing information about us that could also destroy the Maliviziati, our way of life, and our ability to be a force in helping mankind grow as a free society on its own. Without our interventions, the evolutions of the Illuminati and groups like them would have placed the entire world under slavery controlled by a one world order forever."

"I know why we've fought groups like the Illuminati and other one world orders forever, I know history. I know our place in the world–"

Her father raised a hand to interrupt. "Never forget that these groups I will always refer to collectively as the Illuminati have another fear. One of you and Bjorn uniting. As a team you would be very powerful, but the children you would've produced would have been even stronger. They understand that and it scares them. I'm sure they would love to hear we're considering other men for you."

"I'm glad I'm actually being given a choice of

323

who I'll marry. This is a big break in our traditions. When will you let me know who these three are?"

"There will be a meeting soon. This is a major decision that has major consequences for our future here."

She knew what he was talking about. Being given a choice was a major change for everyone. When she becomes queen, however, she planned to make many more changes, allowing her children to freely pick their mates. She forced her mind back to the present. "You know I'll be back on Bjorn's trail as soon as I'm able."

"I know." His face turned stern. "I was saving this for later, but I'll let you know now. You have to promise me you'll wait until you're well and completely ready to complete this mission."

"What?"

"There has been a rumor that Bjorn had developed a super helicopter, one that's stealth and capable of extreme firepower. I think you may have seen it in action."

"If this is the black one, then yes I did. It's super quiet, very fast and was undamaged by a full blast from my Glock."

"This . . . I'll not share with the others. There's no sense in making them more jittery than they are. Word is . . . the Illuminati had stolen it from Bjorn."

"If I had known more about it, I might could've stopped them from making off with it at Eagle Mountain."

"We only learned much of the details on this recently, but there's more. We have a photo of the copter heading across the bay in San Francisco not long after the assault on Eagle Mountain."

"Interesting."

"Very much so. The best we can tell is that it landed on a mega yacht there that we know departed out into the open Pacific. We highly suspect it belonged to Bjorn. As such, it appears he has reacquired it."

"If that's the trail, I need to get after him immediately." Suddenly, Matalina pushed back in her chair. "I understand. You're telling me that Bjorn may have also reacquired his copter."

"Yes, it would appear so." Her father lowered his head. "That would also mean he may've been the guy who shot Mario as you entered the mine on Eagle Mountain. Now why he shot him instead of you is confusing."

Matalina placed her purse on the table. "There's more." She opened the purse and retrieved the single red rose that had been delivered to her. "This is the second time in my life I received such a gift."

"Bjorn!"

"Yes, he did the same thing when we had a disagreement many years ago. I know this is a sign from him."

"And?"

"I loved him once . . . and yes, I may still love him. How am I to know? But, when I find him–I will kill him."

"I know." The tears forming in his eyes reminded her of the last time she saw him cry. The day his daughter, her sister, was murdered. The day Bjorn became a traitor.

TO BE CONTINUED

DRONES   JOHNNY RAY

www.ingramcontent.com/pod-product-compliance
Lightning Source LLC
Chambersburg PA
CBHW071059250626
47159CB00002B/526